KILLING ICARUS

PAUL KEMPRECOS

SUSPENSE PUBLISHING.

KILLING ICARUS
by
Paul Kemprecos

PAPERBACK EDITION
* * * * *
PUBLISHED BY:
Suspense Publishing

Paul Kemprecos
COPYRIGHT
2021 Paul Kemprecos

PUBLISHING HISTORY:
Suspense Publishing, Paperback and Digital Copy, July, 2021

Cover Design: Shannon Raab
Cover Photographer: Shutterstock.com/ mw2st (Gull)
Cover Photographer: Shutterstock.com/ nednapa (Dirt Background)
Cover Photographer: Shutterstock.com/ xpixel (Dirt)

ISBN: 978-0-578-87681-8

BOOKS & SHORT STORIES

NUMA FILES
(co-authored with Clive Cussler)
SERPENT (#1)
BLUE GOLD (#2)
FIRE ICE (#3)
WHITE DEATH (#4)
LOST CITY (#5)
POLAR SHIFT (#6)
THE NAVIGATOR (#7)
MEDUSA (#8)

ARISTOTLE "SOC" SOCARIDES
COOL BLUE TOMB (#1)
NEPTUNE'S EYE (#2)
DEATH IN DEEP WATER (#3)
FEEDING FRENZY (#4)
MAYFLOWER MURDER (#5)
BLUEFIN BLUES (#6)
GRAY LADY (#7)
SHARK BAIT (#8)

MATINICUS "MATT" HAWKINS
THE EMERALD SCEPTER (#1)
THE MINOAN CIPHER (#2)

SHORT STORIES
THE SIXTH DECOY: AN ARISTOTLE "SOC" SOCARIDES
SHORT STORY (NOTHING GOOD HAPPENS AFTER
MIDNIGHT: A *SUSPENSE MAGAZINE* ANTHOLOGY and
THE MYSTERIOUS BOOKSHOP PRESENTS THE BEST
MYSTERY STORIES OF THE YEAR: 2021)

DEDICATION

To Clive, who taught me all I know, and then some.

ACKNOWLEDGMENTS

Special thanks to guide and historian Beth Chapman, owner of Hopper House Tours, for her willingness to share her expansive and insightful knowledge of Edward Hopper and his art. To the Truro Historical Society for pulling together the splendid Jo and Edward Hopper exhibition at the Highland House museum. To fellow newsmen Arthur Gaskill and Jack Johnson whose firsthand accounts of the record-breaking Peter Hesselbach flights planted the seed for this book so long ago. To the Truro folks who shared their memories of the dashing pilot. And to my wife and research partner Christi whose keen eye was such a great help as we wandered over land and sea in search of scene settings.

PRAISE FOR
KILLING ICARUS

"The suspense builds like a burning fuse to a bundle of dynamite in another first-rate mystery from Paul Kemprecos."
—Dirk Cussler, #1 *New York Times* Bestselling Author

"Kemprecos proves again why he was Clive Cussler's first choice for a co-writer. *Killing Icarus* is taut, lean and a whole lot of fun."
—Jack Du Brul, #1 *New York Times* Bestselling Author

"From the first line to the last page, *Killing Icarus* is a spectacular and moody mystery. In the capable hands of Paul Kemprecos, we get a story crafted with the intricate precision of a Swiss watch. The windswept hills of a small New England town provide a wonderful setting. Art historian Abi Vickers and lawyer turned cop, Ben Dyer are characters you'll find yourself rooting for as the pages turn and the dark secrets of an old mansion loom over them like a shadow.

Paul's style and authenticity are second to none. He's like Cape Cod's version of Tony Hillerman. I urge you to pick up *Killing Icarus*, and when you're done, go back and read Paul's other mysteries. You won't be disappointed."
—Graham Brown, *New York Times* Bestselling Author

"It takes a writer of skills and talent to weave an impressive mystery involving Nazis, a famed American artist of the 1930's and 1940's, stolen artwork, a historical glider reenactment, and so much more, but Paul Kemprecos pulls it off with skill and panache. *Killing Icarus* is a stirring tale of secrets and betrayals, of old history coming to life, but more importantly, it's a love letter to the beauty and past of Cape Cod. Highly recommended."
—Brendan DuBois, Award-Winning and *New York Times* Bestselling Author

"Art historian Abi Vickers is an intriguing and refreshing heroine, and *Killing Icarus* is a fast-paced blend of mystery and suspense set upon the idyllic Cape Cod coast—which leaves me with one question for author Paul Kemprecos: When is the next Abi Vickers book coming out?"
—Robin Burcell, *New York Times* Bestselling Author of *The Wrath of Poseidon*

"*Killing Icarus* is a tension-filled thriller that puts the reader on edge from the first page. Paul Kemprecos places you on a roller coaster ride of action and suspense that will leave you breathless and have you begging for more. His characters are richly described and his plotting impeccable. Don't miss this novel from a master writer at the top of his craft."
—Joseph Badal, Military Writers of Society of America 2020 Writer of the Year

KILLING ICARUS

PAUL KEMPRECOS

PROLOGUE

Boston, Massachusetts, 1946

The Four-Faced liar was up to its old tricks.

The quartet of clocks at the top of the Boston Custom House Tower displayed a different time on each face, a common occurrence that had earned the liar its scornful nickname.

Otto Klaas looked up at the tower from behind the steering wheel of the battered black Ford pickup truck making its way along Atlantic Avenue and shook his head. The time was slightly before or after four in the morning, depending. A public display of such imprecision would never be tolerated in Germany.

Klaas was weary after hours behind the steering wheel. His shoulders and neck ached and his pale eyes were burning from lack of sleep. Despite his discomfort, he could hardly contain his euphoria.

As he neared the harbor, gray fingers of fog reached out and enveloped the battered vehicle in a woolly grip. Klaas turned on the wipers to clear the windshield and flicked the headlights to high. The twin streams of light produced a reflected glow that was practically useless.

He slammed on the brakes. His thin lips spat out an exclamation. *Verdammit!*

Anger and frustration welled in his chest. He had come so far in the last few months, trekking over miles of war-torn landscape, living in constant fear that a sharp ear might detect his accent. Questions would then be asked. Papers demanded. The forger who sold him a new identity was good, but he'd been rushed and might have made a mistake.

The worst part of his journey was having to part with the boxes he had carried across Europe. He had placed them on a freighter bound for Boston and traveled separately on a passenger ship headed for New York. He'd been given no choice if he wanted to hide among the hordes of refugees desperate to escape from the continent.

Throughout the Atlantic crossing, as he lay in his cramped bunk, he had been haunted by the specter of possible failure. His ship made port two days before the cargo vessel reached the U.S. The truck he'd been promised was waiting for him, but it needed repairs. He bunked out in a flophouse until he got word that the cargo ship had docked. Within hours of the ship's arrival, he was on his way to Boston to retrieve the boxes.

When the fog showed no sign of lifting, Klaas extracted a sheet of paper from a breast pocket. He carefully unfolded the bill of lading and held it close to the dim light coming from the dashboard. With his forefinger he traced the route on the street map he had drawn in pencil on the reverse side.

He put the truck into gear and drove at a walking speed, the wheels only inches from the curb. He stopped, consulted the map again, and then drove the truck around a corner.

A four-story granite building loomed from the murk. The letters painted on the worn wooden door spelled out Bay State Shipping and Receiving, the same words that were on the letterhead.

He parked the truck and got out, then walked up to the warehouse and pressed the doorbell; after a short wait, he rang a second time. The door slid partially aside and a stocky workman with a face the hue of a boiled beet stuck his head through the narrow opening.

"Warehouse doesn't open until eight," the workman said.

His breath was heavy with the sour smell of whiskey.

Klaas unfolded the bill of lading and thrust it in the workman's face.

"Now," he said in the tone of someone accustomed to having his orders followed.

His lustrous silver-gray eyes gazed at the warehouse man like twin opals from behind a thin nose that angled down sharply over a tapering chin, emphasizing his resemblance to a hawk.

The warehouse man wilted like a flower under the heat from the unrelenting gaze.

"Wait here," he croaked.

He went back into the warehouse. Minutes later, he rolled the loading door fully open and pushed out a dolly that held some wooden boxes stacked vertically. Each container was around four feet square and six inches thick. Printed on the outside were the words: 'Fragile' and 'Product of Switzerland'.

"Gotta sign a receipt," the workman said.

Klaas ignored the request. He easily picked up the boxes and layered them in the back of the truck. He covered the boxes with a canvas tarp and tied the load down with manila rope to keep it from shifting.

The workman shrugged. "No skin off my nose," he muttered before he went back into the warehouse to continue his nap.

The sun was rising over the harbor, its rays shredding the fog, as Klaas set off in the yellow light of dawn. He drove back onto Atlantic Avenue and merged with the first vestiges of morning traffic. He headed south out of the city into the countryside, passing neat farms that reminded him of home.

A few hours later he crossed a bridge that arched high above a wide canal and continued on a winding, two-lane road past velvety marshes and antique houses. The air that came in the open windows smelled of saltwater and fish. Occasionally, there was a glimpse of the sea.

It never occurred to Klaas, as he enjoyed the bucolic scenery that he was participating in one of the most heinous crimes of the twentieth century. In his mind, he was a cultured German, a Nazi of convenience. He looked down upon the savage methods of his friends in the SS, even though they had actually enabled his criminality.

His actions harmed no one, he reasoned. The victims of his crimes were already dead and the future generations he was robbing of their heritage were yet to be born.

After driving nearly seventy miles along the inside curve of a peninsula shaped like a curled arm, he came to the narrowest part of the promontory, where the land was only a mile or so wide. He stopped for gas at a Mobil station with three red pumps. The man who pumped gas said he was his first customer of the day.

Klaas forced a smile and continued on his journey. A few minutes later he turned off the main road onto a narrow lane and followed it to a sandy, overgrown driveway flanked on both sides by pitch pine and scrub oak woods. He wheeled the truck onto the driveway which led to a low-slung, silver-shingled house.

Behind the house was a white barn. Colorful lobster buoys hung from nails pounded into the clapboards. He stopped in front of the house and tried the doors. Finding them locked, he drove the truck further and parked in front of the barn door.

Klaas got out of the truck again and walked through knee-high grass to a high bluff. A sea breeze blew in his face from the sun-sparkled bay. Nearly twenty years had passed since he'd stood on this spot, but the seagirt solitude was as he remembered.

He looked off at the gulls hovering over the cliffs, remembering how he had studied their flight for hours. He lifted his arms and moved them slowly up and down as if they were wings. A beatific smile came to his narrow face.

Klaas filled his lungs with fresh air. The smell of the over-crowded passenger ship decks still clung to his nostrils. He could have tarried at this windswept bluff for hours, letting the breeze blow the stink away, but he had work to do. Reluctantly, he tore himself away from the cliffs and went back to the barn.

The padlock on the door was rusted shut and would have been impossible to open even if he had a key. He took a switchblade from his pocket, stuck the point into the soft wood under the latch, and easily pried the sturdy lock and screws from the wood. Then he slid the door open and stepped into the barn.

He walked between the empty stalls that still smelled faintly of livestock and manure, then went back outside and strolled around the perimeter of the property. The farm was mostly surrounded by forest, except for the side nearest the barn where the land gently sloped down to a neglected apple orchard and a copse of red cedar trees.

All was quiet. The only sounds were the whisper of the wind in the trees and the plaintive call of the gulls. Satisfied that he could work unobserved, he went back to unload the truck.

The tranquility was deceiving, because Klaas was not alone. As he removed the boxes from the back of the truck and carried them into the barn, curious eyes studied his every move.

Extending far out to sea, away from the belching smokestacks of mainland factories, the Outer Cape was known for the peculiar quality of the sunlight that knifed through the crystal-clear atmosphere and carved objects into sharp relief.

It was this clarity that had drawn the artist to the edge of the sea. He liked to paint subjects best seen in the full light of day, skillfully applying strokes of paint to the canvas as if he were using a sunbeam for a brush.

On this day, he demanded a golden light, so he had waited until the afternoon to paint the house and barn. He also wanted the reflection of the sun glowing like fire in the windows.

The artist was a well-built man several inches over six feet in height. He wore baggy cotton slacks, an old dress shirt and a beat-up sports jacket that was practically threadbare. A crumpled fedora was pulled down over the observant blue eyes that had been absorbing the lines and textures of the old buildings.

Something bothered him. There were two wells on the property. One was near the house, the other close to the barn. He was an artist who often painted not what a scene actually was, but how he felt it should be. Sometimes he composed parts of other scenes into his finished work.

The lobster buoys symbolized a local way of life, but they hadn't been used in a long time. He liked the solitude and quiet of the scene, along with its hint of mystery. Had the lobsterman grown too old to work? Or had he died from the toil and struggle of everyday life?

The artist loved the play of shadows and sunlight on simple buildings, especially on white and yellow. To him, the exterior of a building was like an unpainted canvas. But the wells stood between the artist and his subject, so he simply sketched the scene as if the little walls and cupolas were not there. He thought about putting the wells off to the side but decided that would spoil the composition.

The artist had finished a sketch of the farmhouse and barn, when he heard the grumble of an exhaust and the crush of tires on the shells in the driveway. His full lips tightened. He tucked the charcoal pencil behind an ear, turned and strode briskly on long legs toward the stand of red cedar trees. Seconds after he had melted unseen into the woods, a pickup truck came around the farmhouse and parked in front of the barn.

Hidden from view in the trees, the artist felt a twinge of embarrassment for bolting like a scared rabbit.

Technically speaking, he was trespassing, although the house had been vacant for years. More important, he hated to be watched while at work. He was a private man. The last thing the artist desired or needed was someone peering over his shoulder as he made the quick pencil sketches that would lay the foundation for an oil painting.

Vanity played a role as well. He didn't want observers to think the rough sketches were anywhere near the final product. In fact, the sketches often looked far different from the picture he would paint in his studio. He had planned the sketch session days before he'd even sharpened his drawing pencils, and had made a number of treks to the scene from his house to study the effect of light at different times of day. He had hiked some distance across the grassy downs from his house and come onto the property from the rear.

The artist was celebrated for his bleak portraits of the city. His most famous work showed the denizens of a cheap restaurant late at night. But the artist loved to paint old houses and rolling dunes, and he was attracted by people doing their jobs, like a man tending a gas pump at night. Or office people working late in the day. He was equally intrigued by the pickup truck now parked near the barn doors. The long, pointed hood and the grill reminded him of the baleen smile of a whale.

A man got out of the truck. He wore the tan, belted, one-piece coveralls of a workman. A navy knit cap was pulled down over his forehead. The artist liked his pictures to project an air of mystery. In this case, he envisioned the delivery man making his last stop of the day. Maybe someone was moving in and the truck was delivering furniture. But why here, to the dilapidated old Snow farm where no one had lived for years?

The artist watched the man walk to the edge of the cliffs. He could have made his escape while the man gazed off at the bay, but he was curious now what the stranger was up to. After a few minutes, the man turned from the cliffs and, with purpose in his stride, walked to the barn door and slid it open after briefly fiddling with the lock. He went inside, then emerged and came back to the truck, dropped the tailgate and whipped aside a tarpaulin.

Reaching onto the truck bed, he slid out a crate and guided it slowly until one edge rested on the ground. The crate was hinged at the top and fastened with a padlock. The man squatted slightly, spread his arms, his fingers curling around the edges of the box, and then carried it into the barn.

He came out and repeated the action with five more boxes.

As he worked, his labors were caught on the artist's sketch pad. After he'd carried the last box into the barn, the man sat on the tailgate and lit up a cigarette. He took a drag, then removed the knit cap. Seeing the opportunity for a clearer view of the man's face the artist side-stepped a few yards. In the process, he stepped onto a fallen branch.

The noise of wood breaking was only a snap, but the man slid off the tailgate, dropped the cigarette to the ground, then walked to the edge of the woods and stared into the trees.

The artist was dressed in brown and a broad-brimmed hat was pulled down low on his forehead, so he was hoping that in the afternoon light he blended in with the cedars. At the same time, he was in a good position to see the man's narrow face, the silver eyes, gray skin that looked as if it seldom saw sunlight, and the thin nose with the lower half that angled down from the bridge.

It was one of the most frightening faces he had ever seen.

The man's hand slipped inside the front pocket of his coveralls and came out with an object that caught the flash of reflected sunlight. He took a few steps toward the trees.

The artist felt a coldness in the pit of his stomach as he saw the knife pointing straight out at waist level. He stood as still as a statue. He remained in this position for what seemed like hours before the man closed the knife and tucked it back inside the coveralls. He went over to the barn, stepped inside and slid the door closed.

Although the temperature was cool, perspiration beaded the artist's forehead. His heart beat like a jack-hammer. His knees were weak.

He glanced at the notepad in his sweaty hands and realized that despite his fears, or maybe because of them, he had sketched the man's face. His hand seemed to have acted on its own, directing the pencil in quick, short strokes.

It was time to leave…before the man emerged from the barn. He tromped through the woods, then loped over the rolling heath land. Although he was winded from exertion, he didn't stop to rest until he returned to his simple studio at the edge of the sea. He quickly ducked inside; his shaking hands bolted the door shut.

CHAPTER ONE

Truro, Massachusetts: The Present

The eight-thousand-square-foot pile of concrete slabs Eddy Baron built at the edge of Cape Cod Bay as his summer house was considered a monstrosity by everybody except its owner.

The mansion had inspired Baron's unhappy neighbors to impressive heights of creativity. Most of the terms they used at summer cocktail parties to describe the house weren't the kind usually heard in polite company. The one that stuck was Fort Baron.

Much of their ire was directed at a rectangular tower jutting from the mansion's flat-roofed second story. People who knew Baron agreed that the rude architectural gesture was no accident. He knew that a feature suggesting a concrete middle finger was bound to antagonize his neighbors.

The town fought the house project from the minute the blueprints landed on the building inspector's desk. Baron had hired the best engineers and the meanest snake lawyers. The plans met all the legal requirements or came close enough to slip by.

Also upsetting townspeople were Eddy's plans for the old Snow farm buildings. The nineteenth century house and barn would have to come down to make way for the new building. Legal counsel for the town tried to block the demolition of the house, citing its age and historic value. Their argument might have prevailed if the house hadn't burned down one night. Cause unknown.

Baron's acquaintances said that was typical Eddy, too. What they found surprising was that the barn didn't go up in flames as well.

The town was still bleeding cash from an earlier lawsuit involving a different property. Baron had deep pockets and the legal fight against his house plan stretched on until the town depleted its legal budget. They got one concession; a judge ruled that the barn was historic, too. Baron simply resorted to the demolition by neglect. The white paint had mostly peeled off, showing splotches of brown and gray.

Surrounding the Baron estate was a high chain link fence topped by electrified razor wire more typical of a maximum-security prison than a vacation retreat. Baron amplified the penitentiary comparison when he often patrolled a path that ran along the inside of the fence. He made it known he had permits for two pistols and a military assault rifle and wouldn't hesitate to use them on trespassers.

Baron had earned a fortune in the car business. He sold low and made up the difference with financing contracts and a service department that charged top rates for inferior parts. Since selling his car dealerships for millions of dollars, Baron spent a lot of time alone at the house.

His three marriages all had ended in divorce. He had no children and didn't trust his relatives, with good reason. He dabbled in old motels, fixing them up slightly and running them as housing for indigents, winos and sex offenders. When people complained, Baron pointed out that he only rented to level one, the lowest risk offender.

When he wasn't patrolling the perimeter, he loved to sit in his high tower office and make deals. His latest scheme involved the purchase of old cottage colonies, replacing them with multi-level condos that cut off the neighbors' view. He was at his desk, going over the latest venture, thinking how much fun it would be to rile up the locals again, when he heard a strange *thunk* sound above his head.

He looked up at the ceiling and a frown crossed his wide face. The noise had come from the observation deck on the top of the tower above the office. He took a gulp from the beer he'd been drinking, let out a loud belch, then glanced at the television monitor displaying images from the network of security cameras on the property.

Using his remote control, he checked out the screens that showed the fence, the swimming pool and tennis court. Nothing.

Baron was a bull of a man. Big shoulders and bone-crushing hands. He stayed in shape, and was dressed in a work-out suit, having come to his office from his private gym. But Baron always liked to have insurance. He slid a Glock 9mm out of his desk drawer and climbed down the stairs to the terrace surrounding the house.

Seeing nothing out of the ordinary, he decided to investigate the observation deck.

The deck was accessible by way of the inside stairs from his office or a ladder running from the terrace up the side of the tower. He tucked the pistol into his waistband and climbed the outside ladder. As his head rose a few inches above the level of the roof, he saw a blur of movement on the observation platform and reached with his right hand for the gun.

Too late. Something hard smashed into his face, splintering his nose, driving the shards into his brain. His head snapped back. The gun dropped from his hand onto the terrace and Baron pitched backwards off the ladder.

His body made a soggy thud when he hit the terrace. The impact broke his ribs and fractured his skull. As the life drained from his burly body, Baron's glazed eyes saw a shadow pass overhead and his ears heard a soft fluttering sound. By the time the evidence of his senses reached his brain, he was already dead.

CHAPTER TWO

Boston: Three Weeks Later

Something was wrong.

Abi Vickers could tell the news was not good as soon as the door opened, and the mediator stepped back into the conference room. The paste-on smile the retired judge wore on her perfectly made-up face when she'd gone out the door five minutes earlier had vanished. Instead, her lips were compressed in a tight red line.

She settled primly into her chair at the head of the table and placed a yellow legal pad down in front of her. Abi noticed only a few brief notes written on the top page.

"Well," the mediator said, glancing at her pad. "The other party refuses to budge on the extension."

"You told them I was prepared to go to trial on this?" Abi said.

"I did. They think they'll win if you do."

"But they might lose. I don't get it. Why doesn't their insurance company pressure them to settle?"

The mediator rolled her eyes. "They have no insurance. They never renewed it."

"I was under the impression that they had insurance."

"That was the original creditor. We're talking about the company that bought them out. Even if you won at trial, I'm afraid you'd get nothing." She raised her hands palms up in a gesture of helplessness.

Nothing. The last word in the mediator's pronouncement seemed to echo off the walls of the small room. Three years of litigation, a hundred thousand in legal fees, dozens of court hearings and depositions, a subpoena tucked in her front door practically every Friday, countless sleepless nights and a marriage on the rocks. And a once-thriving art business that was in shambles.

Not to mention the twelve hundred dollars the mediator was being paid to walk back and forth between two rented conference rooms.

"Nothing?" Abi said, barely able to say the word.

The mediator nodded. "The property is going on the market immediately. The good news is they've given you a week before you have to vacate your apartment."

Abi felt as if she were about to sink into the floor. Tears welled in her hazel eyes.

"But that's not fair," she said to the mediator.

The mediator must have heard similar complaints before, because without missing a beat, she said, "Fair is a four-letter word you will never hear uttered in the mediation room."

Abi's mouth dropped open in an expression of disbelief. "What are you saying?"

"Your lawyers can explain it. I'll give you a few minutes to talk about what you want to do." She rose from her chair, picked her legal pad off the table and glanced at her watch. "I'll be outside if you have any questions, but I've got another mediation scheduled in exactly ten minutes."

She exited the room leaving a cloud of perfume hanging in the air behind her. Abi turned to her two lawyers who had been typing into their cell phones on the other side of the table. *Probably dealing with other clients*, she thought.

"You heard the mediator just tell me that 'fair' is a four-letter word that no one says in this room. Please explain."

The lawyers stopped typing and looked up, then at each other, then at Abi.

"It's not a question of fairness," the male lawyer said. "It's a question of law."

"Okay," Abi said, struggling to keep her voice steady. "Let's talk about the law. And why no one told me before I wasted tens of thousands of dollars and three years of my life that the legal system is rigged."

"That's not exactly how I'd put it," the female lawyer said.

"That's *exactly* how I'd put it. In fact, I'd go so far as to say flat-out that the system is nothing but a criminal enterprise. It's totally dishonest. It's not about finding the truth or righting wrongs. It's about everyone making a buck. The clerks who handled the endless filings, the stenographers who sat in for hours of depositions, the half-wit judge who allowed this case to go forward even though there wasn't a legal leg to stand on." She paused and added, "The lawyers who enable it."

"We agree that the system isn't perfect," the male lawyer said.

"Actually, it *is* perfect at what it does, which is to suck the last drop of blood from people like me, then kick them out to make room for the next juicy victim," Abi said. "We all know the judge should never have allowed this case to go to the next step."

"We were surprised at that ruling, too. But, unfortunately, once you're in the legal vortex it's hard to get out."

"Let me tell you something about that little ol' vortex of yours. It should have protected me. Instead, I got depositions scheduled on birthdays, subpoenas timed so my weekends would be miserable, my friends and family dragged in, paper dumps of tens of thousands of emails to sort through, and endless hearings. All just to make my life hell so I'd cave. And when I finally get the mediation after months of asking, I'm told I get nothing for all my time and trouble and anguish."

"We understand why you're upset," the female attorney said. "But this isn't all bad. You're sitting in the catbird seat. You don't have to accept the mediation. You can go after them. What they did borders on the criminal. You can drag them into court and I can almost guarantee that a jury will find for you after they hear the evidence."

"How long a trial? And when?"

"There would actually be two trials, lasting about a week each. With the right judge we can schedule them in about six months."

"Half a year?"

"Right."

"How much is this catbird seat going to cost me?"

The lawyers put their heads together, and the male finally said, "About a hundred thousand dollars."

"And if I win, will they be required to pay me back, plus legal fees?"

"Well, no," the female said. "Then they could appeal. That may take months depending on how many hearings and what judge we get."

"Judges almost never award legal fees," her colleague said.

Abi said, "No. We are done. Finished."

"Are you sure?"

She brushed away a strand of auburn hair from her forehead, then firmly crossed her arms. The lawyers got the message, because the male attorney reached into his briefcase and pulled out a sheet of paper, which he slid across the table. "This is the final bill for our services. No hurry," he added as an afterthought.

Abi glanced at the bill, which was for $978, then slowly stood, placed her palms flat on the tabletop and leaned forward. She told the lawyer to do something with his body that was anatomically impossible for anyone except a contortionist, then smiled at his female colleague.

"No hurry."

She stormed out of the room without a glance at the mediator talking on her cell phone in the hall. She took the elevator to the ground floor of the building on Federal Street, one of the vertical hives infested by scores of lawyers who rented space by the hour. She walked toward Boston Common, crossed the Public Garden and made her way several blocks to the South End, finally stopping in front of an empty storefront.

The 'For Sale' sign posted on the window had the added sales pitch: *Suitable for Art Gallery*. There was further information on the sign that the commercial space included an apartment. Her gallery and her apartment.

Abi had always loved art even if she wasn't very good at creating it, and her mother was a high school art teacher. She wanted to study art history in college. Her father was a hard-driving corporate executive who said he would pay for her art history courses if she made it a minor and business her major.

She agreed, discovered that she had a flare for business and joined an investment firm where she worked for ten years. She stockpiled enough money, which with an inheritance from her parents, enabled her to quit business and indulge her love of art as a gallery owner. She opened the Boston gallery and another on Nantucket.

She met her husband on Nantucket. He was a good-looking and charming commercial real estate broker who wanted to become a property owner. He persuaded her to put the gallery and apartment up as collateral. The deal sounded shaky, but what the heck, he was her husband and she was in love.

Her instincts were sound even if her judgment in husbands was not. He got in over his head, started drinking heavily, had an affair with his secretary, and then ran off leaving her holding the legal bag. And a heavy bag it was, filled with troubles she hadn't dreamed existed. She had lost her business. Even more heart-breaking, she had lost her parents' hard-earned savings. The Nantucket gallery was only a rental space, but the South End property was hers. Now she was about to lose her home.

Her cell phone rang. The caller ID showed the name Andrew Waldstein, a professor from her days studying at Williams College in Western Massachusetts. They had kept in touch after she graduated.

"Hello, Professor Waldstein. It's wonderful to hear your voice. How are you?"

"I'm fine, Abi. But more important, how are you? The last time we talked you were optimistic that today was when the lawsuit would end in your favor."

She glanced at the 'For Sale' sign. "It ended today, but not the way I wanted. I'm still reeling from the settlement, which gives me nothing."

"Oh dear. I'm so sorry. Maybe this is a bad time to bother you about helping me with a project."

"Actually, it's a very *good* time to take my mind off things."

"Wonderful. Can you come and see me at the museum?"

"I'll be there in fifteen minutes," she said.

She hung up and tapped the phone to call up an Uber driver. A car arrived almost immediately and minutes later she was walking up the wide stairway into the Greek revival-style edifice that houses Boston's Museum of Fine Arts. She showed her membership pass and followed a hallway until she came to a door. She knocked, was told to enter, and then stepped into the office of her old college mentor.

Professor Waldstein sat behind a big wooden desk that was crammed into the office with filing cabinets and stacks of art books and paper folders. Waldstein got up and edged around the desk to give her a hug. He located a folding chair, set it up in front of his desk and invited her to sit down.

"It's so good of you to come. I'm sorry you've had a rough time."

Andrew Waldstein was in his seventies. He was still an avid jogger and exerciser, and had long ago exchanged his jacket and tie for a closet-full of stylish running suits and high-tech shoes. He kept his body, and more importantly, his mind, in shape. His energy and full head of silvery hair knocked at least a decade off his apparent age.

"Thank you. But the worst of it is over," she fibbed. "You've got me excited with this project you have in mind. Please don't keep me in suspense."

He leaned back in his chair and spread his arms wide.

"*This* is the project."

Abi looked around the office. "I'm not sure I understand, Professor."

"As you can see by the chaos that surrounds us, my files and records are completely out of control. I need everything in this office to be put right. I've been offered a two-week teaching job in Paris, at the Sorbonne, and I can't pass it up. I'm looking for someone to organize my files and catalog this mess into a computer."

"I'm not sure if I'm the person for the job, Professor."

"You're *exactly* the one for the job. I trust you. You've got a background in art history and business. And since there is a bit of both in this sea of chaos that I am sinking into, you'd be perfectly suited to get the good ship Waldstein afloat once more. I can pay you a small stipend, and I won't be using my cottage in Truro. I can have my files shipped and you can work there."

Abi had visited the professor a couple of times at the cottage, now part of an art colony. It was a beautiful location, high on a hill overlooking Cape Cod Bay seated around a hundred miles from Boston. Maybe, she thought, an infusion of beauty was just what she needed to counter the ugliness of the last few years. She wondered if Waldstein was using the job offer as a charitable gesture. Judging from the mess in his office, he could use some help. She didn't have any choice, but she did have her pride.

"Okay, I'll do it, but not for pay. As a favor for a friend."

"That's very kind of you, Abi. I insist on one condition, though. I have a credit line at the local food market. I'd like you to use it to stock up the cupboards at the cottage." He smiled. "They also have a good wine selection."

"How can I resist an offer like that?" Abi said. "I'll take it."

CHAPTER THREE

Truro, Massachusetts: One Week Later

The white Porsche Carrera zoomed past the darkened restaurant in a spectacular example of bad timing. It was two o'clock in the morning and the convertible was the only car on Route 6, except for the black police cruiser pulling out of the restaurant parking lot.

The police car swung onto the highway with roof lights flashing, and pulled the sports car over to the berm.

Patrolman Ben Dyer got out of the cruiser, and with a glance at the orange and black New York plate, he walked over to the driver's side and asked for license and registration.

After he scanned the papers, Ben said, "Did you know you were going more than sixty in a forty-five mile per hour speed zone, Mr. Handler?"

"No, I didn't, Officer," the driver said with contriteness. "I guess I wasn't thinking about how fast I was going."

"It's pretty late. Where were you headed in such a big hurry?"

"Nowhere," the man said, lowering his voice almost to a mumble. "Just trying to cool off. I had a fight with my wife." He smirked. "Bet you haven't heard that one before."

"A few times. What was the fight about?"

"We're here on vacation with the kids. First time in months. I'm a lawyer. I got a call from my office in New York. They want me back on a case. She exploded. Didn't buy my excuse that my work pays for the nice beach cottage and her Mercedes SUV. I went flying out of the house. Lost track of my speed. No one on the road this time of night."

"Did you have anything to drink?"

"Hell, no. I'd be happy to take a breathalyzer test. Stone cold sober."

"It doesn't matter how sober you were, Mr. Handler. There could have been someone else on the road. Maybe another angry guy with wife and kids who's so pissed off that he doesn't see a stop sign and comes out onto the highway just in time for you to T-bone him."

"I know, I know, Officer. I'm sorry."

"Tell you what, Mr. Handler," Ben said. He ripped a sheet of paper off a pad and handed it to the driver. "I'm going to give you a warning this time. Slow down. Go back home and talk things over with your wife."

The driver took the printed warning and said, "Thank you, Officer. You must have been a marriage counselor before you became a cop."

"Actually, I was a lawyer."

"A lawyer? Where did you practice?"

Ben gave him the name of a Boston law firm.

"Now I'm really impressed. That firm only takes Harvard Law guys."

"You got it. We had a Yalie. Don't know how he snuck in."

"What's someone like you doing playing summer cop?"

"Long story, but it'll have to wait, Mr. Handler. I'm on the job and you've got to get back to your wife and kids."

"Thanks again, Officer. This must be my lucky day."

He cranked the ignition and drove off at a snail's pace. Ben watched the red taillights disappear around a curve, and murmured, "Mr. Handler, you don't know how lucky you are."

He got back in the cruiser and stayed on Route 6, driving as far as the town line shared with Provincetown to the north, then crossed near the promontory known as High Head to the Cape Cod Bay side of town. He passed through the intersection that marks the tiny village of North Truro and turned left at the general store.

Minutes later he pulled into a parking lot with a view of Highland Light, the oldest lighthouse on Cape Cod.

He watched the blue-black sky lighten to a dark gray over the golf links built near the bluffs that overlook the Atlantic. After a few minutes, he drove out of the parking lot and rejoined Route 6 south, which bisects Truro, until he came to the town line for Wellfleet, where he turned around and headed back. He detoured off the highway through Truro's blink-of-an-eye town center and then rejoined Route 6.

With its high cliffs and miles of beaches, moors and heath, Truro bore some resemblance to its namesake on the Cornwall coast of England where some of its early settlers came from. Although it was only twenty-six square miles in area, much of it protected by the federal government, Truro had miles of back roads that dead-ended at the bay or ocean.

Ben could have done his entire shift with his eyes closed. He had grown up in the town, and he knew every inch of the Narrow Land as the poetically inclined called it. In school he'd been taught that it was a water stop for the Pilgrims, was settled in the 1600s and was a thriving fishing town before it became a summer resort.

It was eerily quiet in early June, but once school let out the weekends would become busier, culminating in a big crush of people and cars on July 4th weekend.

Truro had a split personality. The year-round population was only around two thousand, but that swelled eight-fold in summer. Many people come to enjoy the town's miles of beaches, although its unique and remote geography attracted artists, writers, intellectuals, and psychiatrists.

His shift was almost over. He headed back to the low-slung gray clapboard police building on State Road, pulled into a parking space and went inside.

Chief Bill Sisson stepped out of his office and intercepted him on the way to the locker room. "How did the shift go last night, Ben?"

"Quiet as the grave."

The chief was a tall man who still wore his hair cut short and shaved on the sides, military style, a hold-over from his days as a

Marine, and later, a State Police officer.

"The calm before the storm," Sisson said, shaking his head. "Hey, Ben. I've got a favor to ask. I'd like you to check out a special duty job. Joe Quinn was supposed to run the detail, but he got the flu or something and will be out for a few days. We're not at full shift strength yet, so I need someone to fill in for him. You can work around your night schedule."

Quinn was a long-time veteran on the police force. "Sorry to hear about Joe. Sure, what's the assignment?"

"Some folks are going to be flying a glider off the cliffs near Corn Hill. We need a traffic detail to keep people and cars from getting too close to the action. Thought with your experience flying planes it'd be right up your alley."

Dyer had done a few flights since getting his pilot's license, which hardly qualified him to man the space shuttle, but he'd always been fascinated by aircraft of any kind.

"Sounds interesting. What are the details?"

The chief handed him a paper. "Press conference is this afternoon. Info is in the email. Thanks for doing this, Ben. Let me know how you make out." He went back into his office.

Ben didn't need the special detail, but he was reluctant to bother the busy chief with small stuff. Sisson had been kind to him, in part because his own wife had died a few years earlier, and he knew what Ben was going through.

Ben read the email, which announced a press conference at the Provincetown Inn at 3 PM. He'd have time to get a nap in.

He left the cruiser, got into his white Ford 150 pickup and drove onto the main highway heading south until he turned off on Pamet Harbor Road. Before he got as far as the harbor, he drove down a short driveway to a white clapboard Cape Cod house with black shutters, set on a low hill back from the road.

The house was the style known as a full Cape. It had two windows on either side of the front door, as opposed to a half Cape, which had two windows on one side, and a three-quarter version, with three windows in all. The house had come down through his family. The Dyers went back generations in Truro.

He went in through the side door, stepped into the kitchen

that ran most of the width of the house, then climbed a steep set of stairs to a bedroom on the second floor. The house was a wreck when they got it, but he and his wife, Loren, had restored it to its original simple glory. Like most Cape Cod houses, it faced south, and their bedroom was on the side where it received first light in the morning.

"I'm home," he said to no one in the quietness of the two-hundred-year-old house.

Loren had been such a strong presence in his life, especially when they were in the house that she loved more than anywhere else. He could easily imagine, even hope maybe, that someday she would answer him. It was probably mentally unhealthy, but thinking that she was in another room helped him cope.

He stripped down to his underwear, hung his uniform in the closet, set the alarm and slipped under the cool sheets, alone, into his empty bed.

CHAPTER FOUR

Boston: The Present

On the last night Abi would spend in her apartment, three friends took her out to dinner at her favorite Italian restaurant in Boston's North End. The gathering was supposed to cheer her up, but the small size of the group only highlighted what a train wreck her life had become.

The hugs and well wishes at the end of the meal helped, but when Abi went home after dinner she polished off a half a bottle of rosé wine on top of what she drank at the restaurant.

She spent a sleepless night tossing and turning in her bed. When she came fully awake at dawn, her mouth felt like a vat of fermented grapes.

After brushing her teeth she showered, got dressed in jeans, a beige cotton sweatshirt and running shoes. She had purposely left everything until the last minute. She should probably have packed the night before and left her place as soon as she got up. Like ripping a bandage off a wound, the pain would only have lasted an instant. Instead, she had procrastinated for as long as she could.

She unplugged her computer and printer and put them in boxes. On top of the boxes she set the long plastic case containing her Japanese bow and arrows. She had developed an interest in Zen archery as a way of diverting her mind from her troubles, but hadn't picked up her bow during the litigation's final phase.

Waldstein had promised to ship his files to the cottage. Her personal belongings were in storage. What was left of the furniture would join those articles when the movers showed up later that day. There was really nothing for her to do except walk aimlessly from room to room. She took one last sad look around, then left the apartment, shutting the door on the enviable life she had once enjoyed.

Before leaving, she put the key under the mat. It took a couple of trips to carry her bags and computer down to her 1982 Land Rover parked in an alley behind the house. The paint on the vintage vehicle had mostly faded, but there was still a trace left of the original light green. Enough so that she could still combine the words Green Rover into its nickname. Grover.

After a stop at Starbucks to pick up a double latte she got on her way. She felt emotionally dead. It had nothing to do with her hangover. The weeks since the lawsuit sank into the swampy muck of mediation had been a whirl of activity that kept her busy during the day and dog-tired at night.

Abi was amazed at how quickly things were wrapped up once the blood-sucking tentacles of the civil court system were detached so they could squeeze the life's blood from another poor soul. She had to deal with the business, or what was left of it, making calls for employees who had lost their jobs and needed references. Even more painful was dealing with the artists.

A handful of men and women who had showed their work regularly at her galleries had become homeless when the doors closed. Some of the better-known ones had found new galleries, but the artists who were on their way up in their careers were still without a home.

Abi made good time out of the city and finished her coffee and a protein bar long before she sighted the parabolic framework of the Sagamore Bridge arcing over the Cape Cod Canal. She stopped for a refill at a coffee shop near the canal, then drove over the bridge.

Cape Cod is an arm-shaped peninsula of dunes and beaches that curls back toward Boston and holds Cape Cod Bay in its embrace.

She had nearly another hour behind the wheel before she reached Truro where the cottage was located.

Abi used to visit galleries and artists in the nearby town of Provincetown, the old fishing and art colony at the tip of the Cape. On those occasions she flew Cape Air or took the fast ferry out of Boston. This was the first time in years she had taken the land route.

As she drove past sun-sparkled blue water coves and inlets, the burden she had been carrying seemed to slip from her shoulders with each breath of salty air. By the time she arrived in Truro and turned off Route 6 onto a narrow, snaking road, Boston—and all the troubles it represented—seemed far behind her.

She might have driven by the row of mailboxes at the entrance to a driveway if not for the Google Maps voice on the phone telling her she had reached her destination. She braked the Land Rover to a stop. The name Waldstein was printed neatly on an aluminum mailbox. The driveway was marked by a sign that read: Flower Cottage Colony.

A wooden barricade with a 'No Trespassing' sign on it blocked the driveway. She wasn't sure what to do, but she was a guest of a cottage owner, which meant she wasn't a trespasser. More importantly, she hadn't stopped anywhere to use a restroom after finishing the second coffee.

Nature's call made the decision for her. She got out of the Land Rover, pushed the barricade aside, then got back behind the wheel and steered Grover up a driveway for about a quarter of a mile to a line of six cottages trimmed in ornate scroll woodwork. Their front porches faced the bay. Between the cottages and the brow of the hill was an expanse of scraggly grass, roughly circular in shape and a couple of hundred feet across.

The one-and-a-half story white-trimmed gingerbread cottages were built in the 1930s as an artists' colony. Wind and sun had turned their cedar shingles a silver gray. Nailed to the weathered trim over each porch was a quarter board inscribed with the name of the cottage. The buildings were named after common local flowers and other plants.

She backed the Land Rover up in front of the cottage named Beach Plum, got out of the car and stepped onto the porch. Waldstein had given her an old-fashioned skeleton key. She opened the door, stepped inside and breathed in musty air that set off a coughing spell.

The knotty-pine living room was furnished with a wood-framed sofa and two matching chairs, all with orange cushions, gathered around a fieldstone fireplace. In front of the hearth screen was an old-fashioned braided rug.

She poked her head through a door on her right into an office containing metal filing cabinets and an oak desk with an office chair that faced the front window. The walls were lined with bookshelves holding a combination of art and Cape Cod themed volumes written by authors, like Joseph C. Lincoln and Henry D. Thoreau. Stacked in a corner were at least two dozen cardboard boxes. The professor's files.

"Dear God," she murmured. She'd need two years, not two weeks to organize the files.

Beyond the office was what she was looking for; the door to the bathroom. When she came out she explored the living room and its adjoining kitchenette. In between the bathroom and the kitchenette was a back door and a spiral metal stairway that went up to the bedroom. She went through the door and discovered it led from the kitchenette to a small backyard that overlooked low hills covered with low vegetation. A path led from the yard into the rolling heath land that was largely open except for a few houses in the distance.

Next, she brought her computer and printer in from the Land Rover and set them up on the desk. Then she brought her archery case and suitcase in. She leaned the bow set up against a wall and carried the suitcase up the stairs.

Sunlight was pouring in through the windows on three sides of the room onto the blue and white coverlets of a pineapple-style poster bed. There was a maple and cushioned chair with matching upholstery and a white painted dresser with blue knobs. The floors were covered with shag rugs.

The front windows looked out on a small rail-lined porch. There was no door to the porch so anyone using it would have to crawl through a window. She opened some windows and left the door ajar to air the place out, then put her clothes in the dresser or hung them in a closet. Next, she went back downstairs and hooked up her computer and printer.

After setting up her workstation she checked the refrigerator and found that it was empty. Abi realized she hadn't thought about food. The grocery store where the professor had a credit was in Wellfleet, a fifteen-minute drive from the cottage.

For the first time in months—years, maybe—she actually looked forward to something even if it was as simple as buying groceries. Not complicated like a lawsuit, with a mob of lawyers in dark suits, endless hearings before irritable judges who would rather be presiding over a murder trial, mindless depositions meant to wear down or play *gotcha* with testimony.

She had been crushed by bankruptcy and kicked out of her apartment, but with the lawsuit behind her she could concentrate on restoring her life and her reputation. First, she had to find something to eat.

Abi had never particularly cared for ABBA, the Swedish rock group, but as she drove down the driveway the song "Dancing Queen" popped into her head. She was living in borrowed accommodations, with no hint of where she would end up or what she would be doing in the future. But as she hummed the tune she realized that it was the first time in a very long while she was feeling good about herself.

CHAPTER FIVE

The alarm clock woke Ben up at two o'clock in the afternoon to start his new career as a traffic detail officer. He got out of bed and stretched, then washed away his residual sleepiness in the shower.

Another short nap was in his schedule before going on duty at midnight, so he didn't get back into uniform. Instead, he dressed in jeans and a blue short-sleeved shirt. He pinned his badge to his front pocket. He brewed coffee in the French press, poured it into a travel mug and got behind the wheel of his truck.

Less than ten minutes later, he crested a hill and was greeted by a sweeping view of Provincetown. The town was hemmed in between the rolling dunes of the Province Lands and the long curving shore of the harbor. The granite spike perched high on a hill above the old fishing village was Pilgrim Monument, a 252-foot-tall replica of a tower in Siena, Italy, built to honor the *Mayflower* and its Pilgrim passengers who anchored in Provincetown Harbor after arriving in the New World.

Ben turned left off the highway onto the shore road and drove past weathered beachfront cottages and waterfront motels. At a fork in the road he went right onto Bradford Street, bypassing the commercial waterfront strip of galleries, restaurants and bars.

Eventually he came to the Provincetown Inn, a sprawling resort complex built on an artificial peninsula at the very tip of Cape Cod. He parked near a long breakwater and went through the resort entrance into a lobby decorated with murals depicting scenes from the town's long and salty past.

A sign with the words *Wings Over Cape Cod Press Conference* stood on an easel in the lobby. He followed the arrow on the sign down a hallway to the conference room named on the sign, opened the door and stepped inside. About a dozen people sat in rows of folding chairs in front of a low platform. Quietly shutting the door behind him, Ben took a seat.

Three people faced the audience from behind a table on the platform. The two men and the woman sitting between them wore sky-blue T-shirts. Behind the table was a projection screen.

The image on the screen was divided into four triangular sections. The top middle space enclosed a black-and-white photograph of an odd-looking plane with narrow wings and a high tail. In the space directly below the photo, the cover of *Sky Technology Magazine* displayed a picture of the same aircraft. Logos with the words Wing Tech and MAC filled the other sections.

The woman smiled and said something to the man on her right who tapped the microphone in front of him to make sure it was live.

"Hello, everyone," he said, flashing an easy grin. "Thank you all for coming. My name is Kyle Magnus. I'm the owner of Wing Tech." He turned toward the screen and pointed to a logo. "On my left, handling the PowerPoint presentation, is Melissa Winslow, editor of *Sky Technology Magazine*. Sitting next to Melissa is Hank Aldrich, president and owner of MAC, which stands for Motorless Aircraft Corporation. Like Wing Tech, MAC designs and builds unpowered aircraft."

As a lawyer, Ben had become adept at sizing up jurors, judges and opposing attorneys with a quick glance around a courtroom. Old habits are slow to die. He studied the panel and guessed that Magnus was in his forties. A thick mane of platinum hair framed the tanned face. With his brawny arms and shoulders straining the seams of his T-shirt, Magnus looked as if he'd stepped out of an episode of *Baywatch*. Melissa could have come from the same cast. Blonde and rosy-cheeked, she acknowledged the introduction with a flash of perfect white teeth.

In contrast, Aldrich looked like a candidate for the 'Sourpuss of the Year' award. He was older than the other panelists and was slightly balding. The lips in his pale face were pursed like a disapproving schoolteacher. The T-shirt sagged on shoulders that were slightly hunched forward. He blinked through thick-lensed glasses and nodded politely at the mention of his name, but showed no more emotion than a fence post.

Melissa clicked the laptop computer mouse. The screen montage disappeared and in its place was a grainy, black-and-white photo of a man wearing a close-fitting leather pilot cap and round goggles.

"The gentleman on the screen wearing the Snoopy cap is Peter Hesselbach," Magnus said. "He was one of the leading fliers of the Darmstadt Academic Flying Group in Germany. In May of 1928, he arrived in the U.S. with two German colleagues, Captain Paul Franz Roehre and Dr. Paul Lubethal. They were in America at the invitation of J. C. Penney Jr., heir to the department store fortune."

Melissa added, "In July of 1928, Hesselbach broke two world flying records for non-motorized flight a few miles from where we're sitting. The first flight was on July 26 at the Highland golf links overlooking the Atlantic Ocean on the easterly shore of Cape Cod. He stayed in the air for fifty-eight minutes in a three-hundred-pound glider. The flight broke the record set in 1911 by Orville Wright, who had soared for nine minutes and forty-five seconds at Kitty Hawk in a box-glider. This is a video of Hesselbach's first flight."

Melissa clicked the mouse again. The video on the screen showed the long-winged aircraft flying low over a crowd of people. The video ended after a few seconds and was replaced by a photo showing what looked like the same glider in the air above a sandy cliff.

"Hesselbach followed a two mile course above the beach and as far as fifteen-hundred-feet out to sea before coming back to fly over the spectators."

She turned to Kyle, who said, "A few days later, on July 31st, Hesselbach flew a glider off Corn Hill on the west side of the Cape. He was attempting to beat the world soaring record of fourteen hours, twenty-three minutes set by another German pilot. Bonfires were stretched along the beach in case Hesselbach went into the night. He had to land early because of wind conditions, but still managed to set another new U.S. record with his flight of four hours and five minutes.

"And this week," Melissa said, "we will attempt to reenact this second flight. Yes, I see a raised hand."

The man wearing a lurid Hawaiian shirt would have been hard to miss. He was well over six feet in height, and his shoulders were slightly hunched, as if he spent a lot of time talking to people who weren't as tall. His unruly black hair looked as if it had been combed with his fingers and his drooping mustache gave him an almost melancholy look.

Speaking with a slight accent, he said, "Thank you. My name is Marty Weber. I am a pool reporter for the Southern Germany News Syndicate based in Darmstadt, here to cover the reenactment." He smiled. "Pardon my Teutonic insistence on precision, however, which prompts me to point out that this is now June, not July."

"Good catch, Marty," Magnus said, giving Weber a quick smile and a thumbs-up. "Thanks for the question. Doing the flight on the exact date would have put us smack in the middle of the tourist season, making it impossible to get around with the traffic and the summer crowds. We scheduled the event a month earlier. A greater disappointment was not being able to use Corn Hill itself, which has become built up since the 1920s. Instead, we've rented private property that resembles the original launch site. The glider is a replica, but it is the same in every respect to the aircraft used to set the record. We hope Peter Hesselbach will forgive us for the deviations from the historical record."

"I'm sure he will," the reporter said with a smile. "And I believe my readers, too, will overlook these discrepancies. Thank you for honoring a pioneering German aviator."

"You are very welcome. The real thanks should go to our backers, like Melissa's magazine, our prime sponsor. She'll fill you in on how this project started."

Melissa brushed a flaxen strand away from her forehead and said, "One of our magazine writers, who was doing an anniversary story on the flights, came to me with the idea for the reenactment. I can't think of another person who knows more about soaring and gliding than Phil Mead. Stand up and take a bow, Phil."

A stocky man rose from his seat in the front row. Like the panelists, he wore a blue T-shirt. Ben figured he was in his fifties, and his straight-up posture and silver-gray hair cut close to the skull suggested a military background. His ruddy complexion could have been from an outdoor life or a booze habit. Maybe both.

Mead acknowledged the applause with a quick wave and a lopsided grin. Speaking in a southern drawl, he said, "I really appreciate that, Melissa. This reenactment is a way to tell a wider audience the story of this amazing moment in the history of aviation, but it's you folks who deserve a pat on the back for pulling this event together." Before sitting down, he added, "I get to do the fun part; writing about it."

"Thanks, Phil. I won't deny it has been quite the project," Melissa said with a shake of her head. "If not for the gentlemen at this table, it never would have gotten off the ground." She paused, an impish grin on her face, to acknowledge the laughter at her joke, then said, "*Sky Technology Magazine* organized the event, so you can blame me for anything that goes wrong. Kyle and Hank contributed the materials and labor to build the replica of the Hesselbach glider."

A reporter with the *Provincetown Banner* asked, "Do I understand correctly that there will be only one reenactment?"

"That's right," Melissa said. "Only the flight off Corn Hill. We canceled the Highland event because of cost and logistics issues."

"Who will be piloting the glider for the reenactment?"

It was an obvious question, and Ben was surprised when no one answered it. Magnus gave his shoulders a slight shrug. Hank crossed his arms and stared into space. Melissa glanced at both men. There was a quick compression of her lips, then a forced smile. "We had a lot of discussion about that."

"In fact, we're still discussing it," Aldrich said in a monotone.

Melissa's cheeks flushed. Leaning into the mic, she said, "Our initial plan was for Kyle and Hank to each make a flight, depending on the flip of a coin. Now we're down to the Corn Hill flight, which means only one of these gentlemen will be at the controls. We'll let you know when we decide who it will be." She flashed a brilliant white smile. "You'd probably like to see the actual glider.

We'll caravan over to the airport, where we're keeping the aircraft. We can take further questions at the hangar. We'll also go over the flight schedule."

The reporters got up and filed out of the room. Ben rose from his chair and ambled over to the table to introduce himself to the panelists. Phil Mead, the magazine writer, intercepted him.

"Hi, Officer," he said, glancing at the badge pinned to Ben's shirt. "Are you Sergeant Quinn?"

"The sergeant is out with the flu. My name is Ben Dyer. Chief Sisson asked me to work the traffic detail."

"Glad to have you aboard, Ben." They shook hands. "I'll introduce you to the rest of the gang."

Ben's thanks were drowned out by loud voices at the table.

"What's this 'we'll decide' crap?" Aldrich was saying. "We agreed that I would take the glider out over the bay and you'd do Highland."

"That was before we canceled the Highland flight. You agreed to that," Magnus said.

"I didn't agree to getting me kicked off my flight."

"You've got to admit that I'm the more experienced pilot, so there's less chance of anything going wrong."

"Are you saying I'm going to screw this up?"

"I didn't say that, but we agreed that we'd leave it up to a vote by the organizers. Melissa and I have been talking."

Aldrich looked as if he had been punched in the gut. He stared at the editor. His mouth was open, but he seemed unable to get a word out of it.

"I'm sorry," Melissa said. She looked truly stricken. "We've all put so much work into this. I'm just trying to do what's best for the project. Even with the help of sponsors and the money we hope to make with a documentary, the magazine is having a hard time paying for accommodations and food and rental of the launch site."

Hank turned back to Magnus. Speaking in a low, quavering voice, he said, "What's good for this project is for Magnus to pay the money he owes me."

"That's not what this is about," Kyle said.

"Damned true. It's about you trying to harm me financially so I won't be able to compete with you for bigger things. The agreement said you and I would split the costs, evenly, for building the replica. So far I've shouldered the entire burden for material, to say nothing of my time. When do you intend to pay what you owe me?"

"I intend to pay you back soon, Hank. I promise."

"And I promise that I am done with this whole damned project," Aldrich said.

He got out of his chair and stormed out of the room.

Kyle got to his feet and went around the table as if he were going to chase after Hank, but Mead said, "This is Officer Dyer, who will be in charge of traffic and security for the launch."

Magnus managed a smile and stuck his hand out. "Hello, Officer Dyer. Sorry you had to hear that stuff. Don't take it too seriously. We've all been under a lot of pressure lately."

"No problem. How can I help relieve some of that pressure?"

He glanced at the door Aldrich had used then nodded his head. "We're mainly concerned with people interfering with the launch and landing. Maybe they could be encouraged to stay on the beach where they would have a far better view of the flight."

"That shouldn't be a problem. Could I take a look at the launch site?"

"I can give you a tour," Mead said.

"Thanks for helping out," Melissa said. "Sorry we can't chat now. The press is waiting. Phil will take good care of you."

After the others had left, Mead chuckled softly.

"Never a dull moment. Like Kyle said, everyone's been under a lot of pressure, but we're really like a big family. You'll love working with this crew."

Ben wasn't so sure. This was no family spat. Mead could sugarcoat the argument all he wanted, but there was obviously deep animosity between the two pilots. The look Hank gave Melissa when she sided with Kyle was a mixture of jealousy and betrayal. *Whoa there, Nellie!* The voice of experience was reminding him not to be nosy and to stop thinking like a damn lawyer. If he weren't careful, he'd be whipping out his business card.

"I'm sure I'll have a great time," he said.

CHAPTER SIX

Abi stopped at the bottom of the cottage hill driveway after coming back from shopping. *Maybe I should slide the sawhorse back across the entrance*, she thought, only to decide against it. Moving the wooden saw barricade every time she went in and out would be a royal pain.

She drove past the barricade to the top of the hill, backed the Land Rover up to the cottage porch and carried the bags of groceries inside.

Next, she stocked the refrigerator with eggs, fruits and vegetables and used an old-fashioned tin breadbox to store a loaf of freshly baked multi-grain. In the cupboard she stacked quinoa, seeds, oatmeal and granola. She'd also bought two bottles of wine, a French rosé, and an Oregon pinot noir.

She figured she deserved a reward. It had been a tough day, starting with the hangover and the trauma of leaving her apartment, then the long drive to Truro. She poured a wine glass more than half-full of rosé, thanking whoever invented the screw-top that allowed bottles to be opened with a quick twist. Abi gave the wine a couple of seconds to breathe before carrying the glass outside.

The sun was slowly descending to the horizon on a ladder of gold and pink clouds. The beauty of the scene drew her to the edge of the hill. Standing on the bluff high above the beach, she toasted the sunset and took a sip of wine. Then she closed her eyes and drew in a heady breath of air perfumed with the scent of the salt spray rose bushes that fringed the hilltop. The breeze caressed her cheeks.

The crackle of tires on gravel cut short her beatific trance. She opened her eyes and turned around as a dark blue van and a white pickup truck emerged from the top of the driveway and parked side-by-side. The truck door opened; a tall man got out and strode over to where she was standing.

Relaxed by the wine, she smiled and said, "Hello. Just in time for the sunset."

"Did you move the barricade aside at the bottom of the hill?" the man said.

The jarring tone wiped the smile off her lips. "Yes, I did. Is that a problem?"

"That barricade was there for a reason, ma'am. This is private property and you are trespassing. I'll have to ask you to leave immediately."

It was the wrong thing to say to someone who had recently vowed to herself not to be pushed around. "I have no intention of leaving. I just got here," Abi said. "I don't even know who you are."

"My name is Ben Dyer. I'm a police officer."

Abi was unimpressed. She had nothing but contempt after three years for any subdivision of the law. "I know this is a small town, but can't they afford to give you a uniform or a police car?"

Ben glanced down at his jeans and sneakers. Lady had a point. After the press conference he had taken the badge off and put it in a pocket. The weight had been sagging down the front of his shirt and he had no jurisdiction in Provincetown anyway. He pulled the badge out of his pocket and pinned it back on, sticking himself in the chest in his haste.

He grimaced and said, "Sorry ma'am. I should have identified myself right away."

"Thank you, Officer Dyer. Now I'll do the same. My name is Abi Vickers. Please tell me what this trespassing talk is all about."

"You don't know about the reenactment?"

"No," she said. "I don't know what you're talking about."

Mead had been standing near the bluff. Ben waved him over. "That gentleman is part of a group that has rented the cottage property this week. They're planning to launch a glider off the bluff and reenact a historic flight made back in the 1920s."

Gesturing toward Beach Plum, Abi said, "That's my cottage, where I'm staying while I do some work for the owner, Professor Waldstein. He didn't say anything about a glider flight."

Before Ben could answer, Mead came up and extended his hand. "Hi, my name is Phil Mead."

"Mr. Mead is a writer with the magazine that's the main sponsor of the flight," Ben said. "This is Abi Vickers. Ms. Vickers was the one who moved the barricade. She's staying at one of the cottages."

"Nice to meet you, Mr. Mead," Abi said, shaking hands. "I'm a guest of a cottage owner. Professor Waldstein is in Paris right now, but I can give Officer Dyer a number to call if he wants to verify what I've told him."

"That won't be necessary," Ben said. "Afraid I got a little confused. I was told that all this private property had been rented for the reenactment."

"It *is* private, but the cottages are individually owned," Mead said. "The property manager notified every cottage owner that the association had made a deal to rent the open space. All the owners will get a cut of the rental fee. Looks like the notice didn't get to everyone, but Miss Vickers has every right to be here."

Abi remembered the chaotic scene in the professor's office. The rental notice could have been buried under a pile of paper. She'd probably find it in one of the boxes.

"It's possible Professor Waldstein got the rental dates mixed up," she said. "Thanks for explaining the situation, Mr. Mead."

"My pleasure," he drawled, his mouth widening in a lazy grin. "But I'd feel a lot better if you called me Phil."

She nodded and turned back to Ben. "I guess that's that. Unless Officer Dyer has anything more to discuss."

"No, that's all," Ben said. "I was a little abrupt earlier. I apologize for the mix-up."

Softening her tone, Abi said, "That's all right. You were just doing your job."

"Thanks." He pointed to the wine glass. "And I also apologize for disrupting your happy hour."

A slight smile returned to Abi's lips. Officer Dyer was the most un-cop-like cop she had ever encountered. "When is this reenactment going to take place?"

"Day after tomorrow," Mead said. "There's a break in the weather when the conditions will be perfect. Steady southwest breeze, temperature in the seventies. You'll have a front row seat to the show from your porch."

"How long will the flight be?"

"The original flight was four hours and five minutes. Hoping this one will be longer. Just so you'll know, we'll be bringing in trucks and cars on launch day. Porta-potties. Areas for the media and so on. We'll be filming the whole thing for a documentary to be aired in the U.S. and Europe, so it's a pretty big deal. Hope it won't intrude on you too much."

Abi wouldn't admit it, but she was secretly pleased at the distraction. Professor Waldstein's files were daunting, and she had no idea where to start. The quick jump from the busy city art world to a lonely cottage was going to be difficult as well. The glider reenactment would be exciting, and having all those people about would help her phase from one reality to the other.

She was telling the truth when she said, "One day won't make a difference. I'm looking forward to it."

She shook hands with both men, then sauntered back to the cottage to pour herself some more wine.

CHAPTER SEVEN

What a jerk.

Ben wished he could kick himself in the butt. He couldn't believe he'd channeled Barney Fife, the bumbling small-town police officer in the Mayberry TV series. Abi had deftly put him in his place.

He watched her disappear into the cottage, his 'suspect' analysis skills quickly coming into play. She was in good shape, trim without an ounce of fat. Evidently self-disciplined, didn't skimp on exercise and watched her diet. Maybe she had a job working in public where it was important to look your best. Bright, hazel eyes were framed by arching brows. She had a nicely-shaped nose and a strong chin.

Abi was working for a professor so it was possible she had ties to academia. She was well-spoken, with no regional accent he could detect, but he found it hard to picture her in front of a blackboard. With her windblown auburn hair and lithe figure, Abi looked like someone who'd be constrained by four walls. No wedding band on her finger. Single or simply independent. Not afraid to stand up to a cop.

Mead had been thinking about her, too. "Interesting lady," he said. "Pretty…smart, too."

Ben felt a twinge of annoyance. Then he got annoyed at himself for allowing Mead's words to stir up feelings of male competitiveness.

Changing the subject, he said, "Tell me about the launch."

"Hell yes, the launch." Mead nodded. "Okay, the day after tomorrow the glider will be snapped off the hill like a stone out of a slingshot. Pretty much the same way Hesselbach got launched into the wild blue yonder."

"What's the flight plan?" Ben said.

"You know much about gliding or soaring?"

"All the planes I've flown had propellers."

"Hell, props are for sissies. No offense."

"None taken. Using thermals to keep aloft must be the purest type of flying."

"Got that right." Mead bent down, pulled a clump of grass from the ground and tossed it off the hill where it was carried upward momentarily by the breeze. "The locals caught onto the wind currents long before the Germans arrived. They say men and boys used to run and jump off the cliffs with their jackets spread like wings, and the updrafts would blow them back."

Ben pointed to a hovering gull. "I'd say some of the other locals caught on long before humans."

"You're not the first to notice the gulls. The Germans would sit at the edge of a bluff for hours and watch how the birds used the updrafts created when the wind is deflected vertically up the side of the hill. Once the glider is in the air, the pilot steers it over the cliffs, catching the updrafts that carry it higher. After he gains altitude, the glider pilot can swoop out over the water and back indefinitely."

"He must have had an amazing knowledge of air currents," Ben said.

"That was the key to success. The hills are strung out along both sides of the coast hereabouts, meaning there is usually an ascending column of air on one side. A change in the terrain below means a change in those air currents. A good pilot can gain altitude by facing his plane into the wind. At higher levels, the air currents are even stronger, so the plane can stay aloft for an indeterminate amount of time while being flown by a savvy pilot."

"A pilot like Hesselbach."

"He was one of the best. The Germans led the world in glider design and flying, thanks to the Allies at Versailles after the armistice ending World War One. They were worried about Germany being bad boys again, so the treaty limited engine power on the planes they built and flew." He shook his head. "Guess you know how that turned out."

"Badly. It didn't stop the Germans from building up their military air force in time for World War Two."

"Not only that, the treaty unintentionally promoted development of German aeronautic science and engineering and pioneered single wing design that replaced the old bi-planes. There were 15,000 glider pilots in Germany at one time and most of them could step from a glider into a powered plane and fly it without a lot of training. And it got even worse."

"In what way?"

"All the German sporting glider clubs were under an umbrella organization called Rhön-Rossitten Gesellschaft. It was the first glider association in the world. After the Nazis came in the association broke up and the clubs were partly absorbed into the Hitler Youth. You had a whole bunch of young pilots coming along as the next generation of pilots for the Luftwaffe."

"Or Lufthansa, as it turned out."

Mead laughed. "Good point."

"While we're on the subject of pilots, from what I heard after the press conference, Hank Aldrich isn't happy that Kyle is the one who'll be in the cockpit. Is that going to be a problem?"

"He could quit the project, but it wouldn't solve anything and he's got time and money invested in the reenactment."

"Sounds like Hank is stuck with the arrangement," Ben observed.

"Yeah, I'm sorry about that," Mead said.

"Why did things go sour?"

"It got off to a good start. The deal was Hank would build the glider, Kyle would pay for the work, and both men would take a turn piloting the plane. Turned out to be more expensive than expected—with publicity, travel and so on—so only one flight got okayed."

"Which Kyle will fly, thanks to the vote by Melissa."

"That's a whole other thing. Kyle and Melissa tried to keep it quiet, but everyone knows they're an item. Hank thinks Kyle hooked up with Melissa just to torpedo him."

"It could be less complicated. Kyle is a handsome guy, and Melissa is a nice-looking woman; they might have naturally been attracted to each other."

Mead chuckled. "Hell, I've been divorced three times, so I'm not exactly what you'd call an expert on women, but you may be right. Final result is the same, though. Melissa voted against Hank and for Kyle. Maybe I woulda thunk twice about the reenactment if I knew then what I know now."

"What's that?"

"That these guys are like fire and gasoline. I knew Kyle was a show boater, but I didn't figure he'd use his good looks to snag Melissa's vote and take control of things. Their little ol' romance poisoned the whole project."

"Explains why Hank was so enraged. Maybe he has a secret crush on Melissa."

"Every guy on the crew has a crush on Melissa. Hey, that's a pretty good call for someone who just stepped into this mess. Did you learn psychology in cop school?"

"I went to law school before I became a cop. And I became an amateur psychologist while sizing people up in the courtroom."

"I'm a dumb scribbler," Mead said thoughtfully, "but I can see how something like that would come in handy."

"You don't have to be a shrink to know that Hesselbach is a fascinating figure. How did J. C. Penney get involved?"

"Penney was the son of the chain store owner. He was a twenty-four-year-old playboy looking for fun and excitement. He'd graduated from Princeton and decided to promote unpowered flight in the U.S. He sponsored Hesselbach and the other Germans who'd been flying gliders for around ten years."

"How'd they end up here in Truro?" Ben asked.

"They tried the Palisades on the Hudson River, but that wasn't great. They heard about the excellent wind conditions in Truro. After their flights, they said they were some of the best flying conditions they had ever experienced."

"Penney must have been pretty happy with the way things turned out."

"He was. Building on the success of the flights, Penney and the

American Motorless Aviation Club promoted the idea of starting the first glider school in America in Truro. It would be the start of a network of glider schools established across the country. He and his backers decided to move the school to the Atlantic shore south of here. There was more space available than on Corn Hill. A syndicate named the Motorless Aviation Company of New York leased the land with an option to buy. Bad timing. Wall Street crashed a year later and the school folded."

"Thanks for the history lesson," Ben said. "I can't wait to see the glider."

"Swing by the airport. The reporters will probably be gone. Hank can fill you in. Give him a call first, though." He rattled off a number and Ben jotted it down in his cell phone. "I'm heading back to the resort to work on publicity stuff."

Ben glanced at his watch. He had a few hours before he took his refresher nap for the graveyard shift. They walked back to their vehicles. Mead drove off first. A moment later Ben called Hank and explained who he was. Hank told him to come on by and gave him directions.

As Ben drove by Beach Plum cottage, Abi came out onto the porch and gave him a friendly wave. He waved back, surprised, hoping she didn't notice that he had swerved the cruiser slightly.

Oh yeah, he muttered. *Barney Fife.*

CHAPTER EIGHT

Good start, Abi thought. *Only in town a couple of hours and already in trouble with the local police.*

Settling into a rocker, she recalled her encounter with the tall police officer. She had been a little hard on him. She was going to have to strike a balance between acting like a human being and not being pushed around by the law ever again. She turned her thoughts to the professor's files and realized she was simply delaying the inevitable. Heaving a deep sigh, she picked up her glass and went into the house.

The stacks in the office looked no less daunting than on first sight. Abi powered up her computer. She told herself that she wasn't stalling; this was a legitimate use of her time. Of course, once the computer was up and running, she had to check her email. She regretted that decision when she saw the number of messages she had. She scrolled down, deleted the more obvious junk mail, and was pleased to see a message from Professor Waldstein.

"Ma chère, Abi:

"Hope this finds you comfortably settled in at Beach Plum. Thank you again for agreeing to organize my files. You must feel like Hercules when he had to clean up thirty years of bad housekeeping in the Augean Stables in a single day. Hoping you won't have to divert rivers the way he did.

"I am in a comfortable apartment a block from the Sorbonne.

My class consists of pleasant and intelligent young people who speak fluent English and tolerate my fractured French.

"The cottage has a few idiosyncrasies I should tell you about. The foundation is off-kilter, which is why the front door swings shut if you don't stick the rubber wedge under it. That's why it doesn't have a spring like the screen door. If the door locks you out, there is an extra key tucked under the shingle next to the doorknob.

"The other point has to do with fire safety. Look under the shag rug in the upstairs bedroom closet. You'll see a trap door. It opens onto a ladder that takes you down to the ground level behind the house in case of fire. The cottage is equipped with more than the required number of smoke detectors, and there's a sprinkler system on the first floor as well.

"If you'd like to get away from the Herculean tasks and lose yourself in art, I'd advise you to take the delightful Edward Hopper tour. It's right up your alley. I did it when I was researching an article on Hopper and found it quite informative and fascinating to see places that he painted. The contact info is on the kitchen bulletin board.

"Adieu. See you soon!"

Abi went to the kitchen. Pinned to the cork bulletin board was a slip of paper with Hopper Tour written on it, along with a name and number. She called; the pleasant-voiced woman on the line said there was room on the tour for the next morning.

She went back onto the porch and tested the door. First she found the key tucked under the shingle. Then she kicked the rubber wedge out, and the door slammed shut. She unlocked it, put the key back, then climbed the stairs to the bedroom and looked under the shag rug in the closet. The trapdoor was about two feet square. She lifted the metal ring on top and the cover swung back on hinges.

She climbed down the ladder and flashed her cell phone flashlight around. The musty-smelling storage space had been used for garden tools. Well-worn spades and rakes hung from nails. A door opened to the backyard with its view of rolling heath laced with a network of intersecting paths.

She walked behind the row of cottages and rounded the last one in line to an outlook where she had an uninterrupted view of the cliffs that curved along the bay.

The slanting light of the lowering sun defined the hills and dunes with deep shadows. She remembered what she had read about Edward Hopper and how he focused the effects of sunlight to convey drama. This was classic Hopper country except for one thing:

Looming above the treetops less than a mile from where she stood was the top of a gray tower. The hard-faced exterior glowed orange in the reflected rays of the sun, like a phantasmagorical fortress in a Tolkien novel.

She went back into the house, got a bottle of water out of the refrigerator and then put it, along with a compact pair of binoculars she'd brought for bird-watching, into a small backpack with her cell phone.

A stairway led from the cottage hill down to the beach. At the bottom of the stairs she removed her sandals and put them in the backpack. The cool sand between her toes felt good. She trudged along the shore, walking in and out of the wavelets, until she came to a stairway twice as wide as the others she had passed.

Judging from the distance she had traveled, she guessed that the stairway led up the side of the dunes to the tower house.

The sun was dropping fast. She probably should head back to the cottage, but her curiosity got the best of her. A 'No Trespassing' sign lay half-buried in the sand under the stairs. Since the sign had fallen off and was detached, she rationalized, it no longer referred to the stairway.

What the heck? she thought.

Abi climbed to the top of the stairs. The tower she had seen from a distance was part of a gigantic flat-roofed house. The massiveness, hard lines and imposing size reminded her of the so-called Brutalist architectural style that came into being in Europe after World War II.

Two stories were built atop each other. The wraparound windows were small compared to the house, more like those on a bunker, designed to keep prying eyes from looking in.

What an absolute monster, she thought. The gross structure aroused her ire and her disgust, but also her curiosity. She wondered why the builder hadn't torn down the white barn a few hundred feet from the house that dwarfed it.

Surrounding the entire property was a tall chain link fence topped with strands of razor wire. A sign hung from the fence. Reaching into her backpack, she pulled out the binoculars and peered through the lenses. Her fingers adjusted the focus. She could read the words: Baron Realty, Inc.

The sun was an orange blob on the horizon by the time she made her way back along the beach and climbed up to the cottages. She saw that she had company. The dark blue van that had followed Ben's pickup truck earlier was parked next to Grover. Sitting on the porch was Phil Mead, the magazine writer. He got out of the chair and met her halfway across the lawn.

"Afternoon, Miz Vickers," he said, flashing a friendly grin. "Thought I'd drop off the flight schedule. Saw your car here, so I figured you'd be close by. Hope you don't mind me making myself at home."

"No, not at all. Nice of you to think of me."

"No problem."

He handed her a brown envelope. "This has the press kit with the info for the event. It's got some historical stuff inside that will help you figure out what's going on when the show starts the day after tomorrow. You have a nice walk?"

"Very nice, thank you. The countryside is beautiful except for that huge house overlooking the bay about a mile from here. Do you know anything about it?"

"A little. Guy who built it is dead. Fell off the tower and broke his neck."

Abi was too kind to say anything about poetic justice, but she couldn't help herself from thinking it. As they walked back to the cottage, she said, "How did the town allow a monstrosity like that to be built? There must be zoning bylaws that could have prevented it."

"The folks I talked to said the builder had deep pockets. The town had to cave after spending tons of money in a lawsuit involving another house."

"Did they say who owns the tower house?"

"Place is managed by a realty company. That's about all anyone knows."

"I wonder why the builder left the barn standing."

Mead shrugged. "Danged if I know. Looks like we're having a nice sunset."

The sun had dropped below the horizon, splashing the sky with orange and painting the cottages in a purple light.

Abi smiled. "I think I'm going to like seeing this at the end of each workday," she said.

"Not bad at all. I heard you say you were working for a professor?"

"That's right. Mainly organizing his research material. It's going to be a bigger job than I expected. I should be in there working on it now. He let things get out of control."

"Nice that you could give him a hand. You had dinner yet?"

"No, I haven't. I don't even think I had a real lunch."

"You gotta be hungry. There's a place in town that serves great chow."

Abi realized that Mead was asking her on a date. He seemed nice enough, but the last thing she wanted to do was sit in a restaurant making small talk.

"Thanks for the invitation, Phil. But it's been a long day and I'm getting up early tomorrow. Things are going to get busy around here from what you have told me, so I'd better use my time to get settled."

"Probably just as well," Mead said. "You're right about tomorrow being busy. Mostly press people setting up for the launch. The glider will be coming in too. Matter of fact, I should get back to the inn and see how things are going."

They shook hands and he got in his van. After he drove off, she headed for the cottage, relieved Mead hadn't tried to pin her down on another dinner date. She wasn't kidding about being tired, as well as hungry.

Back in the kitchen, she got a salmon fillet out of the refrigerator. She seasoned the fish with paprika and garlic powder, basted it with olive oil and slid the pan into the oven. While the fish was cooking she prepared a Greek salad. She ate alone at the table, listening to Mozart being played on a local classical music FM station.

After she cleaned the dishes, she began a preliminary sort of the boxes. Before long, her eyes grew tired. She took a shower and got into a short nightgown, then climbed to the upstairs bedroom. Before turning in, she went to the window and looked out at the bay.

The night stars were like sequins on blue-black velvet. Clouds floated like ghosts in the background.

As she was watching, a funny thing happened. She thought she saw a shadow against the quarter moon, and a second later the stars rippled and blinked out for an instant as if something had passed over them. Odd, she thought. A little spooky, too.

Exhausted after a long day, she got in bed and slipped under the cool sheets. For the first time in three years of nights lying in bed, staring at the ceiling, waiting for sleep to come, she fell into an untroubled slumber.

CHAPTER NINE

Aldrich had seemed cordial on the phone, but Ben remembered the angry verbal fireworks after the press conference and wondered if he'd have to use his lawyer skills.

As a lawyer, Ben often had to deal with an angry witness, or even worse, a pissed off client. He'd learned how to stand in front of an emotional blast furnace without getting burned. Be firm. Don't let it get to you. And after the initial heat is expended, be understanding.

He got out of his truck and went into the hangar through a back door. The main doors were open to the tarmac. The glider rested on a metal framework at the center of a ring of floodlights. The single wing lay on staging next to the aircraft. With its lack of propeller and wings, its high tail and open cockpit, the plane resembled a futuristic space vehicle.

Ben was inspecting the stylized head of a woman painted on the rounded nose of the plane when someone said:

"That's Athena, the emblem of the University of Darmstadt."

Aldrich had come in through the main doors and was walking toward him. He had exchanged his T-shirt and shorts for a one-piece denim jumpsuit.

"I like her," Ben said. He gave the mahogany-colored fuselage a sweeping glance. "What's with the flying goose painted on the tail?"

"The symbol represents the flying group that designed the aircraft."

"They did an amazing job."

"I think so, too. You must be Officer Dyer."

Ben could hardly believe how different Aldrich was from the enraged man whose temper had exploded at the end of the press conference. His sour expression was gone. In its place was a friendly smile.

"That's right. As I said on the phone, I'm leading up the traffic detail for the launch. It was a last-minute assignment. I was hoping you could fill me in on what's going on."

They shook hands. "No problem," Aldrich said. "You can call me Hank."

"I answer to Ben. I just came from the launch site. Phil Mead was kind enough to show me around. With access so limited, the traffic arrangements should be mostly a matter of directing spectators to the beach where they'll have a view of the launch and the flight. We'll position an officer to make sure staff and crew can come and go to the site as needed."

"Sounds like you've got things under control, Ben. Tomorrow is moving day. We'll lift the bird onto a flatbed truck and haul it to the site."

"I'll talk to the Provincetown police about having an escort for the truck."

"That would be a big help, Officer."

Ben turned his attention to the glider. "I've flown powered planes, so I'm in awe at any kind of aircraft that can fly without an engine. This is a pretty sophisticated design for a plane that set records more than ninety years ago. It's hardly what I expected."

Hank smiled, lightly placing his palm on the highly varnished reddish fuselage.

"This little baby is a long way from the glorified box kites the Wright Brothers were building. The early gliders would take off from a hilltop and glide a couple of hundred feet. Planes like this can stay aloft for hours. Even back in its day the Darmstadt 17 was considered a high-performance sailplane." He pointed to the detached wings that rested on the staging. "When we remount the wings on the bird, they'll be sixty feet from tip to tip."

Ben whistled. "That's quite the spread."

"Think about it in terms of bird design, especially soaring birds like gulls and hawks. She only weighs around three hundred pounds. Like the original aircraft, the replica is constructed of four-ply birch wood and linen. Check out the controls in the cockpit. You've got a simple pedal arrangement for manipulating the ailerons, and a stick for the rudder, just like a powered plane."

Ben stepped back and ran his gaze along the fuselage from nose to tail. "It looks as if it just came off the assembly line."

"Thanks. It was a labor of love. I was tempted to use synthetic materials. But I felt like I'd be cheating if I used modern-day technology. Canvas and wood construction give the little plane a soul it wouldn't have otherwise. It was in a bird just like this that Hesselbach smashed the previous record. Took off in the morning into a brisk southwest wind, flew over the white-capped bay, headed south along the shore, then inland, and north again. He reached an altitude of three-hundred-fifty feet and a speed of fifty miles per hour."

"You've got the route down pat."

"No surprise. I was planning to fly the same course before I got fired."

Ben heard the edge in Aldrich's voice and changed the direction of the conversation. "How's she handle?"

"Like a dream. My shop is in upstate New York, not far from the National Soaring Museum. Worked with a consultant named Heller, who's associated with the museum. He's an expert on vintage aircraft design. We ran a number of test flights using a motorized plane to get her aloft. She's even prettier in the air."

Ben started to say something about an American breaking the German record, but he remembered the unsettled and emotional question over who was going to pilot the plane.

Instead, he side-stepped the touchy subject. "I understand that the launch method is the same as the original."

"Exactly the way they did it in Hesselbach's day. It's called a bungee launch. Three people we're calling snappers, will pull back on either end of an elasticized rope that's stretched out in a V from a hook hitched to the glider's nose—just like a kid pulling back the rubber bands on a slingshot. Another snapper is positioned at a wingtip to hold the plane steady. A second team holds onto the tail. When the pilot gives a signal, the pullers will run forward until there is enough tension on the rope. Then the tail team lets go, the glider is catapulted into the air, the rope unhooks from the nose and the pilot takes control of the aircraft."

"Breaking the old world record and setting a new one," Ben said.

"Whether or not it breaks the record, this little plane will create a big splash." Catching himself, Hank said, "Sorry. Didn't mean it the way it sounded. I want this to succeed. I just thought that I would be the one winning glory and gold."

"I can see about the glory, but no one mentioned gold."

"Magnus and I are competing for a contract that could be quite lucrative. The Navy is expected to make their decision any time now."

"I'm not sure I understand how this flight affects the Navy's decision?"

"They're the same as anyone else. They'll be impressed by all the press coverage the photogenic Magnus will get out of this, especially if he breaks the German's record. It could tip the decision his way. Not saying that it should, but that it might. The actual aircraft builder—that's me—the guy who's been working to build the glider and doesn't have a great tan, will be relegated to the sidelines."

"Sorry. You've got to have some satisfaction, though, just from building this magnificent replica."

"Oh, I do, but even without the Navy contract that's at stake, I'm the one who should be piloting this pretty little bird."

"You must have some leverage as a builder. Any chance of getting a re-vote on the pilot decision?"

"You sound like a lawyer."

"I am. Or...I *was*. I'm taking a sabbatical for my mental health."

Hank gave a nod of understanding. "I'm afraid Melissa would vote with Kyle again." A sad look came to his eyes. "She turned out to be a disappointment. Smart woman like that falling for his beach boy looks. At this point, the best I can settle for is getting paid."

"You said at the press conference that he owes you money."

"Yes, for half the cost of the glider. I'm not even counting labor. I'm not optimistic that I'll get it. He's got family money but it's tied up in trust."

"Well, let me know if I can give you any legal advice, Mr. Aldrich. No charge. I'll get back to you on that police escort. Maybe I'll see you at the launch site."

"I'll be doing a dry run with the volunteer launch crew tomorrow morning. Hesselbach almost crashed on one attempt using inexperienced volunteers. The launch can be a little tricky."

Ben thanked Hank again for his time, and headed back to the police station. He checked in with the chief and gave him an estimate of the number of special duty officers he'd need. With access limited to the site by one road and a single driveway, it would be easy to divert traffic.

On the drive home, Ben thought about Abi. It would be a mistake for him to fixate on a natural gesture like a good-bye wave, but she did smile, he mused. He didn't expect that, especially after their awkward introduction. He missed female company, but admitting he was lonely would suggest he'd made a mistake to move from the distracting hustle and bustle of a busy city law practice to become a summer cop in a small town.

The best thing to do for now was fill his days with work and his nights with sleep. His psyche was as fragile as crystal. It wouldn't take much of a complication to shatter.

He drove home, got undressed and crawled into bed after setting the alarm. He was pleased that the special detail would give him a break from the night shift. Some people enjoy working late at night, but he was starting to feel like a vampire.

He stretched an arm across the other side of the bed. He did it out of habit. Instead of Loren's warm skin, his fingers felt the empty sheet, but he said goodnight anyhow.

CHAPTER TEN

The alarm woke Abi from the soundest and longest stretch of sleep she remembered having in months. She rolled out of bed, stood in front of the window to look out at the shimmering blue waters of Cape Cod Bay, threw her arms back and inhaled the breeze tossing the white cotton curtains.

Her joy at an ordinary thing like getting out of bed after a refreshing sleep demonstrated how fully the lawsuit and her husband's betrayal had consumed not only her every daytime moment, but the nights as well—like a *Nightmare on Elm Street* movie where victims Freddie Krueger kills while in their dreams, die in the real world.

After a quick shower, she dressed in white shorts, a turquoise patterned tank top and sandals. She padded down the stairs to the first floor to rustle up a breakfast of Greek yogurt and blueberries topped with coconut granola. After she cleaned up the dishes, Abi stuffed a notebook, pen, camera, binoculars and a couple of bottles of water into her backpack. She got in the Land Rover and headed out the driveway onto the road.

A couple of SUVs were coming from the other direction. The set-up crew was arriving to prep for the launch, Abi surmised.

The rendezvous with the tour was about a ten-minute drive from the cottage. Abi sat in a rocking chair on the front porch of the Highland House Museum, a two-and-a-half story gray-shingled building trimmed in white. As she rocked, she imagined she was a turn-of-the-century summer guest who'd ridden the train from Boston to take in the sea air at the former hotel.

The guide showed up at 9:30 AM sharp. The friendly, middle-aged woman behind the wheel of the red Subaru Outback introduced herself as Beth. Since Abi was the only one taking the morning tour she had the front passenger seat.

Beth handed Abi a loose-leaf notebook of pictures encased in transparent plastic envelopes.

"That first photo is the watercolor Hopper did of the lighthouse," she said. "He painted it from the water side." As they drove off, she asked, "Are you here on vacation?"

"I'm staying in town to do some work for a friend. Do you know Professor Waldstein?"

"Oh sure. He's up at the flower cottages."

"I'm staying in Beach Plum. Professor Waldstein suggested I take this tour."

"Well, that was a good suggestion. My family has lived in Truro for decades, including the time when Hopper was at his shack and later after he built his dunes studio. We'll see a lot of what he painted, and more."

Beth lived up to her promise. The Subaru followed winding two-lane roads from one end of the town to the other, nosing into driveways, past marshes and beaches, up the sharp-ridged hills known locally as hogbacks, and down sandy tracks that were once railroad right of ways.

Hopper was partial to railroads, Beth explained; he loved painting tracks, signs or depots. As they drove around, Abi flipped pages to keep pace with the actual scenery. Beth explained that while Hopper didn't like impressionism, he flirted with it on more than one occasion.

"Some of the South Truro hills he painted early in his career are right out of the realist style of Thomas Hart Benton, but later he flattened the rolling dunes he painted, going back and forth between realism and impressionism." Beth stopped the Subaru in front of an old farmhouse. "See anything different from the painting?"

Abi looked at the picture in the notebook. "The color in the painting is different from the house," she said. "And the addition is on the wrong side of the main building in the Hopper work.

"Hopper loved shadows, but they don't work with gray shingles. He painted all houses white or yellow whether that was their color or not. He especially liked the backs of barns. He often used artistic license when it came to his subjects and manipulated scenery when it suited his aims. I'll show you other examples."

They drove to the top of a high road in North Truro. Beth pointed out how the road in the Hopper painting dropped off more sharply than the real one. At the nearby Truro Vineyards, he painted out the three-hundred-year-old mulberry tree because the massive trunk and foliage obscured the view of the house. Another house had a fat chimney, which Hopper didn't like, so he painted a skinny one instead.

They visited the pile of firewood and gas pump lights that were all that remained of the iconic painting of a gas station at night. Beth said *Gas* was a combination of three different gas stations. And in the painting of a house he did, when he may have been depressed, the road was covered with grass, suggesting remoteness and isolation.

On the drive back to Highland House, Beth said, "The critics thought his Cape Cod work was unimportant compared to his city paintings, like *Nighthawks*. What do you think?"

"The critics were crazy. I love *Nighthawks*. Who are those people and what are they doing in the café so late in the evening? They are all in one place but isolated at the same time. His cityscapes were wonderful, with their loneliness, geometric structure and mystery, but that was Cape Cod light streaming in through the windows of his office and apartment buildings."

Beth smiled. "Glad to hear you say that, because I agree wholeheartedly."

"Could you tell me how to get to his studio?"

"Sure. Go to the beach at the end of the road we were just on, take a left and walk for about twenty minutes. You can see the house from the beach. There's a very large, contemporary house not far from the Hopper place."

"Is it as big as the one near the flower cottages?"

"Probably not. That's the Baron house, built while the town was involved in lawsuits having to do with the house near the Hopper studio. The town spent more than two hundred thousand dollars in legal fees on that case, and didn't have the will or the resources to fight another builder with deep pockets."

"That's a shame," Abi said, shaking her head. "The Baron place is so imposing and it has that awful tower."

Beth told Abi about local speculation, that the tower represented a middle finger making a rude gesture at the town.

"Why would someone be so mean?" Abi said.

"A lot of people in town have asked that same question."

Abi recalled her conversation with Mead. "I understand the owner is dead."

"He died several weeks ago. Fell off that tower and broke his head."

"That was certainly ironic," Abi said.

"Yes, it was. Unfortunately, we're stuck with that thing whether Baron is alive or dead."

A thoughtful expression came to Abi's eyes. "Wouldn't it be nice if someone bought the property and tore it down?"

"That would be nice. Don't see it happening, though. The property is worth millions. I'm not even sure who owns it. Eddy didn't have kids and he was divorced from his wife."

"I wonder why he left the barn standing."

"The town allowed him to build the darn house, but he'd have to keep the barn. Baron said he didn't want to waste money on another lawsuit, but I have my own theory."

"I'd love to hear it."

"I think Eddy Baron was meaner than anyone could have imagined. He already showed he didn't care about spending money. He was going to let the old barn rot to the ground because he could."

Beth dropped Abi off at Highland House. Abi didn't feel like going back to the cottage because of the launch set-up activity. Instead, she walked out past the lighthouse to the observation platform that overlooked the ocean. She sat on a bench and watched the endless ranks of white crested waves roll onto the beach, and listened to the whisper of the surf.

"Ms. Vickers?"

Abi turned at the sound of her name. She smiled. Meaning every word, she said, "Hello, Officer Dyer. How nice to see you."

CHAPTER ELEVEN

Ben had arrived at the lighthouse by a roundabout route which started at the flower cottages earlier in the day. He'd been disappointed to see that Abi's vintage Land Rover was gone. Several vehicles were parked in front of the cottages and porta-potties had been set up. The hill was being transformed from a peaceful old artists' colony into a circus-like stage for a media event.

On the grassy open space between the flower cottages and the brow of the hill a group of men and women pulled the strands of a long, yellow, rubber rope taut, while another group released it.

Kyle and Melissa were talking with a film crew. Watching them was Phil Mead, the magazine writer, who was scribbling in a notepad. He saw Ben get out of the cruiser, tucked the pad in a pocket and strolled over.

They shook hands and Ben looked around the hill. "Busy place."

"It's going to get even busier. Weather's looking good for tomorrow. Everyone wants to make sure the launch goes off like clockwork. Those folks with the rubber rope are doing a dry run with an invisible glider, so they'll be ready for the real launch tomorrow morning."

"Hank told me he's moving the glider onto the site today," Ben said.

"That's right. Well, what did you think of him?"

"Passionate and knowledgeable. Not as fierce as I expected."

"Glad he's calmed down. He knows that little plane better than anyone, for sure. Once the camera crew wraps up here with the interview, they'll go to Provincetown and film the glider being loaded and transported. The wings will be attached on site, so the bird will be ready to take flight first thing in the morning."

"Hank did an amazing job building the replica."

"Hank is a true genius," Mead said. "I went up to Elmira, New York for the test flights. Real pretty."

"I can't wait to see it fly. The Provincetown police will escort the truck to the town line. I'll meet the truck and make sure the glider arrives safely on the hill. How long do you figure before things get moving at the hangar?"

Mead glanced over at Kyle and Melissa. "I'd take my time if I were you. Hard to turn Kyle off once he's switched on. We'll take a break after this, then head to the hangar. Couple of hours at least."

Ben got back in the cruiser and called the Provincetown police department to ask for a heads-up when the glider was loaded on the truck and ready to go. Then he drove to the Box Lunch to pick up a turkey rollwich, basically a sandwich rolled up in pita bread. He ordered an ice coffee, got back in the cruiser and headed for Highland Light.

He and Loren often strolled out past the lighthouse to the observation platform that overlooked the Atlantic. Like his habit of talking to dead air, his frequent return to places they loved was another futile sign of his refusal to accept that she was gone.

He drove into the parking lot near Highland House and pulled up next to a faded green Land Rover. *Couldn't be,* he thought.

What now, Sherlock? Say it is Abi's car and I bump into her; will it be a repeat of the first meeting? Maybe I should eat my lunch in the cruiser. But she did wave at him. He took a deep breath and got out of the cruiser, then walked past the lighthouse, between the Highland Links golf fairways to the observation platform overlooking the ocean.

Abi was sitting on a bench gazing out at the ocean. When she became aware of him standing there, to Ben's relief she smiled and said she was pleased to see him.

"Hope I'm not interrupting you," he said.

"Not at all. I was enjoying the beautiful view." She eyed the paper bag in his hand. "Having a picnic?"

"The glider is being moved from Provincetown to Truro this afternoon. I'll be escorting the flatbed to the launch site. I thought I'd better grab lunch while I had the time. What about you?"

"Taking a rest. I had a fascinating, but exhausting, tour this morning of houses and places Edward Hopper painted. The tour ended at Highland House. I strolled over here and was jotting down notes so I could go back and visit the Hopper sites on my own. Big mistake. I can't stop looking off at the ocean. This is my new favorite spot."

Dyer gazed toward the horizon. "It was one of my wife's favorite places, too."

Abi turned back to Ben. "Your wife?" she said.

Ben hadn't meant to come across as the grieving widower. He had found it best to be direct and honest in awkward situations. "That's right. Loren died last year. She put up a good fight, but cancer got the best of her."

"I'm so sorry to hear about your loss," Abi said.

"Thank you. She was pretty special."

"It's nice that you've kept coming here."

"I swing by a few times a week. Sometimes when I'm on the night shift as well. I think it helps."

"I can see how it would, being in such a lovely spot."

Ben saw an opening to exit the conversation before it got too awkward. He hefted the bag in his hand. "Have you had lunch?"

"No, but—"

He shook the bag again. "Turkey rollwich, big enough for the both of us."

She hesitated, then gestured toward the bench. "Thank you. Have a seat."

Ben sat down, opened the bag and handed her half a roll-up. The bench was narrow, forcing them to sit close to each other.

"Did you see the Hopper studio?" he said, unwrapping his sandwich.

"That's for another day. The guide told me about the controversial house near the studio." She unwrapped her roll-up and took a bite.

"Yum. Thanks again."

"My pleasure," Ben said, taking a bite of his own. "A lot of people were upset because of the house's design and location. Some neighbors wanted to tear it down but the court found they waited too long to take legal action."

"Speaking of big houses, there's a real monster within walking distance of my cottage."

Dyer rolled his eyes. "You must mean the Baron place."

"The tour guide called it Fort Baron."

"It's been called worse than that. Even my genteel wife used choice adjectives. She compared the house to her cancer. She'd say the house is killing the land. It needs to be surgically removed."

"Your wife sounds amazing. The guide and I fantasized about someone with lots of money buying the Baron property, demolishing the house and returning the site to its natural state."

"The only people who would miss it are the fishermen who use the tower to navigate by. We're talking millions of dollars, even if that were possible," Ben said.

"Purely as an intellectual exercise, I wonder how I could find out who actually owns it."

"If it interests you that much, I'd be glad to chase down the ownership. It's my area of expertise."

"I don't understand. You'd do this as a police officer?"

"No, as an attorney. I used to practice real estate law in Boston. After Loren died, I took a break from my practice to play rent-a-cop."

Abi opened her mouth. She seemed to be struggling to speak. Finally, with great deliberation, she placed her half-eaten sandwich down on the bench.

"I'm sorry," she said. "I really must go. I just remembered an appointment. It was nice chatting with you. Thanks for the lunch."

She gathered up her phone and notebook. Ben watched her stride along the path between the golf links.

What the hell was that all about? A wall of ice dropped between them as soon as he said he was an attorney. He'd run into people who didn't like lawyers, but he was surprised at the intensity of her reaction.

He dissected their conversation in the moments before she dashed off like a frightened rabbit. Her wishful thinking about someone buying the Baron house and tearing it down was not a bad idea, really.

Ben gazed off at the ocean. She had planted the seed of an idea in his mind. What if he could establish a real memorial that paid tribute to Loren's love of beauty, by exorcising the land of a malignant growth? And what if this time the treatment was successful?

When he worked as a lawyer, Ben thought he was on top of the world. Successful career. Beautiful wife. Beacon Hill townhouse. His world fell apart when Loren died and he realized material success counted for little because of the hours and days spent away from her.

Ben had felt utterly helpless in the face of Loren's relentless disease. Maybe this time he actually had the power to do something. She loved the Snow property. Restoring its beauty wouldn't bring Loren back, but it would honor her memory.

His phone chirped. He'd have to put his thoughts aside. The Provincetown police were calling to say the glider was on the flatbed.

CHAPTER TWELVE

Abi's head was spinning as she drove away from Highland House. She couldn't believe how quickly her mood of sunny optimism had shifted to a simmering anger and then deep depression. All it had taken to send her off into a blue funk was a single word. *Lawyer.*

She actually liked Ben. His obvious grief over his wife's death made her feel even guiltier about stiff-arming him. *He must think I'm crazy.* She thought of going back to explain, but that would make her seem even more insane. It was generous to offer his legal expertise, but she couldn't get past the fact that he represented to her, through no fault of his own, all that had gone sour in her life.

What now? Launch preparations were under way at the flower cottages. Maybe she'd stay away a while longer. She pulled off to the side of the road and called up a map of Truro on her phone. The image reminded her of what an oddity the town was, starting with its location about where the wrist would be on the arm-shaped peninsula that is Cape Cod.

Bounded on the northwest by Provincetown, the fist-like tip of the Cape, and by Wellfleet to the south, Truro was only a few miles across at its narrowest, sloping down from the high cliffs overlooking the Atlantic on the north and east, to the rolling hills bordering the bay to the west.

She wondered if she could get close to the Baron house. Using the map as a guide, she drove across town and got onto a meandering two-lane road sporting a cracked surface that looked like a blacktop jigsaw puzzle. She went down a couple of dead ends that terminated at bay beaches, but on her third try she braked Grover to a stop in front of a driveway.

The black wrought iron gate guarding the entrance was decorated with a large gilded 'B' and flanked by square brick and marble columns. A large 'No Trespassing' sign hung on the gate.

The road continued past the driveway. She put the Land Rover in gear and drove a quarter mile to a cul-de-sac. By then, the road was all sand.

Abi wheeled Grover in a U-turn, and was about to head back the way she came, only to bring the vehicle to a halt near a faint path that led off into the thick oak and pine forest. She parked next to the path, got out of the Land Rover and followed the trail into the woods.

Scrub oak and pine forest eventually gave way to larger trees spaced further apart and easier to navigate. The still air trapped under the canopy of branches was as hot as a sauna. Squadrons of voracious mosquitoes attacked her. She held her breath so she wouldn't inhale any insects. Only when she broke out of the woods and into the open did she allow herself to take a gulp of air.

She was standing on a strip of cleared land that bordered the chain link fence. Looming beyond the fence like a medieval outpost was Fort Baron. Some mosquitoes had followed her from the woods. She waved them away from around her head and started walking along the outside perimeter of the fence.

After a few minutes she came across a fallen oak tree, probably uprooted by the fierce winter storms. The trunk was about a foot-and-a-half in diameter, and its weight had crushed a section of fence.

Abi clambered onto the upended root ball, then climbed onto the tree trunk. The oak lay almost at a horizontal angle. Most of the leaves had died, leaving the branches bare.

She used lower branches as handholds and made her way along the trunk until she was past the crushed fence. Using her telephoto lens, she shot a number of photos of the house and barn, then sat on the tree trunk and thought about what to do next.

After a few minutes of reflection, she got up and made her way back down the tree trunk. Her decision not to trespass had nothing to do with what was proper or legal. In dealing with a crime against nature like the Baron house, a little law-breaking was justified in her mind. But it would take hours to survey the property and the bugs were driving her crazy.

After a mad dash through the pine forest to the Land Rover, she got behind the wheel and turned on the air conditioning. She waited until the air had cooled down her sweaty body, then drove back along the narrow road, and a short while later parked at the town hall. She went inside and found the assessors' office.

Every property in town was recorded in a database. She located a picture of the Baron house along with tax details. The name of the owner was the same realty company listed on the fence sign.

"I'm trying to track down the owners of this property," she told the assistant assessor. "Any idea how to go about it?"

The assistant smiled when she saw the page Abi was pointing to.

"You must be new in town," she said.

"I arrived this week. How could you tell?"

"All the locals know this property belonged to Eddy Baron. I did a Google search once just for fun, and got nowhere. Guys like Baron don't make it easy for people to know about their business. Maps are all online. A real estate lawyer might be able to help," she said.

"Thanks," Abi said. She paused, "I think I may know where I can find one."

CHAPTER THIRTEEN

Ben stood on the observation platform and stared off at the ocean, absorbing the restorative power of the vast blue expanse, and decided that he was going to help Abi look into the Baron property whether she wanted him to or not.

If not for Abi, then maybe for Loren.

Bringing the land back to its former beauty would be a far better way to honor his wife's memory than wandering around the old house, gazing morosely at her photos. He dug out his cell phone and tapped a number on the contact list.

"Hi, Ben," a man's voice answered. "What a nice surprise. How are you?"

"I'm fine, Nathan. And you?"

"Up to my ears in depositions and hearings, but I'm well otherwise. I'd feel even better if you were calling to tell me you'd like to come back to the firm."

"I'm not quite ready to give up my shiny new badge, Nathan. Although, I do miss everyone."

"And we miss you, too, my friend. I don't blame you for putting me off. It must be a lot of fun driving around in your cruiser with the lights flashing and siren howling."

Ben chuckled. "You make it sound like *Chicago PD*. This is a small town summer resort. I'm on the night shift, so most of my time is spent sitting in my car trying to stay awake." He glanced back at the lighthouse. "Got to admit the scenery is sure pretty, though."

"I simply can't believe you don't miss writing briefs and arguing with grumpy judges." Nathan gave an exaggerated sigh. "Okay, since I can't woo you back, how else can I be of service?"

"You could do me a big favor. I'd like to find out who owns a piece of property here in town." He gave Nathan the name of the property management ownership company he'd seen on the front gate of the Baron house.

"I'll give it a try," Nathan said. "What's going on?"

"I had a crazy idea. I'm thinking of setting up a memorial for Loren that could involve a real estate acquisition. It's all very tentative at this point."

"I understand. I'll be glad to help. You know how much Diane and I adored Loren."

"The feeling was mutual, Nathan. You were great friends, right to the end. No hurry on this. I'm going to be busy for the next couple of days."

Ben asked about his colleagues at the law firm. Nathan told him some funny stories only lawyers could appreciate, but Ben was relieved when they finally clicked off the call. The chat with an old colleague who knew Ben and Loren reminded him how conflicted he was about his life.

A call had come in while he was talking to Nathan. As he suspected, it was the Provincetown police calling to tell Ben that the flatbed had left the hangar and was on the road. He called them back and said he would meet the truck at the town line.

He walked back to the cruiser and drove out onto the highway. At the Truro-Provincetown line he made a U-turn and pulled off to the side of the road.

Ten minutes later he looked in the rearview mirror and saw the front of a large truck traveling his way with its headlights on. The flatbed carrying the glider went past the parked cruiser; the wing was strapped to the side of the fuselage.

A Provincetown police cruiser with flashing roof lights followed the truck. The police car did a U-turn in the highway, the driver gave a whoop of the siren and headed home. Ben whooped back, flicked on his roof lights and got behind the flatbed.

The two vehicles drove at a low speed before turning off the main highway onto the back road to the cottages. The truck driver made a tight turn and drove up the driveway. One of the launch crew directed the truck to a parking space reserved for the glider near the brow of the hill.

Ben parked in front of the cottages. He was walking toward the flatbed when Hank Aldrich emerged from the passenger side and gave him a thumbs-up. Under Hank's supervision, the snappers unloaded the wing and carefully placed them in the grass. Next, they lifted the aircraft off the truck bed.

Hank bolted the wing in place and took great pains to inspect his work before walking over to where Ben leaned against his cruiser watching the plane come together.

"Well, what do you think?"

"As I said before, this is an amazing aircraft. You must be anxious to see it in the air."

"Doubt if I'm going to feel like watching Magnus soar off into the wild blue yonder record books."

"Maybe you'll change your mind before the launch."

"I doubt it. Thanks for your help. I've got to get back to the hangar to take care of a few things."

They shook hands and Hank got back into the flatbed. Ben walked over for a closer look at the glider. He was taking another look at the flying goose symbol on the tail when Mead's van arrived. Mead and Marty Weber, the German journalist, got out and approached Ben.

Mead clamped Ben on the shoulder. "Hi, Ben. Have you met my buddy Marty? He's writing about the launch for a German news syndicate. Thought we'd come by and talk to Hank for a background story."

"You just missed him."

"I caught him out on the road and said we'd see him at the hangar."

Ben turned to the German. "I was at the press conference when you asked about the launch date. I'm in charge of traffic control."

They shook hands and Weber turned his attention to the glider. "Looks like everything is ready to go. Aldrich deserves a lot of credit for building this beautiful replica. Peter Hesselbach would have been proud of him."

Mead lifted the camera hanging around his neck and took a few pictures of the glider from different angles, then pointed to the glider. "How about a photo of you two with the glider in the background?"

"No thank you," Weber said. "I have this journalistic thing of keeping myself out of the story. Besides, I don't want my editor to see what fun I've been having."

Mead's phone chirped. He frowned when he read the name on the caller ID. He put the phone to his ear.

"Hi, Melissa. I was about to interview Hank for the pre-launch. Okay," he said, shrugging his shoulders. "I'll be right over." He hung up and said, "Sorry, gentlemen. Melissa wants me at Highland golf links. They're doing some additional background shots for the documentary."

"Why Highland if the action is here?" Weber said.

"They want me there so I won't talk to Hank. Melissa's decided to build the next issue of the magazine around Kyle. Photo on the cover. Most of the credit will go to him. Hank will be a footnote. Sorry to leave you on your own, Marty. Maybe Officer Dyer can give you a ride back to the inn."

"I'd be glad to," Ben said. "Hop in."

Weber got in the passenger side and Ben slid behind the wheel. As he drove past Abi's cottage he cast a wistful glance at the front door. At the bottom of the hill he stopped to drag the sawhorse across the driveway. Minutes later they were on Route 6 heading toward the tip of Cape Cod.

"How long have you been a police officer?" Weber asked.

Ben furrowed his brow. "About sixty-one days," he said.

"I didn't realize you were so new at this. How do you like it so far?"

"I took the job as a break from the stress of working for a high-powered law firm, so the novelty hasn't worn off yet. Don't know if I'll last through the winter, but it's been fun, especially the last couple of days working with the glider folks."

"Now comes nail-biting time."

Ben smiled. "You've got that right, but things should go well. They've got great weather, top-notch equipment and an experienced crew. Magnus has money and good looks. That's a hard combination to beat."

"Yes, in a way he reminds me of Hesselbach's patron, the J. C. Penney heir. He had a reputation as a playboy, but I think he was sincere in his desire to see soaring introduced to the United States. Like Kyle Magnus, he and the Germans were quite the local celebrities. Both the summer visitors and local people followed their every move and the Germans apparently loved the adulation. When the wind was wrong, they'd hop into Penney's red convertible and he'd drive them to Provincetown for ice cream sodas. Too bad how things turned out."

"Why bad? Hesselbach's flights were a success," Ben said.

"That's true. After Hesselbach broke the Wright Brothers' record, Penney used the flights to attract interest in setting up a glider school in Truro. The syndicate he was working with found a more promising location in South Wellfleet on the Atlantic side."

"Sounds as if he achieved his goal of a school even if the location was changed."

"The future of the school seemed assured. The location high on a cliff was ideal for gliding. The syndicate hired German and American personnel. Gliders were brought in from Germany. A horse team was retained to haul the gliders off the beach to the cliffs. There were dormitories and administrative buildings. The school only lasted a year; however, it would have been longer if not for the crash of 1929."

"The timing wasn't great to begin with, around midway between the end of World War One and the start of World War Two."

Weber chuckled. "I imagine German pilots would not have been as welcome on American soil as they were when Hesselbach was charming his adorers."

"What happened to Hesselbach?"

"He went on to pilot powered aircraft and supposedly was at the Eastern Front destroying bridges, but went missing after the Russians rolled through. The other German school staff were undoubtedly absorbed into the Nazi war machine. Their fates would be an interesting story for another day."

"Sounds like your story has a tragic ending for some of those involved."

Weber gave a shrug of his broad shoulders. "I'll concentrate on the positive aspects. The best glider pilots in the world studying the flight of gulls and dashing off for ice cream with their rich friend."

"I think I like that better, too," Ben said.

They made small talk until Ben pulled the cruiser into the parking lot of the Provincetown Inn. Weber thanked him for the ride.

"The crew is having a lift-off party tonight," Weber said. "You're invited if you'd like to come."

"Thanks," Ben said. "I may pass on the invitation. I want to get a good night's sleep."

"Well then, see you early in the morning. Should be quite the memorable day."

"I don't see how it could be anything else," Ben said.

CHAPTER FOURTEEN

Something was different.

Abi didn't know what it was, only that it felt good. She should have been crippled by disappointment after her unsuccessful visit to Town Hall, but it was just the opposite. She hated the cliché expression, but she felt newly *empowered*.

She owed it all to Edward Hopper. She was going to remove the Baron property from the face of the earth the way Hopper erased natural and artificial features that got in the way of his art.

Rather than head back to the cottage from the town hall, she drove to Fisher Beach, and hiked out to the Hopper cottage as her tour guide Beth had instructed.

The beach was deserted and the loudest sounds were the slosh of waves rippling against the sand. The only sign of life was a cormorant drying its wings on a rock.

The Hopper house was on a low hill about a half mile from the parking lot. She gazed up at the simple white cottage. The large window at the nearest side of the house was shuttered. She tried to imagine the great artist in front of a canvas, paintbrush in hand, as he captured the intense sunlight streaming into his studio.

As an art historian, Abi had studied the life and work of Hopper. She knew that Edward and his wife Jo, who was also an exceptional artist, lived a simple and frugal life. They came to Truro in the 1930s, attracted by the luminous light, the architecture and uncomplicated lifestyle.

They spent half the year on the Cape, going back to New York and their Washington Square apartment in the fall. Hopper roamed the territory around his house, painting dunes and hills; churches and houses. As Beth's tour showed, he liked almost anything that had to do with railroads. He was a private man and sometimes even painted from his car.

Her gaze shifted to a large, slab-roofed building of yellowish brown that stood a few hundred yards from the Hopper house. The contrast between the two dwellings could not have been more jarring. From its size and location, she surmised, she was looking at the controversial house that had stirred up the neighbors and prompted the lawsuit that ended so badly for the town.

It was smaller than Fort Baron. Even so, the house remained standing after hundreds of thousands in legal fees were spent to challenge its existence, proving that a head-to-head confrontation wouldn't work with the Baron house. Getting rid of that monstrosity would require a different strategy.

She trekked back to her car and drove to the cottage, even more determined to remove Fort Baron from the face of the earth. She didn't know how exactly, but the first faint glimmerings of a plan began to materialize in her mind.

Her preoccupation with the Baron property evaporated when she saw the glider perched near the crest of the hill, its nose pointed toward the setting sun. She parked in front of Beach Plum and walked over to take a closer look. Sunlight bathed the fuselage in a golden glow, imparting an almost ethereal aspect to the aircraft.

She knew nothing about aviation beyond the jet airliners she'd flown in during the course of her travels. But she could appreciate the sleek beauty of the glider as an amazing example of form following function.

The streamlined fuselage and the long, wide wing were design features that would allow the aircraft to dance on an updraft, but they also pleased the eye. It was one thing to hear about the glider, but another to see it in the flesh.

She strolled around the glider, taking in the tall tail with its flying goose logo, and inspecting the picture of a woman drawn on the nose.

The aircraft seemed so small. She didn't envy the hours the pilot would have to spend in the cramped cockpit, but the bird's-eye view would help the time pass.

Abi walked back to the cottage, poured herself a glass of rosé, then sat on the porch and watched the sunset.

After the sun bid farewell, Abi went into the cottage and prepared herself a kale and quinoa salad topped with the leftover salmon from the night before. All she had eaten since breakfast had been part of a turkey roll-up. In her haste to get away from Ben Dyer, she hadn't even finished that. After dinner she cleaned up the dishes, then poured another glass of wine and went into the office.

Settling into the desk chair, she connected the camera to the computer and reviewed the photographs taken from the trunk of the fallen tree. She gave the photo of the barn a quick glance, and was about to go on to the next picture when she noticed something.

She squinted at the photo, then opened the file containing the pictures she had taken on her first trek to the Baron house. She put the photos side-by-side and compared them.

The door that had been shut when she first saw the barn was partially open in the second photo, revealing a sliver of blackness that was definitely not a shadow.

Someone had been poking around the Baron property.

She wondered how the intruder got onto the estate. The main entrance to the property had been overgrown with bittersweet vines that would have snapped if the gate had been opened. The only other way in that she knew of was the tree that had crushed the fence.

She shrugged and got back to her main quest: tracking down the property owner. Her fingers tapped the keyboard and she Googled the name of Baron's real estate company. The only entry listed had a contact email address. She wrote a message asking for the name of the property manager, but a message appeared on the screen saying the address was no longer valid. Next, she went to sites that offered advice on how to conceal ownership of real estate.

It didn't take long for her to learn that ownership could be concealed in many ways: Land trusts, limited liability corporations, even phony names and addresses in different countries could hide real estate holdings.

She sat back in her chair and stared at the computer screen until her vision blurred. It was hard for her to admit, but she was playing out of her league.

If she were serious about digging for information on the house she would need professional help. She'd burned the bridge to her old law firm with her intemperate comments and she didn't have the money to hire new lawyers. Which left Ben Dyer.

As she pondered her next step, Abi noticed the glider flight schedule lying on the desk next to the computer where she had put it after Mead had delivered the press kit. She picked it up and read about the next day's events. The actual launch was scheduled for nine o'clock. The set-up crew would arrive an hour earlier. If the glider broke the Hesselbach record of more than four hours and five minutes, at the very least it would be early afternoon before the aircraft landed on the beach in front of the cottage colony.

An asterisk next to the landing time referred to a side note saying it was up to the discretion of the pilot how long beyond the record-breaking time he wanted to fly.

Maybe she could make a dent in the paperwork while things were quiet, she thought. Abi lifted the nearest box onto a chair and removed the cover. The carton was packed with manila folders. Each one was thick with papers. She extracted the folders one-by-one, glanced at the contents, and began a preliminary sorting according to subject. The contents of the files in some cases didn't match the labels. In one folder, labeled 'Office Supplies,' she found travel documents and correspondence.

She'd have to do a rough sorting, then refine it again and again. She stacked the sorted folders on the floor. Luckily, the office had a lot of space to accommodate her improvised system.

The work was like a game of Solitaire, where cards are moved from one stack to the other. As she shuffled papers around, she gathered a pile of metal paperclips and tossed them into a sea clam shell on the desk.

Her eyes were getting tired, and her brain was weary. Abi

surveyed what looked like a miniature city of manila skyscrapers and was glad that she had started the job. The work was tedious and time-consuming, but what else did a bankrupt gallery owner and unemployed art historian have to do?

She placed the clamshell paperclip holder on a carton to mark her progress, clicked off the lights in the office and went into the bathroom to wash up.

Then she climbed the stairs to the bedroom, got into a nightie and slipped under the sheets. She fell asleep almost immediately, and would have slept through the night if she hadn't been awakened by a noise. It was a sharp clatter, definitely not a dream. And it had come from *inside*, not outside. She sat up in bed and remembered she hadn't locked the front door. Lulled by the quietness of the place, she hadn't thought it was necessary.

Abi rolled out of bed and went to the top of the stairs where she flicked on a wall switch, instantly flooding the first floor with light. Her heartbeat ratcheted up as she peered from the top of the stairs, but she saw nothing out of the ordinary. Descending the stairs, she walked quickly to the front door and locked it, surveying the first floor. Again, all was as it had been when she went to bed. She stepped into the office and saw the pieces of the clamshell and some paperclips scattered on the floor.

Abi cleaned up the mess and inspected the rest of the office. Everything else was in its place. Maybe a mouse had disturbed the clamshell, she rationalized, not really believing that theory. Should she call the police? Nothing was missing. She went to the back door and made sure it was locked, then did the same with all the windows. She turned on the porch lights and left the downstairs lights on. Then she went back up to her bedroom.

Before getting into bed she stood by the window and looked out over the bay. The sky was like a sequined brocade. Had her eye not been drawn to the starlight bathing the shiny surface of the glider in an unearthly glow, she would have seen a strange phenomenon. The slight wrinkling of the heavenly tapestry, as if something had once again passed between her and the stars.

CHAPTER FIFTEEN

The first thing Ben did every morning after he got up was tap the antique brass barometer hanging on the wall of his bedroom. The habit was passed down from his father, one of the few non-Portuguese fishermen to fish out of Provincetown. Benji Dyer was tall and rugged-looking, and although his skin was more weathered than his son's, he had passed down his sly grin and dark blue eyes.

In between setting trawl lines and waiting for the baited hooks to catch fish, Benji read a lot. One of his favorite authors was Joseph Conrad. It was no surprise, then, that he'd tap the barometer like Captain MacWhirr in the novel *Typhoon* and quote the captain's words:

"Uncommonly dirty weather knocking about," Benji would declare.

The barometer used to hang in the living room. Everyone in the family knew that it was broken, although the needle could sometimes be dislodged with a sharp rap of the knuckles. It was all a big joke, because his father relied on the weather forecast from the National Oceanic and Atmospheric Administration, but the phrase was absorbed into the family legend and lexicon.

Dirty weather was the farthest thing from Ben's mind as he drove to the cottage hill around seven in the morning. The sun was shining brightly. A steady southwest breeze was coming off the bay. Ben stopped to chat with the police officer parked at the bottom of the hill, whose job it was to turn away spectators and allow crew to pass.

After parking the police cruiser at the top of the hill, he strolled over to the glider and looked out at the jade green waters of the bay. This was far from dirty weather, he mused. The vaulting azure sky was clear except for a few feathery white clouds. The cool morning breeze smelled of salt and schooling fish.

Gathered offshore were a couple dozen boats, including one with a diagonal orange stripe on the hull that identified the craft as Coast Guard.

Ben turned at the sound of tires crunching on the driveway. A Tahoe SUV pulled in next to Ben's cruiser. Magnus stepped out from the behind the wheel. Melissa emerged from the passenger side. The camera operator and sound man exited from the cab and went around to the back to unload their gear.

Ben strolled over and offered a cheery, "Good morning."

Magnus flashed his Hollywood smile. "Good morning, Officer Dyer," he said. "Nice to see you."

He wore a sky-blue, zippered jumpsuit that snugly fit his well-developed physique. Over the breast pocket was a patch with the flying goose logo that matched the one on the glider's tail. A baseball cap, the same color as the suit, was pulled down over Kyle's mane of hair. The jumpsuit cuffs were tucked into soft black leather boots.

Melissa was dressed far less flamboyantly in a pantsuit of oyster white. A matching headband kept her hair in place.

Magnus beckoned to the film crew. "C'mon, guys. Let's get some establishing shots before things get too crazy around here."

The crew set up the camera and sound equipment, then Magnus circled the glider and made a show of inspecting every square inch of the fuselage.

Melissa walked over to Ben. "What do you think of Kyle's flying suit?"

"He looks like he belongs in a *Star Wars* movie, but I like it."

"I like it, too," she said. "Kyle wanted high visibility and comfort. I was more conservative when it came to my wardrobe."

"You did well."

"Thank you. I researched casual wear for women around 1928,

so it's fairly accurate."

Ben's radio crackled. The police officer directing traffic at the bottom of the hill was calling. "Thought I'd give you a head's-up, Ben. Launch crew and press folk are starting to arrive."

"Thanks. Let them up a few at a time so I can get them parked."

"Will do."

"Looks like I've got to play traffic cop," Ben said to Melissa.

"Thank you so much for all your hard work."

"It's been fun. Thanks for bringing some excitement to our sleepy little town."

"You're very welcome," Melissa said. "See you after the flight."

Ben scrambled around the launch site, directing cars and trucks into every available spot until he got word from the other police officer that the traffic stream had stopped. He passed the news onto Melissa. She told Magnus, who kissed her on the cheek, walked over to the glider and placed his hand on the Darmstadt's fuselage. He brought a microphone to his mouth, and his voice came out of two large speakers set up on tall stands.

"Hello, everyone. Kyle Magnus speaking. In a few minutes I will get into this beautiful little plane and ascend into the skies for what I hope will be a record-breaking flight. I'll be broadcasting by radio from the aircraft and you'll be able to hear my comments on these speakers.

"Almost a century ago the German pilot, Peter Hesselbach, flew off a hill near here and stayed in the air for more than four hours, breaking the previous record. This time it is going to be done by an American pilot in an American-built plane."

There was a round of applause from the crowd.

"I'd like to thank all our sponsors, particularly Melissa, editor of *Sky Technology Magazine*. Come over here and say a few words, Mel."

Melissa walked over to Magnus, who handed her the microphone and whispered in her ear.

"Thank you, Kyle," she said. "And thanks to everyone for working to make this a truly awesome event. Kyle has informed me he's going to make a couple of important announcements after the flight. Please stick around to hear what he has to say. Now if you don't mind, we have to clear the area in front of the aircraft so the launch crew can set up."

The crowd peeled away from the glider and gathered in a roped-off section designated as the official spectator area. Mead came over to where Ben was standing.

"Ready to see aviation history made, Officer Dyer?"

"Absolutely," Ben said. "Looks like a perfect day to set a record."

"The weather conditions are almost exactly what they were when Hesselbach made his flight." He shielded his eyes with his hand and moved his head left and right. "Have you seen Hank?"

"Hank? Come to think of it, I haven't."

"Can't say I blame him for being AWOL, after Magnus shoved him out of the cockpit. Hell, if it was me, I'd be in my room at the inn, knocking down a fifth of Jim Beam."

"Too bad. He should be here to see his plane break the record. He deserves a lot of credit."

"That he does. I expect Magnus will beat Hesselbach's record, but it's going to take more than an exact replica of a Darmstadt glider to do it."

"Do you have doubts about Kyle's skill?"

"He'll be okay, but you have to remember, Hesselbach was one of the best pilots in the world. Folks who wrote about that day say he had perfect control of the glider every minute of the flight. Kyle plans to steer into the air current coming off the dunes, then gain altitude by spiraling around in the updraft, hopping from hill to hill, then over the bay and back again. It'll be tricky."

"We'll know soon enough if Magnus can duplicate that feat," Ben said. "Looks like the snappers are getting ready."

The launch crew was laying out the yellow rubber cord in the shape of a V, with the open part nearest the cliff. They attached the point to a hook in the nose of the glider. Magnus inspected the attachment, then climbed into the cockpit. Seconds later, his voice came over the loudspeakers.

"Testing…testing. Can you hear me?"

The spectators applauded.

"Good. I'm tucked into the cockpit now. Quite snug. In the original flight Hesselbach used a whistle to signal the launch crew.

I'll be doing it with radio. Okay, time for the snappers to take their position. Tail crew get ready."

The launch team broke up into two lines, with three people on each side of the rubber cord. A smaller group stood behind the tail of the glider. Another snapper stood by a wing, holding the glider steady.

"Looking good," Magnus said. "On the count of three."

The crew behind the glider grabbed onto the tail and the snappers picked up the cord in front of them.

"One…two…three."

The snappers began running for the edge of the hill, stretching out the cord, with the plane held in place by the tail crew, who dug their heels in and leaned against the pull. At the point of maximum tension, Magnus yelled, "Now!"

CHAPTER SIXTEEN

Abi had set the alarm for an early wake-up. She got out of bed and showered, then got dressed in shorts and a T-shirt and went down the stairs to the kitchen. Breakfast was coffee and a croissant heated up in the toaster oven. She carried her breakfast plate into the office.

Settling down behind the desk, Abi swiveled around in the chair and squinted at the stacks of boxes she had yet to organize. As she nibbled the pastry and sipped coffee, her mind plotted the outline of a plan of attack.

The slam of a car door interrupted her thoughts. She peered out the window. Ben Dyer was walking from his cruiser to the glider.

She wondered if she should go out to wish him a good morning, but instead turned her attention back to the professor's boxes. She barely had time to open the first carton before more doors were being slammed. She looked out the window again. The space in front of the cottages was filling with vehicles and people. Magnus and his crew were emerging from a Tahoe.

Abi's jaw dropped at the sight of Kyle's colorful flying suit and Melissa's 1920s costume. She tried to ignore the activity visible through the window and kept at her filing until the voice of Magnus boomed from loudspeakers and drowned out her thoughts completely. Taking the coffee mug with her, she went out onto the porch.

With all the noise and excitement, it was definitely going to be impossible to get any work done. She'd have to squeeze in some filing before the actual glider launch. Turning her back on the commotion, she went into the office, picked a box at random and began to go through the contents.

In short order, she learned that Professor Waldstein did have a filing system. He simply stuffed folders with papers that in many cases had no connection to each other. It would have been better if he hadn't even tried. The result was confusing and completely useless. Hercules had it easy compared to what she was facing. For starters, he didn't have the distraction of a full-blown media circus outside his window.

As Abi started to sort through the papers, stacking those linked by subject, she kept being distracted more and more. Pulling down the shades shut out the visual distraction, but didn't stop Magnus's amplified voice from coming into the office.

She sighed and sat back in her chair, defeated. If you can't beat 'em, join 'em. She got up and went out onto the front porch again. By then, a couple of dozen vehicles were parked in the front yard and more than fifty people were milling about in front of the cottages.

Ben was highly visible in his lime green vest as he steered people and vehicles like a cowpoke herding cattle. Abi watched from the porch. Ben saw her standing there and during a pause in traffic flow he came over to the porch.

"Good morning," he said. "Sorry for the racket."

"Don't apologize. It's all very exciting."

A grin came to his lips. "Hope you enjoy the show. There's a great view from the press and spectator area."

"Thanks for the tip," Abi said. "See you after the launch."

"We'll have lots to talk about. Got to go now."

Ben excused himself for cutting the conversation short, then trotted over to direct a food truck into one of the few spaces remaining.

Taking Ben's advice, Abi stood in the spectators' section. It was filled with people who were covering the story for media outlets. There was a mix of local press and Boston TV affiliates. Camera crews filmed anchor persons talking against the backdrop. She learned from scattered conversation that other outlets had leased boats to cover the action from the seaward side.

Magnus stood next to the glider, helmet in hand, resplendent in his blue jumpsuit as he posed for photos. He removed the ball cap, put the helmet on his head, gave the press section a wave and climbed into the cockpit.

Seconds later his voice came through the speakers, saying how snug it was in his seat. Then he told the launch and tail crews to get in position. At his instruction, the snappers marched forward, stretching the cords to the brow of the hill while the tail crew held the glider in place.

Magnus began the countdown and Abi and the others on the hill joined in. The tail crew released their grip and the glider shot forward, skimming the ground. The hook in the aircraft's nose disengaged and the glider was catapulted off the cliff as if from a slingshot.

The glider quickly gained altitude and gracefully came around, flew low over the cheering spectators, then followed the ragged line of cliffs until it was a dark speck against the sky.

Magnus's voice came over the speakers. "That was fun. How'd I look?"

A roar went up from the crowd, followed by rolling applause.

The glider turned around and flew above the cottages, then back along the cliffs. Abi watched for a while but once the aircraft had settled into its flight pattern she went back into the cottage. The launch was exciting, but she saw no point in staring at the sky when there was work to be done.

She set her cell phone timer to *bing* every half hour, then dug into the professor's files. Thirty minutes later, she walked outside to check on the glider. It swooped overhead. Magnus was teasing listeners about how long he would stay aloft.

"How about five hours?" he said.

The crowd applauded and yelled encouragement.

"How about six?"

There were yells and whoops mixed in with the crowd reaction.

"All depends on my bladder capacity, folks."

Laughter rippled across the hill.

Abi went back into the cottage, intending to come out in time to see Magnus break the record. Her eyes became bleary from reading files, so she shoved the folders aside and plunked a box of books next to the swivel chair. Like the files, the books were filed haphazardly. She took the books out one-by-one and set them on the top of the desk.

The first book she slid from the box focused on Impressionism. The next was on Picasso. Then came a couple of volumes on the works of Dali, followed by a treatise on Hellenistic sculpture. She got through one box and dug into another.

The volume she picked up was on American Realist artists. She was familiar with the book through her work as an art historian. On the inside cover was an *ex libris* sticker with the name Alden Proctor.

She turned to the title page and read the inscription: "To Alden Proctor, a great plumber and a lover of art. Jo Hopper."

Intrigued, she leafed through the pages and stopped at the chapter on Hopper. There was a reproduction of his iconic painting *Nighthawks*, and she wondered as she had many times before what the back story was for the mysterious couple.

She lingered over a painting on the next page entitled *High Noon*, which showed a blonde woman wearing a revealing shift over her nude body, standing in the doorway of a white clapboard house as if waiting for, or saying farewell to someone unseen. A lover?

On the following page, a woman was seated alone in an urban cafeteria. Something about the page felt funny. It was thicker than it should be. Abi looked closer and saw that the high noon and cafeteria pages were stuck together.

She rummaged in the desk drawers and found an X-Acto knife, then inserted the blade between the pages and sliced them apart. In the painting on the left-hand page, a woman in pink peered out the window of a shadowed house. The work was called *Cape Cod Morning*. The painting on the right showed a man seated in a sun-drenched office in a work Hopper had titled *Office in a Small City*.

What drew her interest were the sheets of textured paper hidden in the pocket that had been formed by the stuck pages. She spread them out on the desktop. Under all three sketches was a title and notes describing the date, subject, colors and the light.

It took a few seconds, but she finally realized what she was looking at. She had seen similar sketches in the ledgers Jo Hopper kept to record Edward's work. Hopper used his drawings not as finished products, but as memory aids to indicate composition and describe light.

She picked up the sketch entitled *Snow Farm and Barn: Truro*, handling it gingerly as if she were afraid it would fall apart. The black-and-white charcoal pencil drawing showed a low-slung house and a barn that looked like the same building she had seen on the Baron property. She studied the sketch for a moment, then put it down and picked up another.

The half-hour alarm went off on her mobile phone. Time to check on Magnus, but she couldn't take her eyes off the images in front of her.

The second sketch showed the barn alone. The door was open, the dark interior sketched with heavy crosshatch strokes of the pencil. An old pickup truck was backed up to the doorway. Between the truck and the doors was the figure of a man with his back to the viewer. He was carrying a rectangular object, his arms spread-eagle. The title was simply *Man and Pickup Truck*.

The third picture showed the man up close, facing the artist, with the buildings in the background. The face was narrow, almost feral, with close-set eyes and an odd-shaped jaw. Like the others, it had been dated September 21, 1946.

The title was simply two words:

Bad Face.

"Zowee!"

The amplified voice of Magnus blasted from the loudspeakers.

"In one more minute we hit four hours and five. Then I'm flying to the moon!"

The sound of wild cheering penetrated the thin walls of the cottage. Abi scooped up the sketches, put them back between the pages and closed the cover of the book, which she slid into a desk drawer. As she made her way to the front door, she could hear the crowd doing the countdown from ten.

Abi burst out of the cottage onto the porch. The glider was hanging about a mile out over the bay as if attached to invisible strings. The excitement in the air was palpable.

"Five…four…three…two."

The crowd was still counting when the glider suddenly, inexplicably, seemed to wobble; it soared for several seconds, then put its nose down and made a long, shallow dive that ended in a white-foamed crash into the sea.

CHAPTER SEVENTEEN

Ben was watching from the beach when the glider fell out of the sky.

Fifteen minutes earlier, he had driven off the hill to talk to the officer who'd been directing traffic away from the launch site. They agreed to split up the traffic duty. Once the flight was over, spectators leaving the beach at the same time would create a traffic jam on the back road between the bay and the highway. The officer would move out to the highway to direct traffic. Ben would see that the exodus from the beach parking lot had some order to it.

He left the cruiser near the exit of the packed parking lot and strolled to the beach. The crowd had grown to a couple of hundred people. The gathering had a party atmosphere. Picnic baskets and coolers were within arm's reach of beach chairs and blankets. Spectators wielding cameras and binoculars lined the shore.

As he wove his way through the crowd to the water's edge, Ben caught a glimpse of Hank Aldrich coming his way. They made eye contact, but to Ben's surprise Hank veered off in another direction and merged in with the crowd.

Hank must have changed his mind about ignoring the flight, but maybe he wasn't ready to talk to anyone. Ben shrugged it off and joined the ranks of people watching the glider go through its graceful aerial gyrations. There was a growing excitement in the air as the seconds ticked by.

Ben checked the timer on his cell phone. Magnus was minutes

away from smashing the Hesselbach record. He steered the glider toward the cliffs, using the thermals to gain altitude, then he dipped a wing and turned toward the bay, putting the glider into a wide, lazy circle over the flotilla.

Halfway through a turn the plane began to wobble like a drunken gull. Ben thought Magnus was going to thrill the crowd with some acrobatic stunts. But the plane yawed steeply to its right, then to the left, its nose dipped and seconds later, the glider dove into the bay.

An anguished cry came from the spectators. People sprang from chairs and blankets. The human wave rolled to the water's edge.

Ben trotted off the beach to the parking lot and got into his cruiser. He drove briskly back up the hill to the cottages. The scene on the bluff mirrored what was happening on the beach. The media people were lined along the edge of the bluff, cameras and binoculars trained on the bay. The Coast Guard boat had broken away from the flotilla and was leaving a high-speed wake as it headed toward a spot where waves were sloshing against the half-submerged plane.

Ben got a pair of binoculars from the cruiser and returned to his viewing spot. The Coast Guard boat was coming to a stop next to the glider. After several minutes had passed, the crew members hauled something out of the water onto the deck. Something blue.

Abi joined him on the bluff. "Can you see what's happening, Officer Dyer?"

Ben lowered the binoculars.

"Looks like the Coast Guard has pulled Magnus out of the water."

"Is he okay?"

"I can't see."

"This is unbelievable," Abi said. "I was listening to his voice over the speakers. He was having a good time, joking with the crowd. Then he yelled something. It was hard to hear what he was saying."

"I'll see what I can find out." Ben handed the binoculars to Abi. "You can use these until I come back."

He got in the police car and headed down the driveway. When he reached the highway, he made a quick stop to tell the traffic officer what was going on. He called in backup, then he drove to the Coast Guard station in Provincetown's west end. The metal gates surrounding the government property were wide open.

Ben got out of the cruiser and was making his way to the station when a car drove into the lot and braked to a stop. The German journalist, Marty Weber, got out of the car and loped after him.

"Officer Dyer, have you heard any news?" he said breathlessly.

"That's what I'm here for," Ben said. He motioned for Weber to follow. He made his way into the building and onto a concrete pier that extended around a third of a mile into the harbor. The Coast Guard boat had entered the harbor and was headed for the floating dock at the end of the pier.

At the same time, an ambulance drove out to the end of the pier. After a few minutes, the ambulance returned with lights flashing.

The ambulance was followed by a Coast Guard SUV which dropped the boat crew off at the station.

"How's it look?" Ben asked a crewman.

"Not good," the crewman said with a shake of her head. "Cockpit was under water by the time we got there. We had a hard time getting the pilot out of his harness."

"Did the glider sink?"

"We got flotation buoys on the wreckage and there's a marker in the water. A salvage boat is on its way out of Provincetown."

Ben thanked the crew member for the information. He saw Weber jotting down the comments in a notebook. "Looks like you've got a scoop," Ben said.

"Unfortunately, yes." The German furrowed his brow. "Were you keeping track of how long the glider was in the air?"

"I was timing the flight on my phone."

"There is something very odd about this. The Darmstadt went down in the ocean one minute short of the Hesselbach record."

"That is odd. And quite the coincidence."

"From what I saw, the pilot was displaying a high degree of skill. Why did he suddenly plunge into the sea exactly sixty seconds short of his goal?"

"Some sort of technical problem?"

"That possibility comes to mind, of course. But the original

Darmstadt design had proven to be sound. Aldrich did a meticulous job replicating the aircraft and Magnus was a skilled pilot."

"If you eliminate pilot error and design flaw, what then?"

Weber shrugged and pulled a phone out of his pocket. "Thanks to the wonders of modern technology I can transmit the story and photographs around the world from my car in an instant. If you'll excuse me."

Ben chatted briefly with some of the local police officers, then with nothing more that he could do, drove back to the Truro police station. Chief Sisson greeted him.

"You've had quite the day, Ben. I've been watching the whole thing on TV. Doesn't look good from what I could see."

"It isn't. I was at the Coast Guard station when the boat came in with Magnus, the pilot. Looks like he isn't going to make it. They're trying to save the glider."

"Damn. That's too bad about the pilot. What a mess! Our little town is going to be on the TV channels for a while. Why don't you take the rest of the day off?"

"Thanks, Chief. I appreciate it."

Ben left the station and drove back to his house. He got out of his uniform and into shorts and a T-shirt. The crash scene was being filmed from a helicopter. He watched television until the reporter announced that Magnus was officially dead. Then he went in the kitchen and poured himself a shot of Irish whiskey. He didn't usually drink this early in the day, but it seemed like the thing to do.

CHAPTER EIGHTEEN

Back at the launch site, Melissa and her crew awaited word from the Coast Guard. She paced along the edge of the bluff; cell phone clutched in her hand.

When her phone chirped all eyes were focused on Melissa's face. Her stoic expression melted. She handed the phone to Mead, then wrapped her arms across her chest and lowered her head, her body racked by sobs.

After a quick conversation Mead clicked off. A grim expression came to his face.

"Gather round folks," he said. "That was the Coast Guard. The news isn't good. They got Kyle out of the water, but I'm sorry to say he didn't make it."

A chorus of moans and outcries of disbelief greeted his announcement. The crew gathered protectively around Melissa.

Abi had been hanging around with the others, but after the bad news she felt like a stranger intruding on a family tragedy. She edged away from the mourners and went into the cottage. No escape there. Even if she lowered the window shades, she'd be aware of what was going on outside.

She could only imagine what Melissa must be feeling. She didn't know what to do. Maybe a drive would help calm her mind. She had always found refuge in art. She had a vague idea of revisiting some of the places from the Hopper tour. Abi went into the office, put the art book into her rucksack, and then went out to her Land Rover.

Abi decided to start at the lighthouse. But as she drove down Route 6 she saw that she was coming up on the road that led to the Baron property. Acting impulsively, she spun the steering wheel and made a sharp turn.

She drove past the iron gate, parked in the cul-de-sac, and made her way through the pine woods to the fence. She climbed onto the fallen tree, crossed over the fence on the angled trunk, and then lowered herself down the limbs on the other side.

Abi kept on the move and quickly made her way through the forest. After emerging into the open, she continued up a grassy slope until she came to the mansion and the barn.

She reached into the rucksack, pulled out the art book and slipped the sketches out from between the pages. Holding the wide-angle drawing of the farmhouse and barn at arm's length, she compared it to the actual scene. In this way, she used the sketch as a guide to position herself where Hopper—if it had been drawn by Hopper—would have been standing.

Hopper had apparently been standing in the cedar grove. It's possible the trees weren't there in his day, but most of the growth seemed mature. Why would he bother to go into the trees if he were going to ignore them in his drawing? He could just as well have sketched the scene in the clear, from a slightly different angle, without having to endure bramble bushes and poison ivy.

She glanced at the sketch of the man unloading the truck, then studied the close-up of his face in the third drawing. It was a terrible face. She knew in an instant why Hopper had been in the woods. He had been hiding.

Again, Abi tried to see the scene as Hopper had sketched it. The massive Baron house stifled attempts to imagine it not being there. Even Hopper would have had a tough time blocking the house from his mind.

The design reminded her of the bunkers the Germans built for the Siegfried line. Fort Baron was constructed of concrete and dark wood clapboard. Windows on the lower level were horizontal slots, further promoting the fortress look.

She walked around the three-car garage to the front of the

house. An asphalt driveway led to a parking area large enough to hold a dozen cars. Walkways branched off from the parking area. The manicured lawn surrounding the house was amazingly green, and appeared to be close cut, in contrast to the unmowed grass around the barn. On closer inspection, she saw that the close-cut grass was synthetic turf.

The house was nothing but a faceless, big fat insult to the beauty of the setting.

She walked over to where the truck would have been parked in 1946, on the day the sketch had been drawn. She went through the motions of carrying a box to the barn which is when she saw that there was no lock on the door.

The door slid open easily. She stepped inside and looked around. There were haylofts on both sides and below them, stalls for animals. Years must have passed since the barn was in use but it still smelled faintly of manure and hay.

Abi took a few steps, then stopped and looked around. The dirt floor was hard-packed except for a rectangular section of softer soil a couple of feet across. Near one edge of the rectangle was what looked to be a partial footprint. Probably made by a man, judging from the size. Sweep marks were visible in the dirt.

Hanging from a nearby post nail was an old broom. Most of its bristles were missing, which may have been why the sweeper missed the footprint.

The light spilling in through the open door only went a slight distance into the barn, leaving the rear section of the interior in shadow. An alarm bell went off in Abi's head. The person who left the boot print could still be there.

Hold on, girl.

Maybe she was over-imagining things and getting freaked out over nothing. Or just maybe she should get the hell out of there. She backed up slowly, her eyes probing the darkness, until she was out of the building.

Turning, she walked briskly for a few steps before breaking into a trot. When she lived in Boston, she ran every morning along the Charles River. She was confident she could outrun anyone short of an Olympian sprinter. She didn't know who that person might be, but as she slipped into the sunless forest, she sensed that this was not a healthy place for her to be.

Her legs broke into a full run even before her brain gave them the order to move. In her panic she lost her bearings. When she came out of the forest she encountered the fence, but the fallen tree wasn't where it should be. She had veered off around a hundred feet from her target. She dashed to the tree, scrambled up the branches and made her way along the trunk. She was breathing hard when she got behind the wheel of the Land Rover and turned the ignition key.

She cast a fearful glance at the gate as she drove by. In her fevered imagination the gate flew open and someone or something burst out to block the road. But a few minutes later she was pulling onto the highway. Her fears slipped away, and her breath became more measured. She chuckled at her madcap flight. She must have looked like a crazy woman running away from an old building.

Well, so what if she did? The footprint was real enough. There was nothing crazy about the intruder who came into her cottage. She didn't imagine the broken clamshell in her office. And she was uneasy about the big bird she saw—or imagined—in the night sky above her house.

Abi was confused about a lot of what was going on, but a couple of things were abundantly clear: She was getting in over her head... and she was going to need help.

CHAPTER NINETEEN

Kyle Magnus got his wish after all. The showy pilot with a flair for publicity had wanted his flight to make headlines around the world, but his name was in the news for all the wrong reasons. Ben was watching television news when the police chief called.

"Hi, Ben," Sisson said. "How're you doing?"

"Fine, Chief. What's going on?"

The chief chuckled. "What *isn't* going on? We've got TV trucks swarming all over the place and choppers circling overhead. It's been like a damned war zone."

"I've been watching the reports. I saw the salvage boat bring the wreckage into the Coast Guard wharf."

"That's what I'm calling about, Ben. A State Police Lieutenant is at the airport hangar where they took the smashed-up plane. He wants to talk to someone from our department who can answer his questions."

"This seems more like a case for the FAA. Why are the State Police involved?"

"I wondered about that, too. Couldn't get a straight answer. You've been the closest to this thing. Hope you don't mind being called back after I gave you time off."

"Not at all, Chief. Glad to help."

"That's great, Ben. The name of the Statie is Lieutenant Curran. He'll wait to see you at the hangar."

"No problem. I'll get right on it."

"Thanks, Ben. Let me know what this is all about."

"Will do."

Ben clicked off and went into his bathroom to wash the sleep from his face. Next, he changed from his shorts and T-shirt back into full uniform. Fifteen minutes later, he was pulling up to the hangar where he'd talked to Hank Aldrich and seen the Darmstadt glider close up.

A couple of State Police SUVs and a Provincetown Police cruiser were parked outside the airport terminal. Several TV trucks emblazoned with logos for Boston stations, each vehicle bristling with antennas and disks, were parked nearby. The TV crews and carefully coiffed male and female anchor persons milled around talking into cell phones.

Ben waved at the Provincetown police officers and they pointed to the entrance door where a State Trooper stood guard.

"I'm looking for Lieutenant Curran," Ben told the trooper.

The officer opened the door to let Ben into the hangar. The interior was brightly lit from the portable lamps placed around the sad hunk of wood and fabric that had once been the Darmstadt glider replica.

The fuselage was still in once piece. The wing had been detached and lay on the floor. He half-expected to see Aldrich mourning the loss of his baby, but the only other people in the hangar were three men in suits.

One man was taking photos and another was writing in a notebook. The third man was talking on a phone. He ended the call and tucked the phone in his suit pocket when he saw Ben and came over with his hand extended.

"You must be Officer Dyer from the Truro PD," he said.

"That's right. Chief Sisson sent me here to talk to Lieutenant Curran."

"That would be me." They shook hands. His grip was as firm as his jaw. "Thanks for coming by, Officer Dyer. Thought it would be helpful to link up with your department, since the flight took off from your town."

Curran was of average height and build, and with his quiet-spoken manner and well-tailored blue suit, he looked more like some of Ben's legal compatriots than a State Trooper.

"Athena wasn't much help," Ben observed.

"Athena?" Curran said, a puzzled expression on his face.

"The silhouette on the nose is the emblem for the University of Darmstadt, the town in Germany where the original glider was built."

"You sound like you know something about gliders."

"Only what Hank Aldrich told me the last time I was here."

"When was that?"

"A couple of days before the launch."

"Your chief said that you were mainly involved with traffic control."

"That's right. I've been running the traffic detail. Yesterday, I escorted the glider from here to the launch site. I stopped by the hangar the first day on the job because I wanted to take a look at the glider. I've got my pilot's license so I'm fascinated by aircraft of any kind."

"I heard Aldrich was disappointed he wasn't flying the plane. Did he say anything about that?"

"Oh sure. He was pretty open about his feelings." Ben gestured toward the wreckage. "He had worked hard to make sure it was an exact replica of the original. He called it his 'baby.' He was disappointed that he wasn't flying the plane instead of Magnus."

Curran tightened his lips in a thin smile. "Turned out to be lucky for him that he wasn't flying."

Ben glanced at the wreckage. "So it seems."

"Did he tell you why Magnus was chosen to fly the plane and not him?"

"As I understand it, originally two flights were planned—one on the Atlantic side, to be flown by Kyle, the other on the bay with Aldrich as the pilot. When the first one was canceled, the project organizers decided to go with Kyle for the bay flight. You can talk to Melissa, who was one of the group that made the decision."

"I already have. She told me about a Navy contract. Did Aldrich say anything about that?"

"Yes. He said not making the flight put him at a disadvantage with the Navy."

"Apparently there was a great deal riding on this flight. Money as well as fame."

"Aldrich thought so, which was another reason he was so disappointed he wasn't flying."

"What did he say that led you to that conclusion?"

Ben hesitated, knowing how bad it would sound, but he always counseled clients to tell the truth. "He said he hoped the glider would make a big splash."

"You're sure of that." It was a statement rather than a question.

"Yes. But I don't think he meant it. He had put in hours of work building the glider and it's unlikely he would have wanted to see it looking the way it does now."

"You sound as if your relationship with Aldrich was more than casual," Curran said, his eyes narrowing.

"Not really. Just two pilots talking shop."

Curran paused, absorbing Ben's reply, then said, "Do you know the current whereabouts of Mr. Aldrich?"

"I haven't seen him since the morning of the flight. He was on the beach below the launch site."

"Did he say why he wasn't at the launch itself?"

"We didn't talk. I only saw him for a second before I turned my attention to the glider. I thought he'd be here inspecting the damage to his plane."

"The Coast Guard guys saw a man answering his description snooping around the wreck after they brought it to the hangar."

"I guess I'm not surprised he'd be interested. He built the glider and would want to know what caused it to crash."

"Maybe that's the reason he's not here."

"Not sure where you're going with this, Lieutenant. What reason would that be?"

"Show is always better than tell. Let's take a closer look at the plane."

Curran walked over to the fuselage and waved at Ben to join him. He took his cell phone from his pocket and handed it to Ben after turning on the flashlight function.

"You said you've got your pilot's license. Poke your head in and tell me if anything catches your eye."

Ben leaned in and flashed the light around the interior of the fuselage. He saw what he thought was a patch of dried seaweed, but on closer inspection it appeared to be something else. Then he backed out and returned the phone to Curran. "There's a hole in the bottom of the fuselage. Dark stains around it. The control lines have been severed."

"That's right. We think that's what caused the plane to crash."

"The control lines could have been damaged in the crash."

"That doesn't account for the stains. We think they were made by the same explosive that blew a hole in the fuselage."

"Explosive?"

Curran nodded.

"You're talking sabotage?"

"Maybe," he said, shrugging his shoulders. "We won't know for sure until the lab finishes analyzing the black stuff on the fabric, but it looks like there may have been a small explosion. What do you think?"

"It's possible, I suppose. But, how and why?"

"That's what we'd like to ask Mr. Aldrich. He would have been the last one to work on the glider."

"If what you're suggesting is true, this is—"

"Yeah, I know. Murder. Got some guys I want you to meet."

Curran introduced Ben to the other men in suits. They were both from the district attorney's office and were working with Curran's investigative unit. They got excited when Curran told them about Aldrich's comment. They handed Ben their business cards with contact information on them.

One man thanked Ben for his help, saying, "We'd appreciate it if you could keep this conversation to yourself for the time being."

"And please call immediately if you hear from Aldrich," Curran said.

Ben tucked the cards in his pocket. "I'll be sure to do that, Lieutenant."

A few minutes later Ben was in his cruiser heading home. His head was spinning. The severed controls could have led to the wild gyrations the plane made before it crashed. But murder? On the other hand, what other explanation was there?

He still hadn't come up with an answer when he pulled into his driveway. Standing in his driveway was Hank Aldrich.

Ben got out of the SUV. "What are you doing here?" he said.

Aldrich wrapped his arms, which had been hanging by his sides, protectively across his chest.

"I think I need a lawyer," he said.

"I agree," Ben said. "Come inside."

CHAPTER TWENTY

Abi had calmed down by the time she got to the cottage hill.

She couldn't believe she had a full-blown panic attack at the barn. Ever since she'd been ground up by the legal mill she'd been acting erratically. Maybe the lawsuit had tipped her over the edge. What could be crazier than dashing over hill and dale at the sight of a footprint?

Back at the cottage, she went straight to the refrigerator and pulled out the bottle of rosé. She changed her mind and put the bottle back in the refrigerator. Alcohol wasn't the only way to steady her nerves. She went into the office and picked up the bow case leaning against a wall and then went out the back door into the yard behind the cottage.

She knelt on the ground and opened the case. Nestled inside was the bow, a sheaf of arrows, a leather finger guard, extra strings and a roll of paper targets. She unrolled a target and looked for a place to hang it. Sections of stockade fence had been erected between the closely-built cottages to allow a little privacy for people using the backyards.

Using tacks from the case, she attached the target to the fence. Next, she pulled the finger guard onto her right hand, then strung the bow and picked up a single arrow.

As a young girl, Abi had practiced archery at summer camp and became quite good with a bow and arrow. The asymmetrical

Japanese bow was far more flexible and longer than the one she had learned on and required a whole different way of shooting.

In Zen archery the goal is to hit a spiritual target rather than a real one. The tsunami of depositions, hearings, and summonses she'd been drowning in would have pulled her under if not for the six-foot-long bamboo bow in her hand.

The archery set was an unexpected gift from a stranger. After a particularly depressing lawyer conference, Abi had taken a ride in the countryside to get away from the litigation. She pulled over at a yard sale in Concord with no intention of buying anything, but her eye was drawn to the open bow case lying on a separate table.

The elderly Asian woman running the sale said she was moving to a condominium and needed to get rid of many belongings, including her husband's Zen archery set.

When Abi asked what Zen archery was, the woman said, "I can't explain. You have to practice it yourself. I can see by your face that you are the right person to have this."

The woman picked up the bow and insisted on presenting it to Abi, along with the arrows, the case and a copy of a book entitled *Zen and the Art of Archery*. When Abi protested, the woman said it would simply not be right to sell the set.

After reading the book, Abi got a couple of bales of hay from a farm outside Boston, and put them in the courtyard behind her apartment to use as a backstop to the target. She even enrolled in a few classes at a *Kyudojo*, where a master instructed her in the ancient art.

It had been hard to wrap her mind around Zen archery. Concepts like aiming at the self, but not the self, becoming the aimer and the aimed, the hitter and the hit, were not easy to understand, but the mystical exercises cleared her mind. Using a *yumi*, or Zen bow was different from western archery. Even the technique differs, with the Zen bow held not at shoulder level, but above the head, a demanding stance that increases concentration.

It felt good to feel the bow's leather handgrip again. She notched the three-foot-long arrow in the *tsuru*, or bowstring, held the bow high in stretched arms, and then brought it down, breathing slowly, drawing the string and holding it until the bow made the decision to shoot the arrow without her aiming or thinking.

The arrow missed the target completely, even from only ten paces. The other arrows came only slightly closer to the bull's-eye, but that was all right because this was Zen. The *thrum* of the string and the *thunk* of the arrow striking the fence were as important as hitting the bull's-eye.

After an hour of shooting, she increased the distance to the target five more paces and improved the accuracy of the arrows. She felt calm enough to put the unstrung bow back in the case, vowing to shoot more often.

It was now clear in her mind what she had to do next.

Abi went into her office, sat behind the desk and took Ben's business card from her wallet. She punched out the number on her phone and a female voice answered. "Truro police department."

"I'm trying to get in touch with Officer Ben Dyer."

"Officer Dyer isn't here today," the dispatcher said.

"Is there another number where I can reach him?"

"We're not allowed to give out that information. Would you like to leave a message in case he calls in?"

"Yes, I would. Please ask him to get in touch with Abi Vickers when he has a minute."

"I'll do that. Anything else I can help you with?"

"No, thank you. That's all for now."

Abi hung up and stared into space, her tightly-compressed lips relaxing into a rueful smile. She had agonized over whether to accept Ben's offer of help. Now that she had made her painful decision, Ben was nowhere to be found. She went out on the porch. Plunking down into a wicker rocking chair, she absent-mindedly placed Ben's business card face down on a side table and gazed off at the bay.

She savored the peace and tranquility. It was as if nothing extraordinary had happened on the hill. Not the launch, or the crash. No cries of dismay or people crowding the edge of the hill for a better look at the fallen aircraft.

A couple of power boats cut wakes across the blue water. A distant sailboat seemed pasted onto the bay. The light from the setting sun streamed skyward from below the horizon to paint the edges of the clouds in gilt.

She glanced at the tabletop, thinking that a glass of wine might not be a bad idea after all, and noticed a phone number written in ball point on the back of Ben's business card. Next to the number was a "C" in parentheses. Ben had jotted down his cell phone number while they were chatting at the lighthouse overlook.

Her fingers plucked the card off the table. She went back into the cottage and called the number. Dyer answered after a couple of rings.

"Hi, Ben," she said. "This is Abi. How are you?"

"I'm fine, thanks, Abi. Nice to hear from you. Hope things have settled down on the hill and you've been able to get back to work. "

"That's why I called. The situation is more complicated than I anticipated. Is your offer of legal help still good?"

"Yes, of course. I'd be glad to get in touch with the real estate division at my old law firm."

"This isn't just about real estate."

"I'm sorry. I thought we were talking about the Baron estate."

"We are, but we aren't. Like I said, it's complicated. I can explain better in person. Can you come to the cottage so we can talk?"

"Sure." After a pause, Ben said, "I can do that."

Abi thought she heard hesitation in his voice. "Is this a bad time?"

"No," he said. "Not at all. I'm wrapping up some business. I'll be done in a half hour and pop right over."

"That would be wonderful," she said with relief. "See you in a bit."

Abi hung up, sat back in her chair and puffed her cheeks out. *Get a grip, girl. Think about what you're going to say, and lay off the sauce.* She needed to have her wits about her. She laid out a plate of cheese and crackers. Then she poured herself a big tumbler of flavored seltzer water and went back onto the porch to wait for Ben.

Forty-five minutes after she talked to Ben the headlights of his white pickup swept the front of the cottages and he parked in front of Beach Plum. Abi got up to greet him. They shook hands and she led him to a chair next to hers. Then she brought out the snacks and another glass of seltzer water.

They clinked glasses. "Thank you so much for coming over to see me," Abi said. "Your day must have been absolutely crazy."

He nodded. "When I joined the police force in April and got assigned to the graveyard shift, the most exciting thing I'd see was an occasional coyote running across the road. But I was the officer at the scene when the housekeeper found Eddy Baron dead. And now we have a fatal glider crash."

"I didn't realize that you'd been on the police department only two months."

"It must have been pretty obvious the first time we met. You probably thought you were talking to Barney Fife, the goofy deputy sheriff in the Mayberry TV series."

Abi threw her head back and let out a laugh "You did seem a little obsessed with that barricade."

A sheepish grin came to his lips. "Dealing with traffic control wasn't something they taught in law school, but I am getting better at it."

"Glad to hear that. It must have been quite the change from law to law enforcement. Do you miss your legal work?"

"Sometimes. I like the structure of the law, and the challenge of untangling a complicated situation. Mostly I miss the camaraderie with my colleagues. Being in the world of law."

She gave a nod of agreement. "It's the same with me. I miss the excitement of an opening, people viewing the work of a talented new artist for the first time."

"I can see how that must have been very fulfilling."

"It was. The day-to-day business of running two galleries was a necessary evil. An art gallery is not a high-profit operation. You have to do it all yourself…bookkeeping, marketing, even catering." She gestured at the appetizer plate on the table. "I got quite good at laying out a cheese and cracker spread, though." She paused, then said, "There is a difference. I got kicked out of my world. You chose to leave yours."

Ben picked up a cracker and slice of cheese, but instead of popping it in his mouth, he put the appetizer down on a paper napkin.

"It wasn't entirely a matter of choice with me. After Loren died,

I threw myself into my practice, but even the most important cases seemed unimportant and trivial to me. I resented all the time I had wasted while Loren was still alive. I thought we were going to be together forever."

"I had the same feeling about my own marriage," Abi said. "We would grow old together."

"Live and learn, I guess. Working as a cop is part of a rebuilding process. Dealing with the everyday problems of people is helping me to become human again."

Damn, Abi thought. *This man is so infuriatingly nice.*

"Before we talk about anything else, I'd like to apologize for being so abrupt when we had lunch at Highland Light. I didn't trust you."

"I don't blame you for being leery. I'm practically a stranger."

"It's more than that. It's because you're a lawyer."

He raised a forefinger. "Correction. I *was* a lawyer. Now I'm a country cop. But I get it. Shakespeare suggested killing all the lawyers."

Shaking her head to emphasize the point, she said, "I don't dislike lawyers. I *loathe* them. For three years, my life was torn apart, piece by piece, by well-dressed gentlemen and ladies in the legal profession. That includes the judges and mediators."

"I'm sorry you had to go through that."

"Everyone knows the system is broken, but they're all enablers who allow it to hurt people rather than help them. My inability to trust anyone was a casualty of that experience. I know it's not fair to transfer my distrust to you, but that's how I feel."

For a few seconds, the loudest sound on the porch was the buzz of insects around a light. Abi held her breath, expecting Ben to bolt from his chair. She was relieved when he didn't. A crooked smile came to his lips.

"Sure, all too many lawyers are bloodsuckers and snakes, but I wasn't one of them. I helped people through difficult situations. And I'd like to help you. If you let me."

Abi stared at Ben's face in the dusky light, as if she were seeing it for the first time. There wasn't a hint of perfidy in the rugged features. She wished she had poured that wine after all. Time to end her self-imposed booze ban.

"Would you like something to drink? All I have is rosé."

"Rosé it is."

She poured two glasses of wine and carried them out onto the porch. Settling into a chair, she took a sip, and said, "I went over to the Baron property again today. I wanted to push the picture of the crash out of my mind. On this visit I went inside the barn."

"The door was unlocked?"

"It was partially open."

"How did you get past the fence?"

"There's a place you can climb across on a fallen tree."

Ben laughed. "You're very determined."

"Foolhardy might be a more appropriate description."

"I don't think so, but please go on."

"I had noticed in some of the pictures I'd taken of Fort Baron the day I moved into this cottage that the barn door had been closed. In the photos I took later, when I first discovered the fallen tree, the door was slightly ajar."

"Are you sure about that?"

"Yes. Which is why I wanted to check it out at close hand. When I went into the barn I saw a shoe or boot print on the dirt floor between the animal stalls. Probably a man from the size. Someone had tried to brush it out, probably the broom hanging from a nail. There were flecks of dirt in the straw and you could see the sweep marks in the dirt. Maybe the sweeper was in a hurry and didn't watch where he stepped."

"Good detective work. Since there is no doubt about the print, the question is who made it? Eddy Baron spent a lot of time at his property. It could be his boot print."

"That's possible, but it goes against what I learned in Girl Scouts. You can tell if a print is fresh if the ridges are raised, as these were." She shrugged. "Maybe I'm overreacting. It was probably made by a security contractor checking on the property."

Ben frowned in thought. "There is no security patrol as far as I know. Representatives for the property manager gave the gate lock code to the police department in case there was an emergency, like a fire. Guess they figured the fence would keep intruders out."

Abi grinned. "It would have kept me out if a big tree hadn't fallen on it."

"The owners could have hired a security patrol and didn't tell anyone. But if that were the case, the breach in the fence would have been fixed. Also, why would someone with a legitimate reason to be on the property sweep away his footprints?"

"That's an excellent point. Thank you, Ben." Abi was even more convinced asking Ben to help was the right decision.

"Was there anything else that didn't seem right to you?"

Abi gave an exaggerated hike of her eyebrows. "Yes. The whole freaky property. Before I went into the barn I took a closer look at the big house. It's even more monstrous up close. Everything about the place gives me the creeps."

"Nothing lonelier than an empty summer house," Ben said. "Especially a place where the owner died."

"Well yes," Abi said. "There's that too." She paused in thought, then said, "Do you know anything about the local bird species?"

Ben wondered why the conversation had veered ninety degrees from the subject of the Baron house, but he answered, "I can tell the difference between a gull and a tern, and I love seeing great blue herons in the marshes. I have a Peterson bird guide on my coffee table, but I rarely use it. Loren was the birder in our family. Thinking of taking up birding?"

She glanced up at the porch ceiling as if she could see through it. "I've heard the sound of wings in the sky at night. They sounded big. I've caught a glimpse of something moving against the stars and cloud backdrop, but couldn't make out what it was."

"This town sticks way out to sea, so we're on the Atlantic migratory flyway. It could be almost anything. We're seeing more southern birds now, like snowy egrets, than in the past. Maybe it's something as exotic as a pelican, which has a pretty wide wingspread."

"A pelican?"

"We've had manatees come this far north."

"Maybe. Like the old limerick says: 'A very funny bird is a pelican.'"

Without hesitation, Ben concluded, "'Its beak can hold more

than its bellycan.'"

They laughed at the joke.

"Sorry to get off track," Abi said. "Back to the main reason I asked you over. I'd like us to work together toward the acquisition of the Baron property. You offered to help dig out the ownership details."

"I'll be glad to give it a try."

He smiled. It was a nice smile, Abi decided. In her anti-legal mindset, she hadn't noticed it before.

"Wonderful! When can we get started?"

"Right away. After we talked the last time, I gave some thought to what you said about buying the property. I asked an old colleague to check around. I'll give him a call and let you know."

He started to rise from his chair. Abi didn't want him to go, not just yet. "Would you like another glass of wine?"

"No, thank you," he said. "I've got duty tonight." He settled back into his chair as if he were reluctant to leave. "How is your work going?"

"I haven't done much filing with all that's been going on, but I found something special. It's one of the reasons I went back for another look at the barn."

She disappeared into the house and came out a minute later holding the art book. She placed it on the table between their chairs.

"This was in a box Professor Waldstein asked me to organize." She opened the book, removed the sketches and presented them to him one-by-one. Ben took his time examining the drawings. When he had finished studying the last one, he handed them back.

"Where did you get these?"

"They were in the book between two pages glued together. I can't say for sure if they are real Edward Hoppers. I'm leaning in that direction, though."

She showed him the *ex libris* sticker on the inside of the cover and the dedication on the title page.

He read the inscription. "I can see why you'd think they're originals."

"Apparently, Jo Hopper gave the book to Alden Proctor. My guess is, she didn't know about the sketches."

"The Proctor family is still around," he said. "They run a septic system cleaning and installation company." He handed the paper back. "Maybe they can shed some light on the mystery. I can give them a call if you'd like."

"Thanks for the offer, but I can do it."

"Great. I've got to get going and get a snooze in before I go on the night shift."

"Thank you again for coming by." They shook hands. Ben extended his other hand to enclose hers. His grip was warm and firm. She suddenly wanted to give him a hug. She needed one herself; it had been too long. She and her ex-husband had barely talked after he tanked her business and ran off with his young lover.

Abi felt a strange sense of loss as Ben released his grip, and said, "I'll give you a call later tomorrow morning."

"I'd appreciate that," she said. Abi walked him to his truck and watched the taillights disappear down the driveway. She strolled to the edge of the hill and looked off at the lights of Provincetown, then lifted her gaze skyward to the sequined tapestry of the Milky Way.

Maybe she shouldn't have told Ben about the wings. Her nutty reaction to the footprint was bad enough. Despite his assurances, she wondered if she would ever see him again.

She hoped that she would.

CHAPTER TWENTY-ONE

Ben was having a hard time figuring Abi out. The meeting at the cottage hadn't resolved his confusion. One second she seemed entirely rational. The next, she galloped off into Crazyville, USA. The legal system had really done a head job on her. But he was certain of one thing: He liked her.

He sat in his living room chair, drinking a glass of ice water, thinking about their conversation. It wasn't really as complicated as she suggested. He had offered to help. She had accepted his offer. Simple.

He wished the situation with Hank Aldrich was equally as uncomplicated. He set his glass on the table next to the cell phone, opened the Voice Memos app, clicked the Play/Record button, then leaned back and closed his eyes. He heard his own voice saying the date, time and place, then:

"Hope it's okay with you, Hank, but I'm going to record this conversation to protect us both."

"Fine with me."

"Good. Please state your name."

"Hank Aldrich."

"You came to me looking for a lawyer. Is that correct?"

"Yes."

"Let me state something for the record. I cannot be your lawyer. I am no longer a practicing attorney. I am an officer of the law. And while I don't consider you a fugitive, I am aware that the State Police would like to talk to you regarding the death of Kyle Magnus. Also, I could be ordered to testify about this conversation and anything you say could be held against you. Still want to talk?"

"I have nothing to hide."

"Good. Since I am not a State Police officer, I have no authorization to arrest you. At the same time, I am obligated to inform the State Police that I have talked to you."

"Are you going to put me in handcuffs while you call those guys?"

"Nope. I will make no attempt to restrain you."

"Then I can go out the same way I came in."

"You can dash out that door and I won't stop you. But I would have to report your action to the police and they would chase you down. They might catch you. Or they might not. In any event, you'd be on the run. They would find you eventually. So my advice is to turn yourself in. I can escort you to the police station after we talk."

"Okay."

"To start with, tell me why you were on the beach and not at the launch site with the others."

"I was depressed at being marginalized. I built the aircraft, and was supposed to fly it. I wanted to see how well it flew, but I couldn't bear to see Kyle pilot my plane. I wanted the freedom to come and go, which might have been difficult on the hill, so I went down to the beach."

"How long were you there?"

"The whole flight. Around four hours. The longer I watched the beautiful little plane up there in the sky the calmer I became. I decided I would be a big boy. Kyle would grab the headlines if he broke the record, but maybe people would recognize that I built this amazing aircraft. I decided to watch the whole thing and make sure he landed with the glider in one piece."

"You saw me on the beach."

"Yes."

"Why didn't you acknowledge seeing me?"

"I was surprised you were there and not on the hill. But mostly, I wanted to get away by myself. I walked about a quarter of a mile to where the beach crowd thinned out. That's when I got the call from Kyle."

"Now I'm the one who's confused. You say Kyle called you from the glider?"

"On his cell phone. Late in the last half hour of the flight when it looked like he was going to break the record. He told me he was sorry for the way things turned out. That when he beat Hesselbach's record he intended to pay me the money he owed and make sure I got full credit for building the Darmstadt."

"Did that surprise you?"

"Hell, yes. I was even more surprised when he threw in the sweetener."

"What sweetener is that?"

"The Navy contract. He got word just before the flight that his design won. He wanted me to work with him on the project. We'd be equal partners."

"That was pretty generous of him."

"More than generous. I was euphoric. That's why I took it especially hard when he went into the drink. Not just the loss of the plane, and a life, but of a golden opportunity."

"Okay, you've had the conversation with Kyle. What happened next?"

"The glider crashed minutes later. I was as shocked as anyone. Magnus was doing an amazing job controlling the plane. Then he obviously lost control. The plane yawed and pitched, lost altitude, and went into the water. I didn't see the actual crash because it was obscured by a bunch of boats."

"What did you do next?"

"I got in my car and drove a few miles to a high bluff with a good view of the bay. I had binoculars. I watched the Coast Guard boat move in, then I went back to my room at the Provincetown Inn and turned on the TV. The crash was on every channel. I saw a helicopter shot of the boat heading for the Coast Guard station. I went there to see what was going on. It was only a few minutes from the inn."

"I didn't see you there."

"I saw you in the parking lot, but I stayed out of sight."

"Why didn't you say something to me then?"

"I was half crazy, Ben. Like I said when you came by the hangar, I spent hundreds of hours building that glider. I was devastated to see it crash into the sea. I figured Kyle had been killed."

"What did you do then?"

"I went to the Governor Bradford bar and tossed down a couple of gallons of beer. They had the story on the TV. I finally got the courage to call Melissa. She couldn't talk. Really was pretty messed up. She and Kyle were tight."

"What next?"

"I was still sucking down brews when the wreckage was brought in. The aircraft only weighed three hundred pounds, so it wasn't a major salvage job. I went back to the station and saw them put what was left of the plane onto a truck. I followed it to the hangar. There were a couple of Coast Guard guys there, so no one objected when I poked around."

"The State Police know you were there. It made them suspicious."

"I can't help that."

"No, you can't. Did you see anything at the hangar that suggested why the plane had crashed?"

"Right away. The glider's control cables were severed. Their ends were burnt and there was a ragged hole in the floor of the fuselage that was surrounded by burned material. It was obvious to me that there had been an explosion."

"Any idea how that could have happened?"

"Of course! Someone put a charge in the fuselage. It wouldn't have taken much to do the job. There was no other explanation."

"When was the last time you inspected the glider before the flight?"

"After it was delivered to the launch site. I went over every inch of that aircraft. There was nothing resembling an explosive charge."

"You're sure?"

"I take that as an insult to my professionalism."

"Sorry. I have to ask. Did you report your findings to anyone?"

"Hell, no. I was trashed, but I wasn't so drunk I didn't know that I would be the prime suspect. I built the glider; I was the last one to work on it. Everyone knew there were hard feelings between

Magnus and me. I had to sleep it off. I drove to a motel outside of town, rented a room and crawled into bed."

"After you woke up, you decided you might need a lawyer?"

"I knew for sure that I needed a lawyer. Melissa called my cell phone and woke me up. She was yelling, saying Magnus was dead and I had killed him, that the cops were looking for me and I'd better turn myself in. *Migod*, she made me sound like Jack the Ripper! You said to get in touch if I needed legal advice."

"I was talking about civil law, not criminal. As I said, I'm a cop."

"Oh yeah. That."

"Yes. That. I can call the State Police and tell them you're here. Or I could give you a ride to my police station and you could call them from there."

"Sounds like the same thing. I'd be giving myself up."

"You have no choice."

"I guess that's it," Aldrich said. "I'll turn myself in. I can drive there myself."

Ben said, "That ends this interview." Ben tapped the 'off' button on the phone, stopping the recording.

"Good decision," he said, "but before you leave I'm going to hook you up with a criminal lawyer I know so you will have legal representation."

"Do I have any other options?"

"Sure, all bad. This is the best one. Running would imply guilt, and might get you killed. Cooperating with the police is what an innocent man would do." Ben punched out a number on his phone, talked to someone, and then handed the phone to Aldrich. After a brief conversation, he handed the phone back.

"Your friend says he's in Boston and can't get to the station right now. He's got a local lawyer he works with who can be at the station within an hour." His shoulders sagged. "What do we do in the meantime?"

"I can pour you a shot of Jameson."

"Pour away."

Ben filled a glass half-full of Irish whiskey.

"One other thing," he said. "I never contacted an attorney for you. If you say so, I will deny it."

Aldrich raised his glass and smiled.

After drinking another shot he decided that he'd accept the offer of a ride. The attorney was waiting when Ben drove Hank to the police station. He was a smart young criminal defense attorney who had been racking up a good record of wins for his clients. He called Curran and said Hank was at the station. The lieutenant showed up with a couple of brawny state troopers who must have been the biggest he could find. They arrested Hank on suspicion of homicide.

On the way home from Abi's, Ben got a call from the lawyer saying he would ask for a reasonable bail at Hank's arraignment, which was what prompted Ben to listen to the recording one more time.

The news that Kyle wanted Hank to be a partner seemed too good to be true, but he sounded genuinely surprised by the offer. Ben was surprised as well. One thing was becoming manifestly clear to him, though. Kyle was a much more complex person than you'd figure by looking at him.

CHAPTER TWENTY-TWO

Abi woke up brimming with renewed purpose the morning after her talk with Ben. She rolled out of bed and descended to the kitchen, humming to herself as she brewed a pot of coffee, and carried the steaming mug to her office. She removed the sketches from between the pages of the book and put the close-up drawing of the man's face on top of the others.

Hopper had captured the malevolence in the thin face with a few quick strokes of the pencil. Assuming these were authentic Hopper sketches.

It was probably time to call Professor Waldstein to let him know about the treasure she'd found in his files. The book and the sketches belonged to him, after all. She calculated the time difference and looked up his number. She paused with her finger over the 'call' symbol. What if the sketches were bogus? She'd be getting the professor excited over nothing.

As an art historian, she knew that even the most complex work could be faked. Abi wasn't qualified to say whether the sketches were authentic or not, but she knew someone who could. She scrolled through the contact list and tapped in the number for Celine Benard.

A woman's voice answered, "Hi, Abi. Saw your name on caller ID. How are you?"

"I'm fine, thank you, Celine. How are things in the Provenance

Research Department?"

"Busy. The museum acquired a new collection of Impressionistic artists. Nothing major, but the ownership of a few pieces looks a bit dodgy. We're taking a closer look at them."

The Provenance Research Department at the Boston Museum of Fine Arts investigated chains of art ownership and looked at gaps possibly caused by theft or looting. Provenance is a tool used for better understanding of an artwork, as well as possible theft. The scientific research lab was set up in the 1930s, and the MFA went on to become one of the first museums in the world to use forensic science for authentication and preservation.

When Abi had her galleries, she had occasionally asked the department to authenticate an artwork with a vague history that could have indicated an illegal transaction.

"Sorry to bother you, Celine. Hope you're not too busy to take a look at some sketches that may have been done by Edward Hopper."

"Hopper! No bother at all. Can you fax them to me?"

"I don't have a fax. And you should see them in person. I'd be glad to drive up today, if you have a few minutes."

"Come ahead. It would be wonderful to see you. Where did the sketches come from?"

"They were tucked into a book on American realist painters. I came across it while I was reorganizing Professor Waldstein's office files."

"The professor told me that you were working out of his cottage. Lucky you. How's the reorganization going?"

"You've seen his office, so you know what I'm up against. The professor said it would be like Hercules cleaning out the Augean Stables."

"It's worse than that. Not as smelly, hopefully. I admire your fortitude."

"I was actually making progress. In fact, I came across the sketches as I was digging through the mess."

"Have you told the professor about your find?"

"Not yet. I want to check their authenticity before I let him know his disorganized office may have kept valuable art out of circulation."

"Maybe the scolding will do some good, but I doubt it. I'll be here at my office all day. Can't wait to see what you have."

Abi said she'd be at the museum in a couple of hours. She gulped down her coffee, went upstairs to brush her teeth and take a shower, and threw on a light cotton dress. The art book and sketches went into her backpack and she tossed a couple of granola bars and bottled water into a cooler.

Next, she called Sally Silva, the fundraising friend she saw at dinner her last night in the city, and told her she was driving to Boston for a meeting.

"I was wondering whether we could get together for lunch at the MFA after I'm done," she said. "My meeting shouldn't be too long."

"I'm free all afternoon. Give me a call when you get to the museum and I'll Uber over."

Minutes later Abi was behind the wheel of the Land Rover. Traffic was light and an hour after leaving the cottage colony she was passing over the Sagamore Bridge. Boston was another hour from the Cape Cod Canal.

As she came in sight of the glass-faced John Hancock building, Abi realized that she had only left the city a few days before. So much seemed to have happened since she had pulled Grover up to the front of the Beach Plum cottage.

She parked in the museum lot off Huntington Avenue and called Sally to let her know she'd arrived. Once inside the museum, Abi headed away from the main galleries to a corridor lined with doors leading to various museum departments. She stopped at a door labeled Provenance Research Department, and gave a soft knock. A woman's voice told her to come in.

Celine was sitting behind a contemporary-style metal desk in front of floor-to-ceiling bookshelves. When she saw Abi, a bright smile came to her dark-complexioned face.

"Hi, Abi," she said. "You made great time." She rose from her chair and came around her desk to give Abi a warm hug. "It's so wonderful to see you. You're looking great."

Celine was a trim, energetic woman in her fifties. She lived in Boston's Back Bay and they had been running partners before the legal mess played havoc with Abi's fitness schedule as well as her bank account.

"Thanks, Celine. It must be my rosy cheeks from all that sea air."

"Whatever it is seems to be working. I can't tell you how much I miss our morning runs along the Charles."

"I miss them, too," Abi said with a sad face. "Maybe we can get back on schedule after I wrap up the job for the professor."

"How soon will that be?"

"It's hard to tell at this point. You must have heard about the glider accident on Cape Cod."

"Oh yes, it was in all the papers and on TV. Someone was killed."

"That's right. The glider was launched off the hill in front of the professor's cottage."

"How awful! Did you see the accident?"

"I was inside the cottage working when it went into the water, but as you can imagine, there was a lot of excitement. Things are just starting to calm down."

"It must have been very emotional, nonetheless. That was the last thing you needed after all you've been through."

"I seem to attract bad luck," Abi said.

"Not if what you told me about the Hopper sketches is true," Celine said, cocking her head.

Abi slid her backpack off and settled into a chair.

"I really appreciate your seeing me on such short notice, Celine."

Celine stuck her hand out, palm up. "Are you kidding me? Edward Hopper? I should thank *you*. Don't keep me in suspense."

"I don't intend to."

Abi unzipped the pack, pulled out the folder with the sketches and set it on the desk. She opened the folder and slid it across to Celine, who clapped her hands like a child anticipating a treat.

Bending her head over the sketches, she studied the first one, then the others, spreading them out in front of her. Without taking her eyes off the sketches, she opened a drawer, extracted a magnifying glass and inspected the drawings one-by-one. Then she set the glass aside, sat back in her chair and tented her fingers.

"You said you found these lovelies in a book?"

Abi reached into the pack for the book and set it on the desk.

She opened the book to where she had placed a bookmark.

"This was with some other books in the professor's boxes. There was something funny about one page. It was actually two pages sealed together, creating a pocket. When I pried them apart I found the sketches inside."

Celine ran her finger along the rough edges of the pages. "I can feel the dried glue. Fascinating. The sketches were deliberately hidden."

"That's my guess. I'm less sure about who would have taken the trouble to do this."

"Someone who didn't want the sketches seen, apparently."

"Hopper?"

"That's certainly a possibility."

"Any idea where Professor Waldstein got the book?"

"Not specifically." She opened the book and tapped the yellowed *ex libris* sticker with the name Alden Proctor printed on it. "This is one of a number of art books in the professor's collection that had been owned by this person. The professor was always hitting up estate sales."

"Proctor was the book's owner, so it's possible he could have hidden the sketches."

"Certainly makes sense. It also suggests that he knew the value of what he had."

"That doesn't explain how Proctor acquired them."

Abi turned to the inscription from Jo Hopper to Alden Proctor on the title page.

Celine examined the sketches again with her magnifier. Then she got up and plucked a book off a shelf. She set the book down in front of Abi who saw that its subject was Hopper's paintings and ledger book drawings. On the cover was a sketch of a sailboat and lighthouse, and a finished painting of the identical subject.

"As you probably know, Hopper's wife Jo used ledger books with thumbnail sketches to keep meticulous records of all his paintings for accounting purposes. She kept records for everything except work—sketches, mostly—that never left the studio."

Abi turned to a page showing a house by the side of the road. She compared the script to the inscription.

"The handwriting is very close," she said.

"Compare her writing with the notes on the sketches."

"They're not the same," Abi said.

"The ledgers were written for the most part by Jo. Which means the notes with the sketches you found are not in her handwriting."

"Edward's, then?"

"The writing is similar to what I've seen of Hopper's, but I'd like to know more about the paper used for the sketches. I can have the museum lab look at it."

"Maybe later, thanks. I'd feel better holding onto the sketches until after I talk to the professor."

"Let me know. But sometimes a gut feeling is almost as good as lab work. Let me ask. Do these sketches seem authentic to you?"

"Yes. I know where these sketches were made. The house was torn down, but the barn is still standing. It's the type of subject Hopper would have been attracted to. Also, if someone was going to fake some sketches, he might draw the house and barn. He might even sketch a man with a pickup truck. But I can't see a forger doing something so different from the expressions Hopper usually painted on his human subjects."

"The artist must have been standing close enough to see every detail. I'm intrigued by the description in the notes. *Bad Face*. It certainly impressed him."

"I think that face frightened the crap of him."

"He frightens me!" Celine said.

They both laughed, then Abi said, "Maybe Hopper was so disturbed by what he saw he decided not to do a painting. He tucked the sketches in a book where Proctor found them.

"When you talk to the Proctor family, you might be able to establish a trail of ownership that can tell us who hid the sketches."

"I'll try to do that as soon as I get back to Truro."

"Thanks for coming all this way to show them to me. Let me know what you find out. And what Professor Waldstein has to say when you tell him about the treasure right under his nose."

"Every anguished word."

They broke into laughter. Celine said, "Speaking of the professor, you must be looking forward to your new job."

Abi wrinkled her brow, confused at the way Celine had phrased the sentence. "My Truro gig?"

"No. The curatorship." She brought her hand up to her mouth. "Oh dear. From the look on your face I spoiled the surprise. I'm sorry."

"About what? Please don't leave me hanging."

"That would be unforgivably cruel," Celine said. She explained Waldstein's plan to bring Abi in to take over his duties gradually so he could get away from administrative tasks and do more teaching. She and Celine would share an apartment until she got on her feet.

They talked a few minutes more, until Abi remembered how busy Celine was. She gathered up the book and sketches and tucked them into her backpack. They exchanged hugs, then she followed the signs to the museum's West Wing, the three-story addition designed by famed architect I.M. Pei. The cafeteria was in a courtyard that extended more than two-hundred feet under a glass barrel vault.

Abi took a seat at a vacant table. She was in a daze after hearing Celine's news. She looked around and reminisced about the times she had met artists or buyers for lunch in the impressive setting. She thought those days were gone forever, but, thanks to the professor, she might be coming back to the museum many times in the future.

She still had a smile on her face when Sally showed up. Settling into her chair, she said, "You look happier than the last time I saw you."

"I am. I think I may have a job and a place to live."

"Oh, Abi, I'm so happy for you. What and where?"

"I'm not supposed to know, so I don't feel right sharing. I'll tell you first, as soon as I'm sure it's a done deal."

"Promise?"

"Promise."

They shook hands on it and ordered lunch. "Okay," Sally said. "This news obviously wasn't what you wanted to talk to me about."

"No. It's something completely different."

Sally listened intently as her friend described the history of the Baron property and her proposal to buy it, tear the house down and return the land to its original, pristine state. When Abi was through, she spread her hands and said, "That's it, Sally. Crazy or possible?"

"A little bit of both. But doable. There's money out there. I would just have to convince donors that this is a worthy cause. I'll need more information; the current owners of the property to begin with."

"I may have something soon. A lawyer friend has offered to work on that."

Sally gave a quick, short laugh. "Hard for me to believe that you used the words lawyer and friend in the same sentence. You must be getting over your 'all attorneys are scum' phase."

"I don't think I'll ever get past that completely, but Ben's very nice. And he was a trust and estates lawyer, not a litigator."

"Does nice Ben have a last name?"

"His name is Dyer. He's from an old Cape Cod family. He's interested in helping because the acquisition would be a monument to his late wife."

"Single, too. Hmm."

"Don't read too much into this, Sally. It's an arrangement of mutual convenience."

"Okay, my dear. I'll go with what you've given me. Get back to me as soon as you have more information." She glanced at her watch. "Got to go."

They walked together to the exit and exchanged goodbye hugs. Abi was practically giddy over Sally's encouraging reaction, on top of the good news from Celine. She was feeling so good she considered driving past her old apartment and gallery. Once she got in the car she thought better of her idea. She convinced herself that she didn't have time, but she knew deep inside that she wasn't ready to see what she had lost. It was too soon.

Instead of cruising through the old neighborhood, she got onto the Southeast Expressway and headed back to Truro. Today had been a good day, and she didn't want to ruin it.

CHAPTER TWENTY-THREE

Ben wanted to help Abi, but he wasn't sure he'd been wise when he promised to snoop around Fort Baron. Doubts plagued him as he drove up to the entrance of the estate and got out of the cruiser. He ambled over to the keypad on the concrete post next to the iron gate. As he punched out the numbers that would unlock the gate, he half-hoped it would not open.

It wasn't technically a break-in. He was a cop, and the owners had voluntarily given the police the numerical code that allowed entry to the estate in case of an emergency. But Ben had lifted the code from the police computer without permission. And he definitely wasn't on the Baron property for police business.

The gate swung open. Despite his misgivings, he got back into the cruiser and drove in between the pillars, following a gravel driveway for about a quarter of a mile to the front of the main house. He parked in the same place he'd been the morning Eddy Baron's housekeeper found the broken body of her employer on the terrace. Ben had been coming off his shift when the call came in.

He got out of the cruiser and stood in the driveway, studying the house, wondering what sort of person would build a monstrosity in such an idyllic setting.

Ben had never met the living Car Tzar, as Eddy liked to call himself, but in spite of his financial success—or maybe because of it—Ben concluded, the man who built this house must have been a real jerk.

As a local, he was aware that Truro was no stranger to innovative houses. The town attracted professionals and intellectuals who liked the wild, sea-blown heaths and moors and the ambiance of the old town. Some people preferred flat-roofed modern structures of glass and cedar to the ground-hugging, gray-shingled cottages with small windows; the latter inhabited by people like Ben's forebears, who wanted warmth and protection against the windblown environment in which they labored.

Baron's architect and lawyers must have pushed the local building code to the limit. The Baron house was built mostly of gray concrete and contained little wood, mostly for decorative trim. It was built on the highest part of the property in two tiers, the second floor smaller than the first. The tower was in the middle of the second level, and around its top was a low metal fence. Rungs ran up the outside of the tower.

The first floor entrance was guarded by a menacing steel door. The few windows were small and placed high, as if designed to discourage Peeping Toms. The only water view was from the tower. It was as if Baron had sacrificed the view from the main house for his privacy.

Ben continued on to the barn about fifty yards from the main structure. The door was unlocked, and he rolled it back with less resistance than he expected. He got down on one knee and inspected the rusty rollers. He stuck his finger down into the roller guide and, when he withdrew it, his fingertip was covered with grease. The roller seemed to have been recently lubricated.

He flicked on his LED flashlight, stepped into the barn and swept the beam around the interior. Walking slowly between the stalls, with his eyes glued to the floor, he made his way further into the barn.

Abi had seemed so sure of herself when she'd told him about the footprint in the dirt, but the floor was unmarked. No trace of a boot print or broom marks. He flashed his light into the nearest stalls. There was no broom hanging from a nail as she'd described.

He poked around in the livestock stalls. The first two were empty. Lying on the floor in the third one were some boards nailed together. When he flipped the boards over he saw black letters on the mottled, white-painted surface that read:

FLY LIKE A BIRD

Painted under the message was the flying goose symbol he had seen on the tail of Aldrich's glider and the front of Kyle's blue flying suit. Aldrich had told him the goose was the symbol for the Darmstadt Flying Club Hesselbach belonged to. He recalled what he'd heard about the aftermath of Hesselbach's Truro flights. Sponsor J. C. Penney Jr. wanted to set up a glider school on Corn Hill in Truro.

Could the Baron property have been a third potential site? The land between the barn and the edge of the cliffs could have offered a superb space for take-off and landing.

Ben put the sign down, checked the other stalls, and then made his way back through the barn. Again, he looked for the boot print Abi had reported seeing. Again, he found nothing of the sort.

It was hot and stuffy inside the uninsulated building. Ben fanned his face with his hat, thinking how Abi had said that in her haste to get off the property, she had forgotten to take a photo of the footprint. Was she telling the truth? Or was her loss of memory convenient? Maybe there was no photo because there was no boot print. He wanted to give her the benefit of the doubt. After all, she could have been creeped out by the spooky old building and had seen her own footprint.

Ben plunked the cap back on his head and stepped back out into the sunlight. The door slid shut with an easy push of his hand. He walked around the house to the driveway. Before he got in his car he stopped to gaze at the top of the tower.

He tried to picture Eddy leaning over the parapet after he'd had too much to drink, losing his balance and falling to his death. It still didn't make sense. Eddy was found on his back, head away from the tower, as if he had been climbing the outside ladder when he fell. Why didn't he use the interior stairs to get to the tower platform? The autopsy report mentioned a non-fatal bruise on Eddy's forehead. How did that happen if he'd landed on his back? And why was the Glock lying on the terrace near the body?

The tips of Ben's mouth turned downward in a perplexed frown.

Walking out to the security fence, he followed the perimeter until he came to the fallen tree Abi had used to get onto the Baron property. He pictured Abi clambering along the tree trunk and shook his head, marveling at her determination. He returned to his cruiser and followed the driveway back to the gates. He stopped and got out of the car to punch the code into the keypad. As the gates opened, he blinked in surprise. A car was pulled over to the side of the road across from the gate. Walking toward the car was Weber, the German journalist.

"Good morning," Ben said. "Are you lost?"

Weber stopped in his tracks and turned at the sound of Ben's voice. "Hello, Officer. No, not lost," he said. "I'm looking for the Baron property. Is this it?"

"Yes, it is. Or it was. Mr. Baron is deceased."

"So I understand. I've been waiting for something to develop on the glider mishap and heard about the controversy over the house. I thought there might be a story in it for my readers." He looked past Ben. "Would it be possible for me to gain access to the property?"

"Not today. There arc a number of vantage points that will give you a view of the place, though." He gave Weber directions to a couple of roads that abutted the property, but had to break off the conversation when his cell phone chirped.

Weber thanked him and headed for his car. Ben saw on the caller ID that it was Nathan at his old law firm.

"Hi, Ben," Nathan said. "Good news. We made contact with a human at Baron's property management company. Turns out their attorney is an old colleague of mine from law school."

"Congratulations, Nathan. Did your colleague explain why it was so damned difficult to track him down?"

"Sure. Eddy Baron didn't trust anyone so they set up a corporate maze. As you know, it's common with real estate holdings. Mostly for tax purposes. He wanted to keep everything for himself." Nathan chuckled. "His greediness may have screwed him up. He and his wife were negotiating the terms of a divorce, but he cut the talks short. Said she wanted too much money. Which means they were still man and wife when he died."

"Which means she got everything."

"Correct. The devil is in the details, but I can't see her holding onto that monstrous house. She might entertain an offer so she can make some money to pay off her taxes. It could take a while to put something together."

"That's okay, we'll need time to raise funds. Thank you, Nathan. I owe you."

"Not at all. I'll send a summary of my discussion along with a history of ownership."

"Who owned the property before Eddy?"

"An outfit called the Sunna Corporation. I haven't had time to look into them, but they bought it from the Snow estate, the original owners."

"Thanks again, ol' pal. Talk to you soon."

"I can practically guarantee that, Counselor. We've got an opening for you in the firm."

"There must be lots of people who could step into my old job, Nath."

"We're not talking about your old job. We're talking about a partnership. There would be some out-of-state travel almost immediately, but your salary would reflect that. We really, really miss you."

"I'm stunned. Can I give it some thought?"

"Sure, but you know how fast things move once they get started. I'll email the proposal. We'll need an answer in writing in, say, one week."

"Ouch."

"Yeah, I know. Let me say something off the cuff, as a friend. I can't tell you to stop mourning Loren. I think of her often. But once the summer crowds have gone, that big old house of yours is going to be very lonely."

Ben could have responded that the house was lonely now. Instead, he expressed his thanks and told Nathan he would be getting back to him.

"Great. Tell you what. As a little sweetener, we can assign someone in the office to deal with that property acquisition while you're busy with other cases."

"You're making the offer very hard to resist."

"That's my intention, old friend. *Ciao.*"

Ben stared at the phone. He mustered the arguments against his return to the legal trenches. *Too soon.* Would it ever not be too soon? He couldn't use his obligation to the police department as an excuse. Bill Sisson had told him to stay with the department only as long as he needed to.

And there was Abi. She had asked for his help and finally allowed herself to trust him. If he pulled away he'd be simply another shifty lawyer who wasn't there when she needed him. She was truly worried about something, even if she couldn't define what it was. He could brush off her talk of a phantom boot print, the intruder who came into her cottage, and the rustling of wings in the sky as the ramblings of a troubled young woman. But what if he was wrong?

He shut his eyes and took a deep breath. *Jeez, Nathan.*

One week.

CHAPTER TWENTY-FOUR

Weber was in a cold sweat. He had almost been caught breaking into the Baron estate. Dyer drove up to the gate as Weber was walking to his car to fetch a pair of bolt cutters he'd bought at a hardware store. A rookie mistake could have brought his assignment crashing down.

He checked the rearview mirror. Dyer was leaning against the cruiser, phone stuck in his ear. Thank God for the phone call. Weber's flimsy story about researching an article would have fallen apart under further questioning. Saying he was snooping around the Baron property for a story wasn't a bad cover, but Weber suspected the police officer would have found the actual explanation a lot more interesting.

His mind flashed back a few weeks when he'd been thousands of miles from this country road. He'd been sitting at a window table in the historic old Café Odeon, gazing out at the busy Zurich street scene while he sipped on a double espresso.

He let his gaze drift idly around the dining room, imagining that some of the famous denizens who once frequented the premises had dropped in for coffee. Was that Einstein, and his mustached companion James Joyce at the next table? And were the shiny-scalped gentlemen sitting at the bar with their heads close together Mussolini and Lenin cooking up deadly mischief?

His mobile phone had purred. He cut his musings short and

read the text message:

There's been a house break-in.

He tapped the keypad.

How did the burglar get in the house?

Through an unlocked window in the Salon. When can you come?

Now.

As Weber knew, the house was not a physical building; it was a computer data bank, and the electronic entry point was called a window because like the real thing, it gave the illusion of security but provided little protection. In fact, it was designed to entrap the hacker like a burglar alarm that silently notified the police of an intruder.

He downed the contents of his cup and left some coins in a change tray. A short walk from the cafe he climbed onto a trolley and got off at a stop near the *Bahnhofstrasse*, the ritzy shopping area near the railroad station. He walked briskly along the crowded sidewalks to an ornate four-story building.

Stopping at a door next to a Rolex outlet, he inserted a key in the lock, opened the door and climbed the narrow stairs to a dimly-lit hallway. A few steps from the stairwell was a door that had the words *The Restitution Registry* painted on a frosted glass panel.

Not bothering to knock, he opened the door and stepped into a small office sparsely furnished with a steel desk and a couple of black leather and chrome chairs. The desktop was bare except for a computer and keyboard and a brass name tag that read Leo Bryner.

Seated behind the desk was a middle-aged man dressed in a tailored gray suit. The deep blue tie matched the color of the eyes set in the chiseled face. The man rose to his feet and reached across the desk to give Weber a finger-crushing handshake.

He smiled, showing big teeth. Speaking in Swiss-accented German, he said, "You came quickly!"

"I was at the Odeon having coffee when I got your call. This seemed like an important matter. The Salon, you said?"

Bryner waved Weber to a chair and settled down behind his desk.

"Yes. The motherlode." He clicked the computer mouse and turned the monitor around so Weber could see the text on the screen. "The hacker seemed most interested in this section of the database."

Weber read the name Otto Klaas written in bold face caps and he let out a low whistle.

"This is the first time I've seen this file."

"There has never been a need for you to read it before now."

"Where did the hack originate?" Weber said, knowing even as he asked the question that the hacker could have patched his way in through a dozen different countries around the world, easily disguising his identity.

Furrowing his brow, Bryner said, "That's the odd thing. It came in last night from the U.S. Quite clumsy, as a matter of fact. The sender made no attempt to disguise his location or ID."

"Maybe the hacker is trying to throw us off by being so obvious."

"Always the suspicious policeman," Bryner said. "Of course, you may be entirely correct."

"In that case, this guy must be a pro."

"You wouldn't think so by looking at him."

Bryner tapped the keyboard. The image that appeared on the screen showed a man in his forties whose obviously dyed blond hair was worn long over the ears.

"I see what you mean. Looks like he came from the cast of *Baywatch*."

"*Baywatch?*"

"An American television series famous for its virile men and large-bosomed young women in bikinis. It is very popular in Germany."

"Evidently in Switzerland as well," Bryner said, a bemused smile on his lips. "You watch this program?"

"I found it entertaining. Who is he?"

"His name is Kyle Magnus. He owns an aeronautical engineering and design company that specializes in unpowered flight. Maybe his last name rings a bell?"

"Any connection to the Sunna Industrials Magnus family?"

"One and the same. He's only distantly related to the Norwegian metals manufacturing family, but he's a Magnus, nonetheless. Although from what I found out he's pretty far down in the family pecking order. Which is why it puzzles me that he'd be interested in the more nefarious dealings of his illustrious family."

"Maybe he's just curious about his family's past."

"That still doesn't explain why he wanted information on Otto Klaas. It's not widely known that Klaas was a friend of the Magnus family. And how did he know to come to us? Most people don't even know our organization exists. This is what a casual inquiry into Klaas would produce."

Bryner tapped the keyboard and called up a post from Wikipedia, the online encyclopedia. There was a one-paragraph article under the name Otto Klaas.

"As you can see, Mr. Klaas was only a blip on the radar screen," Bryner said. "I can count the number of inquiries we've had on Klaas on the fingers of one hand. All from scholars after bigger fish in the Nazi ocean. The only reason they asked about Klaas was that no one knew who he was and what he did."

Weber read the article although he knew from previous readings what it said. Klaas had been a pilot and joined the Luftwaffe in 1939. He was on the staff of Hermann Goering, the corpulent commander-in-chief of the Luftwaffe, in charge of the Special Acquisitions department. The article said he died before the end of the war in an Allied bombing raid.

Weber smiled. "Special Acquisitions indeed. The Nazis had a wonderful way of using vague words to disguise their true intent. He was an art thief."

Bryner nodded. "Klaas went to great pains to bury himself and the details of his job deep in Nazi bureaucracy, but as we know, he was Goering's go-to man when he wanted to steal a particular artwork."

"The Americans call that a 'gopher.'"

"Really?" Bryner cocked his head. "Did you learn that on *Baywatch*?"

Weber shrugged. "Perhaps. A more important question is why Kyle Magnus, whose family business profited off the war, is suddenly interested in Klaas?"

"You can ask Magnus that question when you talk to him." Bryner handed Weber a large envelope. "You leave tomorrow for the U.S. Airline tickets and cover information are inside. You'll be posing as a German journalist covering a glider flight reenactment. Magnus is involved in the event."

"How did you learn about this reenactment?"

"Not difficult. It was in a magazine article my hired snoops found when they did a search on Magnus. Your job will be to watch him and those around him every minute. Maybe he'll make a mistake. He already made a blunder when he got caught accessing our database."

"We're assuming he was the only one with access to his computer."

"I've taken into consideration the possibility that others were involved. The envelope also contains a list of everyone who is part of the project. I've been going over the names. I've excluded the film crews and technicians and narrowed it down to a small list at the upper echelon."

"Have you notified the commission of our investigation?"

Weber was referring to the Commission for Looted Art in Europe, a non-profit organization that locates and recovers art stolen by the Nazis in World War II and tries to get it back to its rightful owners.

"In time," Bryner said. "I don't want them *harrumphing* in indignation over our unorthodox methods."

Weber set his lips in a tight smile. He and Bryner were the only full-time employees of The Restitution Registry. He was the chief investigator and Bryner was the organization man. The company employed an army of computer whizzes and unsavory characters to flesh out the company staff, allowing TRR to operate in a twilight zone between what is legal and what isn't.

Its network of informants included art thieves and shady art dealers. It also worked with legitimate entities like the commission, and with police in a number of countries. The police liked The Restitution Registry because art theft was given low priority in their budgets, and TRR allowed them free access to one of the biggest databases of stolen art in the world.

What the police didn't know was that there was a part of the database they couldn't get into. The only one who had access was

Bryner and those, like Weber, he allowed in. The Salon was where the most sensitive files were kept. Like the one on Otto Klaas.

Someone had tried to break into the Salon. And it was Weber's job to find out who.

CHAPTER TWENTY-FIVE

Abi would have loved to have wandered the halls of the MFA to bask in the warmth of the Impressionist paintings, but now that the Hopper sketches had been authenticated, she was eager to find out why they'd been hidden all these years. She also wanted to beat the ferocious Boston rush hour that turns the highway south of the city into a parking lot.

Abi made good time to the Cape Cod Canal. Late in the afternoon she arrived at Beach Plum. Grabbing her backpack from the Land Rover, she went into the cottage and pulled together a Greek village salad for her dinner. Between bites of tomatoes, kalamata olives and feta cheese, she jotted down notes of her Boston conversations while they were still fresh in her mind.

Given her recent history as a bad luck magnet, the offer of a curator's job might never come through. But if and when it did, she wanted to be ready to jump right into the position. Living in a cottage by the sea was none too shabby, but she was eager to resume her career and was tired of eating alone.

Abi decided she would wait to hear from the professor before telling him about the Hopper sketches. She didn't want to upstage his announcement of her job offer. The smart thing would be to have the filing job done by the time Waldstein's call came. She did a quick cleanup then went into the office and sorted out a couple more boxes. Like the earlier material, the folders were chaotic and she soon had piled up several stacks of unrelated paper. Her eyelids began to droop and she realized she was exhausted.

Before she climbed the stairs to the second level, she took the art book out of her backpack. She slipped the sketches from between the stuck pages and found space on a corner of the desk where she laid them out side by side. She paid particular attention to the sketch Hopper had labeled Bad Face. It was evident that Hopper had been both fascinated and repelled by the face he had drawn.

She picked up the sketch in both hands and held it at arm's length. She wanted to know why the man was at the barn and what he was doing. If the man was bad, as Hopper suggested, maybe what he was doing was bad as well.

She gathered up the sketches and put them back into the book, which she carried upstairs and tucked into a dresser drawer. Then she turned off the lights and looked out the window at the sequined glimmer of Provincetown.

The sky above the bay was clear except for a few whisker-like clouds. She could almost count the stars in the Milky Way. She scanned the sky looking for the strange wrinkling she thought she had seen earlier, but everything was normal.

She got into a nightie and slipped under the covers. What a wonderful day it had been, with good news about a job and place to live. Sally's encouraging insight onto the possibility of acquiring the Baron property was the icing on the cake. She fell asleep as soon as her head hit the pillow.

The crackle of tires on the clamshell driveway woke Abi up the next morning. Then came the noise of slamming doors. Abi rose from bed to look out the window. The documentary production crew was unloading sound and light equipment from a van and carrying it to the cliff where Melissa stood looking toward the bay.

Abi sighed. *The drama never ends.* After a quick shower, she got dressed in shorts, blouse and sandals, then grabbed the art book, went down to the kitchen to make coffee and a breakfast of oatmeal with blueberries. She cleaned up the breakfast dishes, brushed her teeth, and then stepped out of the cottage.

Melissa was talking to a young man holding a microphone. They stood in front of the camera with the blue waters of the bay as a backdrop. Mead was nearby watching the interview. He saw Abi and motioned her over.

"What's going on?" she said in a low voice.

"Melissa is telling the interviewer for PBS how Kyle was a great aviation pioneer in the tradition of the Wright brothers. How his tragic death ended the life of one of the foremost designers of motorless aircraft of our time. And how she will miss him…mostly, as a great friend."

"Those are lovely sentiments," Abi said.

"Thanks." Mead grinned like a mischievous boy. "I wrote them. Melissa asked for my help."

"That was nice of you."

"Hell, it was a no-brainer. Kyle was all of the things I said about him. There was more to him than a tan and thick hair. Although as you can see, she's got an eye for the pretty boys."

Melissa was smiling at the interviewer, who was both young and handsome.

"Looks aren't everything," Abi said.

Mead chuckled. "Glad you feel that way. Does that mean you'll say yes this time if I ask you to go out for dinner?"

"I'm sorry," Abi said after a pause. "I'm seeing someone."

"Lucky him. Hold on there. It's not Officer Dyer, is it?"

"We've had a couple of dates."

"Why that sly old dog with his 'aw shucks' routine. That's a big surprise because you and he didn't exactly get off to a great start as I recall."

"Now that I've gotten to know him, I can see that he's a nice man. His wife died not too long ago." That was totally unnecessary, Abi thought. She could feel the heat in her cheeks. "If you'll excuse me, I've got to get to an appointment."

Abi went back into her office and looked up the number for the Proctor office on Google. She tapped the call symbol and seconds later, a woman's voice came on the line.

"Proctor Septic Services. This is Dawn speaking. How may I help you?"

"My name is Abi Vickers. I'm staying at Professor Andrew Waldstein's place up on the flower cottages hill."

"Oh sure, I know the professor. We did a septic system installation at the cottages a few years ago. How is he?"

"He's well, thank you," Abi said. "I'm doing some filing for him while he's teaching in Paris. I was going through one of his boxes and came across a book that included a chapter on Edward Hopper. There was an inscription in the book that's apparently from Hopper's wife, Jo, to Alden Proctor."

"That would be my grandfather. He did some work for the Hoppers."

"Really? I'm an art historian when I'm not helping the professor. I wonder if sometime, when you're not busy, we could talk about your grandfather and the Hoppers."

"Come by now if you'd like."

"That's great. I'll be right over."

Dawn gave her directions to the office. Abi removed the sketches from the book and locked them in a desk drawer. She tucked the book into her backpack and carried it out to the Land Rover. Melissa was still talking to the interviewer. Mead waved at Abi, who gave him a half-hearted wave in return.

Proctor Septic Systems was in a small, white clapboard building on a road off the main highway.

Dawn Proctor was an attractive, slightly plump, middle-aged woman whose short cut silver hair framed a round face and a warm smile. She welcomed Abi, suggesting they sit on a sofa and have some newly-brewed green tea.

"Good for what ails you," she said. "I have six cups a day." She poured hot water into a couple of antique teacups. "You said you were an art historian?"

"That's right." Abi looked around at the paintings and prints hanging on the walls. "From the looks of this office, I'm not the only one who likes art."

"Quite the collection, isn't it? They belonged to my grandfather. Allie didn't just like art. He *loved* it. There were a lot of artists in town. Most didn't have very much money and were glad to trade paintings for work. I heard that my grandmother scolded him for bartering services for art. Said pretty pictures didn't put food on the table."

Abi pulled the book out of her pack, placed it on the table and opened to the title page. "This is the inscription that caught my eye." She read the words aloud.

"To Alden Proctor, a great plumber and a lover of art. Jo Hopper."

Dawn smiled. "There's quite the story behind that."

"I'd love to hear it."

Dawn picked up the book and cradled it in her lap. "Allie did some jobs for the Hoppers," she said. "They were on the tight side when it came to money, and he'd lowball his estimates because he liked to go over to the studio. There was always the chance he'd see Mr. Hopper at work, though that never happened. One day, Mrs. Hopper called to have Grandpop over to fix a leaky pipe under the sink. Unfortunately, Edward had recently died. Mrs. Hopper was in New York tying things up. He didn't charge her for the work—told her that Mr. Hopper had paid him enough by painting his pictures."

"She must have been touched by that."

"Apparently. When Grandpop said he wished he was rich enough to afford one of Edward's paintings, Mrs. Hopper said they were going to a big museum where everyone could enjoy them. But sometime after that a package came in the mail from Mrs. Hopper. It was that book. My grandfather kept it under lock and key, but he'd bring it out to show people."

"I'm wondering how Professor Waldstein got the book."

"My grandfather had a ton of art books like this. When he died, he left them to my grandmother. She kept them up in the attic. After she passed away, the collection went to the next generation. Books take up a lot of space, and no one was as interested in art as much as Alden. The professor heard we were trying to sell the books. He came over and bought almost everything."

"That's a wonderful story," Abi said, although it didn't explain how the sketches ended up between the glued pages. Instead of using the sketches as a guide for oil paintings, could Hopper have tucked the sketches in the book? It was obvious that he didn't like the drawing of the man with the bad face and unlikely he would have turned that into an oil.

Maybe Proctor found the sketches in the book where Hopper had put them. And like Abi, he would have been stunned at his discovery. He could have intended to tell Mrs. Hopper, but he'd have found it hard to let them go. Jo Hopper died soon after her husband, so he resealed the sketches, stopped showing the book to people and kept it under lock and key.

Dawn handed the book back. "I'm glad this is in the hands of someone like the professor. He and Allie would have liked each other."

"I'm sure they would have," Abi said. She returned the book to her backpack. "Thanks for the information and the tea."

"It was my pleasure."

Abi glanced around at the walls again and her gaze froze on a black-and-white photograph mingled in with the paintings and prints. She went over and studied the picture, which was about eight inches by ten.

"I know this place," she said.

"That's the old Snow property," Dawn said. "Or at least that's the way it looked before Eddy Baron tore down the old house to build his fortress."

"This is the first time I've seen the original house. Did Baron buy it from the Snow family?"

Dawn smiled. "Oh no. Around here, we tend to name a house after the original owners, even though they haven't been there for a hundred years. After the last Snow died, the house fell into disrepair and someone bought it cheap. We might have handled the septic upgrade."

"I'm a historian. I'm interested in the past."

Dawn opened a drawer in a gray metal filing cabinet and pulled out a beat-up manila folder that overflowed with yellow sheets of paper. She riffled through the papers and said, "Alden was an old Yankee. He never threw a thing away. Ah, here it is." She handed over a yellowed receipt that proved in 1945, Alden had charged a hundred dollars to open up a well.

"It doesn't say who the customer was," Abi said.

"Allie wasn't good at keeping records. He knew who the customer was, and the bill was marked Paid so that's all that counted."

Abi handed the paper back.

"I bet a job like that would cost a whole lot more to accomplish today," she said.

"A lot more. Funny thing, though. Even before 1945 there was already a working water source on the property; an electric pump that brought water to the house. Both the house and barn wells were filled in when the farm went electric. There hadn't been livestock since the Snow family lived there, so there was no need for the barn well. You can still see the cupolas for both wells in the photo."

Abi examined the house picture again. The circular walls with the roofs built over them were clearly visible, one near the house, the other closer to the barn. There were no wells in the Hopper sketches.

"That is strange. Maybe they liked the old-fashioned look of the wells, simply for decoration."

"I guess the later owners didn't have much use for decoration, because if you go there now, you'll see that the well roofs have been cleared away and the wells capped."

Abi was only half-listening. She was wondering what, if any, the connection was between the man in the sketch and the property owners.

She thanked Dawn again, and headed for the door. But stopped and turned when Dawn said, "Tell Professor Waldstein hello from me if you see him."

"I'll be sure to do that," Abi said.

She returned to the cottages and was pleased to see that Melissa and the film crew, Mead included, had departed. She went back into the office, intending to go through another carton of files, but her mind kept wandering.

Instead of working on the files, she left the office, got her bow case and went behind the house where she had set up the archery target. Slipping into a Zen mode, she notched the first arrow, drew the string and held it back. She tried not to think of the target and let her hands, rather than her mind, make the decision to release the bow string. But when she shot the arrow it was because her arms were tired, and the projectile went wide of the mark.

After a few more shots missed she put the bow and arrows back in the case, left it in the garden tool shed at the foot of the fire escape ladder, and went for a Zen walk on the beach.

She was thinking how quickly things had changed.

When she left Boston, it was like fleeing a haunted house in a horror movie for the sunlit dunes of Cape Cod. Now Boston represented light and hope and her idyllic haven had become a place of shadows and whispers.

CHAPTER TWENTY-SIX

The graveyard shift was unusually lively. Ben helped a couple of young women change a flat tire by the side of the road. Then he broke up a noisy beach party that had gone into the wee hours. He pulled over a driver and gave him a sobriety test, which he passed, thankfully, meaning Ben would not have to appear in court.

Ben was grateful for the diversion.

Suspicious little thoughts had been flying around inside his skull like birds in an aviary. He seemed to suspect everyone and everything. Like his doubts about Abi's stability, the way Baron had died, even the fishy excuse Weber had given him for lurking at the front gate of the Baron estate.

After many boring nights of mostly trying to stay awake, he actually enjoyed doing his sworn duty to serve and protect. He dropped the police cruiser off at the station and retrieved his pickup truck. He was looking forward to flopping into bed for his morning nap. Tired as he was, though, the nagging suspicions returned and sleep refused to come.

Nathan could be right when he said working late at night when most people were tucked into their beds was bad for the psyche. Maybe he should snap up the job. He now had less than one week to decide.

He was finding it hard to focus on the job offer. Questions still gnawed at him, keeping him awake. Finally, Ben gave up trying to sleep, got out of bed and took a hot shower. Then he changed into his civilian uniform: shorts, T-shirt and sandals. He brewed some coffee, poured himself a mug, and was on his way to the patio when the doorbell rang. He made a detour to the front door. Phil Mead was standing on the doorstep.

"Good morning," the magazine writer said, much too cheerfully to suit Ben's dour mood. "Happened to be in the neighborhood and thought I'd stop by to see if you'd heard the latest about Hank Aldrich."

Ben didn't have a clue what Mead was talking about. He had distanced himself from Aldrich after putting him in touch with a defense attorney.

"I've been out of the loop," he said. "What's going on with Hank?"

"Nothing good from his standpoint," Mead said. "He's been indicted for first degree murder."

"Ouch," Ben said. The news snapped him out of his funk. "I'll get you some coffee and meet you out on the patio."

"Sounds good. I take it black."

Ben went into the kitchen and poured a cup of coffee for Mead. They settled into a couple of patio chairs. "By the way, how did you know where I live?" Ben said.

"You mentioned it when we were on the hill."

Ben shrugged. "Okay," he said. "Tell me the gory details."

"The DA's office had a press conference a little while ago. They said that a grand jury had indicted Aldrich on premeditated murder charges."

"Guess I shouldn't be surprised Hank is in trouble," Ben said. "A couple of days ago I talked to the state cop in charge of the investigation. He had Hank accused and convicted and practically headed for the gallows."

"Yup. Sounds like old Hank-boy is screwed."

Switching into defense attorney mode Ben said, "Not necessarily. Depends on the physical evidence."

"They have enough proof to convict, according to the DA. The cops found a remote control in Hank's workshop that could have been used to set off explosives in the glider. Hank says he used it to control experimental glider models."

"That's an explanation a jury might believe. The defense lawyer will say there's no proof of an explosion. The glider could have crashed because of a design or building flaw. This was an aircraft built of canvas and wood, after all."

"Hard to explain how a flaw would account for the burned area around the hole in the fuselage and the damaged controls."

"Maybe it was grease or oil. Coast Guard could have damaged the controls and fuselage when they hauled the wreckage out of the water."

"Not bad, Counselor. Only problem is the fabric around the hole in the fuselage had traces of PETN, the stuff used in primacord."

"The only explosives I'm familiar with are Fourth of July firecrackers."

"Primacord is a plastic tube filled with explosives that is used as a high-speed fuse," Mead said.

"You're saying the same explosive was found in the glider?"

"Not me. The FBI tested the fabric in their labs."

"Begs the question: How does Aldrich get his hands on explosive cord?"

"He doesn't. According to the DA, he makes it himself with plastic tube and chemicals."

"Did they find tubing and explosive chemicals in his workshop?"

"His workshop is in upstate New York near the glider museum. The DA's working with the locals on a search warrant."

"That would change things. If they find the right chemical blend in the workshop, his lawyer could have a tough time mounting a defense. The prosecution would say Hank had the means and motive as well. Kyle had pushed him out of the reenactment. Hank had made threats to Kyle in the presence of witnesses. And since he was the last one to work on the glider, he had opportunity."

"Don't forget the bad blood over the Navy contract. More motive."

Mead apparently didn't know that Kyle had called Aldrich with an offer for a 50/50 partnership. As a defense lawyer, he'd use it to dismiss motive, but he saw no need to get into a discussion of legal strategy with Mead. His mind skittered off on a tangent.

"Something puzzles me, though. The Navy has all sorts of fighter jets and bombers. Why would they be interested in gliders?"

Mead shook his head. "Damned if I know. Hank didn't share any details with me."

"Well, he did with me. It was something to do with the Navy SEALs."

"Do tell." Mead grinned. "You must have a trusting face."

"I doubt that," Ben said. "Remember, I'm a lawyer."

"And I'm a magazine writer working on a cover story about Kyle's life and death for the magazine. Which reminds me, I gotta get back to the launch site. Melissa is doing an interview with CNN. I want to make sure she sticks to the script. Thanks for the coffee."

"Thanks for the update on Aldrich."

They stood and shook hands. Mead plunked his baseball hat on his head. Ben took a closer look at the pin attached to the front of the crown. It was three flying birds linked together.

"That's unusual," he said.

"It's from the old gliding school. The three-gull badge was the top award given to student pilots. I got it on the internet. Spent more than I should have, but I think it's kinda cool."

"It is. That reminds me. I've been thinking of taking a ride over to see the glider school site. I'm not sure where it is."

"Look in the informational packet that was handed out at the press conference. There's a reprint of the magazine article I did, and a map to show you how to get there."

Ben walked Mead to the door and thanked him for dropping by. The night shift blues were starting to catch up to him. He stretched out on the sofa and fell asleep despite the caffeine injection. When he woke up it was after lunch. He realized he hadn't had breakfast so he made himself a grilled ham and cheese sandwich.

After lunch, he found the press packet. Mead's article recapped how J. C. Penney Jr. formed the American Motorless Aviation Club to promote soaring in the U.S. Penney invited Hesselbach to fly gliders in the U.S. with an idea of setting up America's first school of gliding at Corn Hill. The site was changed to South Wellfleet at the top of the dunes on land rented from its owners by a syndicate from Boston. There was no mention of a third site.

Maybe the glider school sign he had seen in the barn was for a Corn Hill school, but that didn't explain how it got to the Baron property.

He read on. The three-gull button went to the students who could stay up five minutes and make certain maneuvers. Five gliders were brought in from Germany. The school planned to train 250 students in ten-day courses.

Mead was a good reporter. He'd dug up quotes from locals who liked the business the school brought in, but they were wary of the Germans who arrived to teach at the school. It had been only ten years since a German U-boat had attacked the coast a few miles to the south of the camp. Five years after the school went under, Hitler absorbed the German glider clubs and schools into the Nazi movement.

Ben folded the article and stuck it in his shirt pocket. A few minutes later he was in his truck driving south on Route 6. After going ten miles, he turned off the highway and headed east until he came to a beach parking lot overlooking the Atlantic Ocean.

He got out of the truck and followed a sloping path to the beach, then walked along the edge of the scalloped white frills that marked the surf line. He stopped from time-to-time to gaze at the cliffs that were similar to those in Truro. It wasn't hard to imagine gliders cruising with the gulls.

He walked along the edge of the surf for another few minutes then hiked back to the parking lot, got in the truck and reread the article. The credits at the end of the article listed the name Lester Heller from the National Soaring Museum in Elmira, New York.

He remembered Aldrich mentioning the name the first time they talked. Heller was the consultant who'd helped Hank build the replica of the Darmstadt. He looked up Heller's number online and gave him a call. He got a recording, and left a message saying he wanted to talk to Heller about the glider school.

Ben headed home. Minutes after he walked into the house, his cell phone chirped. It was Lester Heller getting back to him.

"Sorry I missed your call," Heller said. "I was working on a talk for the museum. Your message said you're interested in the South Wellfleet Glider School?"

"That's right. I saw your name in Phil Mead's article. I also talked to Hank Aldrich, who said you were a big help building his glider."

"Hank was great to work with. Real picky on the details. I don't blame him, after all the time and money he put into that glider. I saw on TV that the Darmstadt had ended up in the sea and the pilot died."

"You heard right."

"Damn shame. What's going on with Hank?"

Ben didn't have the heart to tell Heller his friend was being charged with murder.

"Hank is working out some legal issues."

"Wish him well if you speak to him. I've got a pile of glider school photos. I can email the file to you. Give me a call if you have any questions, and I'll do my best to answer them."

Ben said that would be fine, and gave him his email address.

He checked his computer ten minutes later. Heller had sent him a file containing at least two dozen black-and-white photos. Most of the pictures were of gliders in various stages of a launch. There were also photos showing groups of young men in flying uniform who must have been students. He scrolled through the photos, stopped at one and clicked on it.

Unlike the other shots, this photo showed only three people, all grinning for the camera. A boy in his teens stood between two men. Judging from the facial resemblance, Ben guessed, the man on the youth's right was his father. Pinned to the boy's shirt was a three-gull badge similar to the one on Mead's cap. He turned his attention to the man on the left and stared at the screen.

"Holy crap," he said.

CHAPTER TWENTY-SEVEN

Abi was skipping stones on the water when Ben called with an urgent message.

"I'm sending you an email attachment. Let me know what you think."

The words tumbled out of his mouth far faster than his usual deliberate way of talking.

Abi clicked on her phone's email function, went to the attachment and pulled up a head-and-shoulders photo of three people. The details were hard to see on the small screen in bright sunlight.

"Got it. What am I looking at?"

"Check out the face of the guy to the left of the kid."

Abi cupped her hand to keep out the light. The man in the photo had a full head of close-cropped hair and looked to be in his thirties, but there was something about the narrow face that looked familiar.

"This is a younger version of the man in the Hopper sketch!"

"It's either him or his twin brother. Where are you now?" Ben said.

"I'm taking a walk on the beach."

"See you at the cottage in ten minutes."

Abi hurried back to her office and called Ben's email attachment up on her computer. Then she compared the face in the photo to the Hopper sketch. No mistake. They were one and the same. Ben pulled up next to the Rover around ten minutes later. He entered the house after a perfunctory knock on the door. Abi called out and told him to come into the office.

Seeing the image displayed on the monitor, he leaned over her shoulder and tapped the screen with his finger. "What do you think?"

"There's no doubt that's the same man." Abi motioned for Ben to pull up a chair. "Where did you find this picture?"

"I got it from an aviation historian named Lester Heller. He's with the National Soaring Museum in upstate New York. He worked as a consultant with Hank Aldrich building the replica of the Darmstadt glider. I called him looking for information on the glider school. He sent me a batch of photos. This was one of them."

"Good job, Ben! Maybe Mr. Heller knows Mr. Hatchet-face's real name."

"Worth a try," Ben said.

He called Heller's number and put the phone on speaker.

"Hi, Ben," Heller said. "Didn't expect you to get back to me so fast."

"Thanks for the photo file. I'm here with my friend Abi. She's helping me with research."

"Pleased to meet you, Abi," Heller said.

"And you too, Lester. We were particularly interested in one picture." She gave Heller the photo's identification number.

"Got it. Two guys and a kid. There's a dedication written at the bottom of the photo." Heller read the inscription, "To my young bird man-congratulations on earning your gulls' wings. O.K."

"That's the one. We're interested in the identity of the man to the boy's left."

"He and the kid are in uniform. My guess is that the guy is an instructor and the boy a student. An accomplished one, from the looks of the three-gull pin on his shirt."

Abi said, "The other man is looking proudly at the boy and there's a strong facial resemblance. Father?"

"That would be my guess."

"Do you know anything about the photo credit at the bottom right? Viktor Neilsen?"

"His credit is on a number of glider school photos. The boys at the school came mostly from well-to-do parents who would have had the money to hire a professional photographer."

"We'll Google the name as soon as we're through," Ben said.

"That'll be good. I can go through my files and see if there's a group shot with names attached."

Ben hung up and turned to Abi. "So, Hatchet-face may have been a flying instructor at the glider school."

"Seems that way. Still doesn't tell us why he came back to Cape Cod more than fifteen years after the school closed and what he was doing at the old barn."

Ben said, "Let's try the other lead." He Googled Viktor Nielsen, photographer.

Within minutes they had learned that Nielsen was Norwegian, that he specialized in aircraft photography, and that he'd worked for a number of corporations. One name on the list of employers caught Ben's attention.

"He worked for Sunna Industries, which is owned by the Magnus family."

Heller called back a few minutes later. "Hello again. No picture. I found a list of instructors, though. That won't ID your guy, but it can narrow things down."

Abi had been studying the photo. "This inscription doesn't make sense," she said. "Look at the O.K. It just seems to be tacked onto the original congratulations."

"I wondered about that, too," Ben said, squinting at the screen. "I thought it was short for Okay, but it's O.K. There's a period after each letter." He paused, then said, "Is there any name on that list of instructors with those initials?"

"Only one name fits that description," Heller said. "Otto Klaas. It says he was from Darmstadt, Germany. Not surprising. Darmstadt was a center of glider activity and the school imported German talent with the help of the Rhön-Rossitten group. The chief pilot was Heinrich Knott and his assistant was from Darmstadt. They brought in a combination of German and American instructors."

"Is there any way to find out what happened to Otto Klaas after the glider school closed?" Abi asked.

"I don't know what he did immediately, but I'd guess with his flying skills he ended up in the Luftwaffe. The glider flying clubs were known for their esprit de corps, the feeling that they were different in a special way. The Nazis absorbed the flying clubs and appropriated this spirit into their movement."

"So he was a pilot during the war?"

"Hold on. I can look him up on a list of German World War II pilots." After several minutes, he said, "Sorry for the wait. List is pretty long. I found a number of pilots with his name. None of them is from Darmstadt, however. He could have held an administrative post, although that would have been a waste of his flying skills."

"Peter Hesselbach was from Darmstadt," Ben said.

"That's right. Hesselbach could have recruited him for the school. Let me try something." After a few more minutes, he said, "I may have lucked out. Googled Otto Klaas, Darmstadt and Luftwaffe and came across a link to a news article with his photo. I'll send it to you."

He hung up, and the email link appeared on the screen after only a moment. The story was from *The Nantucket Inquirer and Mirror*. The headline over the story read:

Long-Time Island Resident was a Monuments Man; Inspired Book and Movie

Photos accompanied the article. The larger picture showed a man in his twenties holding a painting of an aristocratic young woman with her hair piled high in the fashion of a bygone century. The man had a broad grin on his face and he wore a World War II army helmet. The caption identified the man as Clint Hammond, and the painting as a work by Rembrandt.

Buried further down in the article was the headshot of another man. The line under the photo in bold face type identified the man as Otto Klaas. He was wearing a uniform and a cap.

"I know him!" Abi said.

"Otto Klaas?" Ben said, confused.

"No. Clint Hammond. He's an old friend." She looked at the picture of Klaas again and this time she read the entire caption. "That's odd."

"What is?"

"According to the note on the drawing, Hopper sketched Klaas at the barn in 1946."

"Yes. I remember. What's odd about it?"

"The caption under the picture says Otto Klaas died in an Allied bombing raid in 1945."

CHAPTER TWENTY-EIGHT

"Now I know why Edward Hopper said Otto Klaas had a bad face," Abi said, handing the print-out of the *Inquirer* article to Ben. "Klaas was one of the scouts the Nazis sent across Europe in the 1930s to inventory public and private art collections they planned to steal."

Ben said, "But if the bombing raid story is true, Klaas could not have been in the U.S. in 1946 unless he came back from the dead."

"Or, unless he didn't die in that bombing. I've got to talk to Mr. Hammond and see what else he knows. I hope he's still alive. He'd be quite elderly, and I haven't seen him since I closed the Nantucket gallery. I may have his name on the list of gallery regulars." She scrolled down the list of contacts on her phone. "Got it."

She tapped the call symbol. A gravelly voice answered the phone: "Clint Hammond."

Abi gave Ben a thumbs-up. "Hello, Mr. Hammond," she said. "This is Abi Vickers. How are you?"

"Abi! What a nice surprise. I'm fine. Wonderful to hear from you. I've missed going to your openings since the gallery closed."

"Those were fun days. I always enjoyed our chats about art."

"Me too. What can I do for you?"

"I read an article in the *Inquirer and Mirror* about your experiences with the Monuments Men. You never told me you were with such an elite group."

Hammond chuckled. "Not many people knew the Monuments,

Fine Arts and Archives Section even existed until the book and movie came out. I did a Veterans Day talk the paper covered, mentioning I was a Monuments Man, so they interviewed me about my service. How did I do?"

"You did great, but there's something I don't understand. You said in the article that Otto Klaas died in 1945."

"Yes. That's correct. That's what the official army investigation showed. Is there a problem?"

"I'm not sure." She paused, trying to figure out how to break it to Hammond that he'd been wrong. "I heard from another source that Klaas didn't die in Germany. He survived the war, and visited the United States in 1946."

There was momentary silence on the line before Hammond replied, "That can't be true, Abi."

"I know it sounds crazy, but I have evidence he was alive after the war. I'd love to show it to you."

"And I'd love to see it. Are you still in Boston?"

"I'm on the Cape. I'll try to get to the island today, if possible. Let me check the ferry schedule." She called up the island boat schedules on her computer screen. "Good news. I can catch a ferry if I leave soon. There's a boat coming back this evening. We should have plenty of time to talk."

"We may need plenty of time," he said.

She hung up and said to Ben, "Feel like going on a boat ride?"

Ben shook his head. "I'm working tonight so I'd better pass on this one, just in case your meeting goes longer than expected."

"Okay," she said. "I'll take good notes and fill you in when I get back."

She ran off copies of the Hopper sketches and put them in the art book which she tucked into her backpack. Then she shut down the computer, grabbed a bottle of water, and told Ben she'd give him a call from the ferry coming back to the mainland.

He walked her to the Land Rover. She gave him a quick hug before she got behind the wheel and drove off.

Ben climbed into his truck and called Lester Heller to thank him for all his help.

"No problem. Give my best to Hank. He's kinda gruff, but a

good guy nonetheless."

"I will. Have you talked to him recently?"

"I called him after I heard about the crash. We couldn't figure what could have gone wrong. Like I told the Swiss guy, that little plane was solid."

"Sorry. Did you say, 'Swiss' guy?"

"That's right. A journalist named Weber. He called to ask about my work with Hank on the glider."

"I see. For the record, though, Weber is German. From Darmstadt."

"Really? Coulda fooled me. I was stationed in Germany and speak German. He definitely had a Swiss accent. Funny that he'd say he's from Darmstadt. The Swiss are very sensitive about being taken for German."

"Maybe he spent some time in Switzerland," Ben said.

"That could be," Heller said. "Well, let me know if you need any more help."

"I will. You've been a great help already. Thanks again."

After they hung up Ben stared into space for a minute, then dug out Weber's business card and Googled the Darmstadt news agency on his phone. He found websites for some news agencies but nothing by that specific name. He expanded the search to German news agencies. None matched the listing on the business card.

Next, he looked under Martin Weber, journalist. Then Martin Weber, Swiss journalist. Nothing. Finally, he called the number on the business card and left a brief message.

"Hi, Marty, or whoever you are. This is Ben. We've got to talk."

CHAPTER TWENTY-NINE

The windowless room was on the fortieth floor of a tall office building that overlooked the East River in New York City. The walls were taken up by oversized television monitors tuned to the major broadcast outlets all around the world.

The chamber's only occupant was a balding man in a dark blue suit who sat in a swivel chair at a computer table in the center of the space, like a spider in its web. The simile would have been apt, because the computer and phones on his desk were connected to electronic strands that extended to every part of the globe.

He stared through rimless glasses at a television screen that showed a crowd of men and women waving signs written in German. They were facing off against a line of helmeted policemen. The volume was turned off, but it was obvious from the angry expressions on the faces that they were shouting.

He turned up the volume and was pleased to hear the decibel level rising. So far, the police were managing to keep control. Without removing his gaze from the screen, the man picked up a phone, murmured a few words and hung up.

After a minute or two an arm reached past the jostling protesters on the right of the screen. At the end of the arm was a hand holding a canister. A stream of brown vapor shot out from the cylinder into the crowd of police officers, who reacted defensively and started swinging their billy clubs. The shouts turned into screams.

The balding man smiled. Nothing like a little pepper gas to light the flame under a tense situation. But the execution was sloppy. The agent provocateur should have been invisible. He would have to take someone to the woodshed.

A phone at his elbow chirped and its red light blinked. He tapped the speakerphone button and said, "Central."

A man's voice, hardly louder than the hiss of a snake, said: "I've been watching."

The director was always watching. He watched everything.

"Yes?" said the man in the blue suit.

"Sloppy work."

The hand with the pepper spray. The smile vanished. "I agree. I'll deal with it."

"Not now. There's been a development in the Nantucket situation."

The computer screen came to life. Displayed side-by-side were two photos: one of an elderly man, the other a woman with auburn hair. The balding man jotted down instructions on a pad, "I'll take care of it immediately."

CHAPTER THIRTY

Abi sat back in her seat on the Nantucket-bound ferry and tried to remember what she knew about the Monuments Men. The best she could recall was that George Clooney played in the movie as one of the team chasing down stolen masterpieces. And that, even with gray hair he was a hunk.

At the entrance to Lewis Bay the ferry picked up speed and headed on a southerly course, twin hulls knifing the waters of Nantucket Sound. The freight and car ferries that kept the island supplied with food and fuel took more than two hours to make the thirty-mile trip but the catamaran did the crossing in less than half that time. She planned to take the slower car ferry back after she had talked to Hammond.

She called up Google on her phone and tapped in 'Monuments Men.' Then she scrolled down the postings on the subject to the website for The Monuments Men Foundation. During the war about sixty, mostly American and British, Monuments Men were mobilized to serve in Europe to protect churches and museums from being damaged during the fighting. But as they made their way into countries formerly under German occupation, they spent most of their time tracking down stolen art.

Abi stared out the window at the rolling seas. She felt as if she were trying to put together a jigsaw puzzle with the key pieces missing. She was no closer to a solution when, about an hour after leaving the Hyannis dock, the ferry rounded the diminutive Brant Point lighthouse that marked the entrance to Nantucket Harbor. Abi disembarked from the ferry and walked along the cobblestone main streets of Nantucket town, taking a roundabout route that bypassed her old gallery. Losing the gallery had been traumatic. She didn't feel strong enough yet to see the property vacant, or occupied by another business.

Hammond's two-and-a-half-story antique white clapboard structure was on a narrow street in a quiet neighborhood a couple of blocks from the bustling center. An attractive, middle-aged woman answered the doorbell. Abi recognized Hammond's daughter Eleanor, who used to accompany her father to the art gallery.

"How nice to meet you again, Abi," she said.

"Great to see you too, Ellie."

She ushered Abi into the house. Lowering her voice, Ellie added, "Dad's sharp as a tack most of the time. Amazing for a man in his nineties, but sometimes his mind wanders. He might doze off at any moment. Not sure that will be a problem today; he's been quite excited since you called."

Abi said she was sure she could keep Hammond's attention. She followed Eleanor through the house and out the back door to a small brick patio bordered with neat flower gardens.

Hammond was sitting at a round metal table reading *The New York Times*. He put the paper down, rose from his chair, leaned on a cane and extended his free hand. Hammond was slightly more bent over and seemed frailer than the last time Abi had seen him, but his handshake was remarkably firm and his voice was strong. He had a full mane of pure white hair and the alert gray eyes in the tanned face sparkled with good humor.

"Thank you for coming all this way to visit me, Abi. It's been a while since we've seen each other."

"Much too long. I've missed Nantucket."

"And Nantucket has missed you. Have a seat."

Ever the gentleman, Hammond sat only after Abi had settled into the other chair. Eleanor said she would be back with iced tea. As soon as his daughter was out of hearing range, Hammond leaned forward and a whispered, "Dang it, Abi, I almost jumped out of my skin when you called about Otto Klaas."

Smiling, Abi said, "You may want to button up your skin before you see the evidence I promised." She unzipped the backpack, pulled out the book and removed the sketches. She placed them on the table with the Otto Klaas drawing on the bottom.

Hammond put on a pair of reading glasses and picked up the sketch showing the house and barn from a distance. He studied it for a second, then raised his bushy white eyebrows.

"This looks like a Hopper sketch and it was in a book on realist artists. Am I correct in deducing that it's a Hopper?"

"You wouldn't be off the mark."

"Where did it come from, Abi?"

"All three sketches were hidden inside the book." She showed him the pages that had been glued together. "The sketches are most likely authentic."

Hammond studied the second sketch of the barn that showed the figure unloading the truck. He set it aside and examined the third sketch with the close-up of Otto Klaas.

"I'll be damned," he said.

"As you can see, the artist dated the sketch."

Hammond read the notes. "*Bad Face?*" he said.

"Apparently, the man made a strong impression on Hopper."

A rueful grin came to Hammond's weathered features.

"Klaas was still alive in 1946!" he said. "That slippery little snake fooled everyone, including me. I guess the story is true."

"About Otto Klaas?" Abi said.

He nodded. "Someone in my unit heard from a Waffen-SS officer that Klaas had faked his death. He figured the SS guy made the story up so he'd have something to bargain with. The Monuments Men had bigger fish to fry and we never followed up. Klaas managed to wriggle off the hook."

"Don't beat yourself up. The Monuments Men had an almost impossible job to do."

"It was *beyond* impossible. More than five million pieces of art were plundered."

"It's amazing the Germans had time to fight a war."

"German efficiency. They had planned their crime long before the first shot was fired. Years before the war, Hitler's so-called art scholars fanned out across Europe. Their mission was to inventory every important piece of art that they could find and list its location in massive catalogs so the object could be stolen easily after a country was occupied by the invaders."

"Sad that anyone with a love of art would be an accomplice to a crime like that."

"Sad but true. And no different than the bankers who collected gold teeth ripped from gas chamber victims or doctors who performed horrible experiments on camp prisoners. Educated, supposedly cultured people were guilty of atrocious crimes. Without these artsy types the Nazis could not have swept art masterpieces back to the Fatherland. Hitler wanted to put the loot in a gigantic museum to be built in his hometown of Lintz."

"Where was Otto Klaas in the scheme of things?"

"Right in the thick of it. He kept a low profile, but he was one of Goering's top art procurers." He paused. "I'm puzzled. What led to your interest in Otto Klaas? Something to do with your art history background?"

"Indirectly. After I found the sketches I became curious about the man in the picture. I wondered who he was and why Hopper had sketched him. The trail led to a glider school on Cape Cod where Otto was an instructor in the 1920s. I was researching the school and read the article you had written for the newspaper."

"You would have made a good Monuments Woman, if there had been such a thing."

"Thank you! I don't understand how Klaas got into art theft on such a grand scale. It's quite the jump from teaching young men how to fly off a Cape Cod sand dune."

"Otto studied fine arts at Darmstadt University. He got interested in flying and joined the university's glider club when it was one of the best in Germany. It's logical that he would have gone on to teach flying."

"He was apparently an excellent instructor." Abi handed Hammond the photo Lester Heller had sent showing Otto posing with his student. "This picture was taken in 1929 at the glider school, the year it closed after the stock market crash. The O.K.

written in the dedication stands for Otto Klaas."

"I'll be damned. Any idea who the boy is?"

"Only one student named Karl was on the list of those who'd been awarded that badge. His name is Karl Magnus. The photographer did some work for Sunna Industries. Have you heard of it?"

"Oh yes. Sunna was one of those international corporations that kept trading with Germany during the war. They supplied metal for weapons used against Allied armies. The company was started by Andsgar Magnus, who emigrated to the U.S. from Norway. He got involved in the metals business and became immensely rich. His son Gunnar took over the company and ran it in the 1920s, about the time the picture was taken."

"The facial resemblance suggests that the man in the photo was Karl's father."

"In that case, we're looking at Gunnar, although I can't be sure. The Magnus family didn't like its picture taken. Where did you get this photo?"

"It was part of a collection that came from the soaring museum in upstate New York."

Hammond sat back in his chair and tented his fingers. "I'm not as sharp as I used to be, but I'll put myself in Otto's shoes. The glider school closes. The world economy crashes and Nazism arises. The German glider clubs are absorbed into the Luftwaffe, led by Hermann Goering, the worst of the art thieves."

"Worse than Hitler?"

"Hitler was a failed artist and he could at least appreciate the magnificence of what he stole. With Goering it was pure plunder, but I guess I owe him one. Goering's greed got me into the Monuments Men."

"How so?"

"I was fresh out of college. The war was winding down. The Monuments unit needed more feet on the ground to help deal with Goering's extensive thefts. I was a cheeky youngster with energy and a law degree. I spoke German and had a minor in arts. Goering was moving stolen art around and I was trying to keep track of it. I kept seeing shipment authorizations with O.K. scribbled on them."

"Just like the initials on the photo."

"That's right. I figured out they were Otto's when I saw his full name on a document. I started paying more attention to O.K. He spent a lot of time in France and the Netherlands, but near the close of the war he went to Poland, then to Norway before coming back to Germany, where he was supposedly killed in the bombing raid."

"You said the Magnus family was Norwegian?"

"Norway was the ancestral home of the Magnus clan. Where they owned a castle. Maybe Otto was renewing his acquaintance with Gunnar and Karl, going back to the glider school. Karl would have been in his thirties by then and running the company." He picked up the sketch. "There's one thing I can't figure out. What was Otto doing on Cape Cod in '46?"

"I can answer that question in part," Abi said. "The house and barn in the sketches were owned by Sunna Industries."

A stunned expression came to Hammond's eyes. "Are you sure?"

"Very sure. The property was abandoned at the time Hopper visited it with his sketch pad. The barn is still there."

"You've seen it?"

"I've been *inside* it. The building hasn't been used in years."

Hammond murmured something under his breath.

"Pardon?" Abi said.

"I was just thinking about the young man."

Abi recalled what Ellie had said about Hammond's wandering mind.

"I'm not sure I understand," she said.

"You will," Hammond said. "Come with me."

He got out of his chair and went into the house. Abi followed him into a room that had a chair and a small table with a banker's light on it. A half-dozen tall, metal filing cabinets lined the walls.

"This is all stuff from my Monument Men days. The key to the Otto Klaas mystery may be locked in these files," he said with a sweep of his hand.

"Where should we start?"

"That's the problem. My body has outlived my mind. It's going to take a while to find what I'm looking for. I remember reading correspondence between Klaas and Magnus regarding a trip to Norway, but I'm afraid I don't have a clue where to look. It's been a long time since I've gone through these records."

"Let's get busy, then. I'll grab another chair."

She suggested that they go through the files one-by-one, using much the same system she used with Professor Waldstein's papers. Starting at the beginning, she transferred the files to the table where Hammond went over them.

It was a slow process. His eyes easily tired and he had to stop often to rest. Or something totally unrelated would grab his attention and he'd go off on a tangent. After a couple of hours had passed Abi glanced at her watch.

"I'll have to leave soon to catch the car ferry to the mainland."

"That's okay. I think I know how to narrow this down. May take a while, though. Tell you what. I'll call you as soon as I have something. Who else knows about this sketch?"

"The provenance expert who authenticated it, but she doesn't know its context. And my friend Ben Dyer. He's a police officer and an attorney. Why do you ask?"

"I can't say for sure right now, but promise me that this will go no further."

She put her hand on his. "I promise."

"Good," he said with relief in his voice. "Because your life may depend on it."

Abi had never seen Hammond look so serious. She would have asked him for more details if his daughter hadn't popped into the office carrying a tray.

"Anyone care for a snack?" Ellie said.

CHAPTER THIRTY-ONE

"*Guten Tag, mein Herr.*"

Weber swiveled in his stool and saw Phil Mead approaching the bar, his mouth stretched in a wide grin.

"Danke schön," Weber said. "I didn't know you spoke German."

"That's my whole vocabulary, except for knockwurst and bratwurst."

"You wouldn't go hungry in Germany, in that case."

"Yeah, but I might go thirsty, since I don't know how to ask for a beer."

"I can fix that," Weber said. He pointed to his near-empty beer glass and raised two fingers in the air. The bartender set a couple of foaming mugs on the bar top. Mead slid onto the stool next to Weber's, and buried his face in the foam.

"Thanks," he said, wiping his mouth with the back of his hand. "How's the reporting?"

"Not much to report. I'm waiting for the police investigation results, but that could take weeks." Weber shrugged. "I'll head back to Zurich if nothing happens soon."

"The snappers are getting together at cottage hill. They're going to do a 'ghost launch.' Melissa asked me to track you down and see if you wanted to come by. Might make a good story."

"It might if I knew what a ghost launch was. American idiom?"

"Nah. It's *my* idiom. You'll have to see for yourself. It's a final

184

tribute to Kyle from Melissa and the crew."

"That does sound interesting. When is it?"

"Forty-five minutes." He chugged the rest of his beer. "Thanks for the brewskie. See you up on the hill."

Weber answered with a nod of his head. He wasn't sure whether it was a good idea to go back to Truro. He'd gone directly to the bar after he listened to the voicemail Officer Dyer left on his phone for Marty Weber or, "whoever you are."

The police officer had seen through the excuse Weber had given for being at the Baron property. His fake press card had been created on an office computer. A quick check of his credentials would reveal he was not the journalist he said he was.

Weber sipped his beer and rehearsed how he should respond when Dyer eventually caught up with him. He could try to lie his way out of it, but Dyer would have no reason to believe him. He cursed in German, loud enough for the bartender to hear, thinking he had ordered another beer.

Weber waved him off and muttered the curse again, more quietly this time. The last thing he needed to complicate his life was a country cop sniffing around while he was trying to do his job. He would have to tell Dyer the truth, or a version of it.

He paid his tab, strolled down the hallway to the section of the inn rented by the glider crew and stopped in front of the door to Kyle's suite. The hacker who attempted to get into the Restitution Registry data base had used a Mac computer. Melissa had used a Mac at the press conference. Magnus had picked up the laptop after the presentation. That was the last Weber had seen of the computer. Magnus transacted his day-to-day business on a mobile phone.

The computer could still be in the room.

Voices were coming down the hallway. He moved away from the door, walked to an exit and went out to his rental car. Fifteen minutes later he drove to the top of the flower cottage hill and parked.

A small group of people stood on the bluff, silhouetted against the orange sun and the shimmering waters of the bay. Weber got out of his car. Mead broke away from the others to greet him.

"Howdo, Marty? Glad you could make it. The crew is going over instructions. We'll start in a minute. What you are going to see is a glider launch without the glider."

"That's a good trick."

"Easy when you know how. Like shooting an empty slingshot only in slow motion. Afterwards, they'll line up at the edge of the cliff. A camera drone will circle overhead, catching them in the light of the setting sun. A hovering gull will be spliced into the final take to represent Magnus's soaring spirit."

"With a soaring soundtrack to match no doubt," said Weber.

"I suggested the *Wind Beneath My Wings*," Mead said. "Hell, what do I know? Think there's a story here?"

"Phil, if there is one thing I have learned about this whole experience, hardly a minute goes by when there is *not* a story."

"Can't argue with that," Mead said. "Looks like they're getting the drone in the air. Excuse me, but I've got to help out. We're short on snappers."

Weber jotted down a few sentences in his notebook describing the scene. The snappers stood in a line positioned well back from the cliff's edge. When they were ready, Melissa, who was off to one side, called out the countdown.

On the count of one, the snappers holding the center of the cord dug their heels in. On two, the others pulled the ends forward so the rope was in a V formation with the opening facing the bay. On three, the tail crew walked forward, dropped the rope, and everybody stood side-by-side in the rosy golden rays of the setting sun.

The drone buzzed over the bay, then came back above the beach to circle the snappers in the dusky light. The whole exercise only took a couple of minutes. Melissa walked over to talk to Weber.

"Hi, Marty," she said. "Thanks for being here. All the other reporters have left town."

"Thank you for the invitation. This is an impressive farewell to Kyle."

Melissa looked off at the darkening waters of the bay. "It's just so unbelievable that he's gone. I know that some people thought Kyle could be a real pain, and he totally used people. Including me. He knew everyone thought he was just an overgrown trust fund kid, but he was going to surprise them after the flight."

"What sort of surprise?"

"It had something to do with the Navy project he was involved in."

"Did he mention any details?"

"Only that the code name was Icarus." A sad smile came to her lips. "How ironic is that? Kyle and Icarus both fell into the sea."

"I'm surprised he didn't use the name of Daedelus, who built the wings for his son Icarus and warned him about getting too close to the sun. Why Icarus?"

"I asked him the same question. He said the Icarus story isn't about a technical achievement. In real life, the wings would not have worked, and the sun's warmth at a high altitude would not have melted the wax used to attach the feathers. The story was a warning about what happens when you get too close to the realm of the powerful."

"Seems there was a lot more to Kyle than anyone suspected."

"Much more. The beach boy personality was pure Kyle, but so was his MIT degree in engineering, which makes it even more of a pity that Hank took matters into his own hands."

"Do you think Hank killed him?"

"Yes," she said half-heartedly "Maybe. He was so angry. The police think he did it." She shrugged. "I don't know. My concern now is preserving Kyle's legacy. After we're through here the crew is going over to the Governor Bradford bar to toast Kyle. Would you care to join us?"

"Thanks. Maybe later. I'd like to type up some notes while the ghost launch is fresh in my mind."

"I'm sure the party will go on for a while."

Weber said he'd try to swing by the bar, but his mind was on Kyle's computer. He got in his car, drove back to the Provincetown Inn, and parked in the shadows away from the building near the breakwater.

Rather than pass through the lobby, he entered the inn through a side door and went back to his room. Hidden under his clothes at the bottom of his suitcase was a plastic case. Inside was an electric lock picker he'd used in a number of European hotels.

He made his way to Kyle's suite, glanced to the right and left, then placed the electronic device against the lock and pressed the button. He heard a click. A second later he was on the other side of the door. He switched on a flashlight and swept the beam around the room. The MacBook was on a desk.

Weber sat at the desk and booted up the laptop. The prompt on the screen asked for a password. He typed the word 'Melissa' and an error message appeared informing him he'd made a mistake. Kyle was trying to break Hesselbach's record. Weber typed in the name of the German pilot and paused, knowing he could be permanently locked out if he kept up the guesswork.

He could take the computer with him and figure out how to get into it later, but someone might notice the laptop was missing. He sat at the desk, holding the useless thumb drive in his hand, and stared at the screen.

Recalling his conversation with Melissa, he held his breath and typed in the word 'Icarus.' This time, icons popped onto the screen. Weber searched for a mention of the hacked art database. Most all of the files had to do with the glider flight.

He inserted the thumb drive and downloaded the files listed under 'Navy Project.' When the download was complete, he pulled out the thumb drive and put it in his pocket. Then he turned off the laptop and closed the cover. He put his ear against the door. Hearing nothing, he stepped into the hallway and headed toward an exit, then out into the parking lot.

The assailant must have been crouched down on the other side of the car because Weber never saw him. He had opened the driver's door, tossed the lock picker onto the passenger seat, and was about to slide in behind the wheel when he heard a footfall behind him. Then, what felt like a ton of bricks fell on his head and fireworks exploded behind his eyes.

The next thing he recalled was waking up with his face against the cold, hard blacktop.

He pushed himself up to his knees, then stood and leaned dizzily against the side of the car. He squelched the urge to vomit, taking several deep gulps of cool air into his lungs. When his blurred vision cleared somewhat he looked around, but he was alone in the parking lot.

He cursed himself for letting someone ambush him, then put his hand in his pocket and got even angrier when he discovered the thumb drive missing. The lock picker was still on the seat where he'd left it. He staggered back into the inn and made his way to Kyle's room. Having broken in once, he quickly gained entrance, and went directly to the table.

Weber picked up the computer and tucked it under his arm. He felt suddenly dizzy and gulped back the sputum in his throat. He needed to get some ice on his head very soon. He opened the door and stepped out of the room into the hallway.

In his haste and disheveled state he neglected to make sure that the coast was clear. It wasn't. Through dazed eyes he saw someone coming toward him.

CHAPTER THIRTY-TWO

It was dark when Abi left the Hammond house. Ellie had offered to give her a ride, but she wanted to clear out her head and she had always loved walking the narrow streets of the old whaling town in the footsteps of Ishmael and Queequeg. She liked late spring on the island before the invasion of tourists, and summer residents who lived in the big shorefront mega-mansions.

On the way to the harbor, Abi summoned the courage to walk by her former business. She could have gone straight to the ferry, but she wanted to reaffirm the memories of her past life. Which sometimes seemed like a dream, and in more recent times, a nightmare. But she was damned if she were going to let a bunch of lawyers and a jerk of an ex-husband run her life.

She gazed through the windows of her old art gallery at the mannequins dressed in resort wear. Hanging on the walls where she had displayed beautiful canvases of sea and shore were beach scenes of lithe young women wearing high-priced dresses and bathing suits.

Once the decision had been made, she was surprised at how easy it was to confront the past. There was sadness, of course, but no regret. Chasing down international art thieves had given her a jolt of reality. Her troubles seemed so trivial. She lost a couple of art galleries and a marriage that had been an illusion. Her experience paled in comparison to the museums and families whose art collections had been plundered.

Hammond's daughter had insisted that Abi have something to eat. She laid out a platter of cold cuts, cheese, and freshly baked bread and they made do-it-yourself sandwiches. They'd put the file search aside, and there was no talk of Otto Klaas and massive art theft. Abi brought them up to date on her work for the professor. She said her prospects for the future looked good, and that she would be doing something having to do with the art world very soon.

Cars and trucks were lined up, waiting to get on the ferry. Unlike the sleek catamaran that carried passengers only, the squat, white-hulled car ferry was a rugged workhorse of a boat, with multiple decks dominated by a butternut-colored smokestack.

Abi bought a one-way ticket to Hyannis and joined the passengers gathered at the loading dock.

She was distracted by thoughts of her conversation with Hammond. Although, even if she hadn't been, it was doubtful she would have noticed the two men who separately entered the ticket terminal after she'd come out. They bought tickets minutes apart and took great pains to stay out of her line of vision.

Passengers were allowed on the boat before vehicles. They were directed through doors on either side of the car deck, then up flights of stairs to the middle section of the boat between the main bow cabin and a smaller seating section at the stern.

Abi headed to the bow observation deck. She sat in a front row seat and chatted with a young couple who were eating ice cream cones to celebrate the end of their day trip to the island.

The loud blast of a horn announced that the ferry was leaving the dock. The boat made its way along the channel to the entrance of the harbor and set a northerly course to the mainland.

Abi was dressed in shorts and a blouse which offered little protection against the cool breeze coming off Nantucket Sound. Her ice cream friends had gone back into the cabin and she was all alone on the deck. She went back inside, grateful for the warm air that enveloped her. She still had a two hour trip ahead. Before she settled down, Abi took a stroll around the boat to pass the time.

She walked along the port side past the restrooms, crew spaces and the stairs that went down to the car deck, continued on into a smaller passenger area that housed a quaint bar, tables and booths, then through a door and out onto the deserted stern observation platform.

The platform was flanked by two lifeboats in davits. She went to the railing, glanced down at the car deck, then looked off at the wide wake behind the boat. She watched, mesmerized, but after a moment she started to shiver. The cold aluminum row seats weren't exactly inviting.

Back inside, she made her way along the starboard side to the bow cabin and took an aisle seat. Only a few dozen passengers were taking the late boat. Some were already stretched out for a nap. She downloaded the Monuments Men book on the phone and read a few chapters before her eyelids started to droop. Using the pack for a pillow, she stretched out and closed her eyes.

She wasn't sure how long she'd dozed before she heard someone say, "Miss? Please wake up."

She opened her eyes. A big, broad-shouldered man was bending over her. She vaguely remembered seeing him in a window seat.

She sat up and rubbed her eyes. "Yes?"

"It's my wife. I need your help."

The man she remembered had been sitting alone, but she could have been mistaken. She said, "What's wrong with her?"

"She passed out on the deck."

Abi looked around the quiet cabin. "Should we tell someone else?"

"Good idea. But she needs first aid now. Please. At the back of the boat."

Abi got up and followed the man toward the stern, thinking that she'd ask the bartender to call for medical help. The bar was empty when they went into the aft passenger section, so she continued through the door out onto the stern deck.

The chill air snapped Abi out of her lethargy. She looked around the deck. None of the seats were occupied. And no one was lying on the deck.

"Where's your wife?" she said.

"Over there," the man replied, pointing to the lifeboat in its fenced-off section.

She took a couple of steps closer to the barrier, still not seeing any sign of the man's wife. What she did see was another man who must have been crouching behind the lifeboat. He came around the boat toward the fence. Like the big stranger, he wore a polo shirt and chinos and his hair was cut close to the skull. The deck lights illuminated a wide face. The man was smiling, but it was definitely not a friendly smile.

Alarm bells went off in Abi's head. She remembered Hammond's warning about her life being in danger. She turned to go back into the cabin. The big man was standing between her and the door. She tried to go around him, but he quickly stepped in front of her and blocked the way.

"It's okay, miss," he said in a voice that was more menacing than reassuring. He held his hand out. "All we want is your pack and then you can go on your merry way," he said.

Before Abi could answer, she heard the gate in the metal fence open behind her. The second man had stepped through the gate onto the deck. "Give him pack," he said, brandishing a metal cylinder. "Then you go to sleep in ocean."

"*Jeezus*," the big man said. "Pay no attention, miss. My friend is just joking."

Abi didn't know what the metal thing was, but it was clear to her that he *wasn't* joking. She slid the pack off her shoulders. Instead of handing it over, she stepped closer to the stern rail and lifted the bag as if she were going to throw it down onto the car deck below.

"Come any closer and I'll toss it over," she said.

The big man chuckled. "See what you've done, Viktor? You've got the lady all nervous. It's no big deal if you throw the pack down there, miss. We can always go after it. Why don't you save us the trouble and hand it over?"

She raised the pack higher, knowing what he said was true. They could close in, deal with her, and then take their time searching for the pack. But it was all she had. She would throw the pack down and try to get by the man guarding the cabin door. If he grabbed her, she would fight. She'd try to avoid his big fists, but there wasn't a lot of space to maneuver on the deck. As it turned out, she didn't have to.

The starboard door opened and the young couple she'd seen

eating ice cream on the bow stepped out onto the deck.

"See, dear," the woman said. "We're not the only ones crazy enough to come out here."

The distraction only lasted a second. It was all Abi needed. She dashed between two rows of chairs, past the couple, then through the door and ran along the starboard side of the ferry.

The bartender was back behind the bar, but Abi didn't have time to explain why she needed help. Nor was she sure that when help arrived, it would be in time.

Her instinct was to put as much distance as possible between her and the two strangers. The bow platform was a dead end in more ways than one. She could dash into the main passenger cabin, maybe try to hide in a restroom or storage area, but she'd be trapped there.

She took a sharp turn amidships at the lifeboat embarkation sign and practically stumbled down the stairway to the car deck. Just before her foot hit the first step, she glanced back and saw the taller of the two men. She was sure he'd seen her.

At the bottom of the stairs she almost crashed into a baggage carrier but regained her footing and went through the doorway onto the car deck. What now? The noise of the boat's engines and the swash of water against the hull were so loud she could hardly think.

She groped her way between the lines of cars and trucks. If she hunkered down on the deck, she'd be nothing more than a mouse in a maze with two hungry cats on the hunt. They would split up, come onto the car deck from both sides, and drive her toward the stern.

Eventually, they'd find her. The noise was so loud she could scream her lungs out and no one would hear. She went from vehicle to vehicle. She tried door handle after door handle and in every case they were locked.

She was desperate and had almost given up hope when she grabbed the handle of a big blue Ford pickup truck. The words Coffin Construction were printed on the door. It was unlocked. She opened the door, slipped into the backseat of the cab, then locked the door and stretched out on the floor.

There was nothing for her to do but wait until the ferry made port. Then she'd have another problem to solve. Getting off the boat.

CHAPTER THIRTY-THREE

The desk clerk at the Provincetown Inn said Weber had come in and might be in the lounge. Ben looked in the bar and saw a few patrons, but no Weber. He was walking down the hallway to the suite of rooms set aside for the crew when Weber stepped out of a room, glanced at Ben with a startled look on his face, then began a slow collapse to the floor on rubbery legs.

Ben rushed over and grabbed Weber's arm, catching him in mid-sag. With Ben holding him upright, Weber managed to steady himself.

"Are you all right?" Ben said.

"I'll be fine after I catch my breath," Weber said, clutching the laptop closer to his chest.

Ben had his doubts. Weber's face was as pale as a sheet. Sweat beaded his temple. His unruly hair was even more disheveled than usual. Weber didn't have the happy, dim-witted look of someone who'd had too much to drink. In fact, he looked decidedly unhappy.

Ben glanced at the door. "Let me help you back into your room," he said.

Weber shook his head. "This is not my room. I'm down the hall. I may need some help getting there."

Ben wondered why Weber was coming out of a room that belonged to someone else, but the man was in no shape for an interrogation. He hooked arms with Weber and they made their way slowly to a room in another part of the inn.

Weber fished a key card out of his pocket and, after a couple of fumbling tries, he unlocked the door. They stepped into the room. Weber sank into a chair and pointed to a plastic bucket.

"There's an ice machine down the hall," he said. "If you don't mind."

Ben picked up the bucket and a couple of minutes later returned with the ice. Weber asked him to put some in a towel. He applied the makeshift ice pack to his head. He winced with pain at first, then he took a deep breath and a faint smile came to his lips.

"That's much better, thank you."

Ben sat down on the edge of the bed. "Are you feeling well enough to tell me what happened?"

"Someone hit me on the head as I was getting into my car. I managed to make it back inside."

"Have you asked the front desk clerk to call the police?"

"No. I didn't want to make a big fuss."

"You were just mugged in a public place. The police might have an interest in that."

"Yes, I know, but I didn't want to sit around answering questions."

"Too bad because I've got one for you. Any idea who slugged you?"

"I'm sure you're quite competent at your job, but I would prefer not to waste my time talking to a village constable."

The German accent made Weber's comment even more patronizing.

Ben tamped a lid on his temper. "Okay, if you don't want to talk about the mugging, tell me why you broke into a room that wasn't yours."

"Technically speaking, it belonged to no one. It had been occupied by Kyle Magnus, and he's dead."

"Okay, we'll forget about the breaking and entering part. Let's talk about grand larceny. Did that computer you're holding in a death grip belong to Kyle?"

"A reasonable assumption."

"But is it true, or phony like you?" Ben said. He crossed his arms, using body language to express his skepticism.

Weber looked Ben straight in the eye. "I listened to your phone message. How did you learn I was a fake journalist?"

"It wasn't difficult. I did an internet search. There is no such thing as the Darmstadt News Agency. Someone who heard you talking thought that you sounded Swiss. I knew you were not a journalist or a German. Either way, you were lying. So, let's try telling the truth for a change."

"Fair enough. Martin Weber is my real name. And as the person with the linguistic ear observed, I am Swiss, not German. Nor, as you so easily discovered, am I a journalist. I'm a private investigator." He smiled sadly. "My cover stories are usually tighter, but we pulled this together at the last minute."

"Thanks for being honest. You said 'we.'"

"I'm working for The Restitution Registry, an organization that finds and retrieves stolen art and cultural objects. Our head office is in Zurich. Most of our work involves current-day theft, but we maintain cold case files containing lists of property looted by the Nazis during World War II. Someone broke into our network and tried to gain entrance to the most secure files." Weber tapped the laptop cover. "Our experts traced the hack to this computer."

"Kyle hacked your files?"

"I don't know for sure. I didn't intend to take the computer. I was in the room earlier to download his files onto a thumb drive."

"How did you get past the lock?"

Weber dug the leather case out of his pocket and tossed it on the bed. "Electronic lock picker. I thought I'd find something that would provide a lead. Whoever attacked me removed the thumb drive from my pocket."

"You could barely walk when I saw you, but you went back to the room. The computer must contain some pretty important material."

"That remains to be seen. My plan was to download the files and return the computer; in the meantime, I didn't want to let it out of my sight. I'm hopeful what's on this laptop can help me in my search for the young man."

"Sounds more like a missing persons case. I thought we were talking about looted art," Ben said.

"We are."

"Then what's this about a young man?"

"Those who inhabit the sordid nether world of art theft would know I'm talking about the *Portrait of a Young Man* by Raphael. The Nazis stole it from the collection of the Polish Prince Czartoryski. It is the most important painting still missing since the war. It disappeared from sight in 1945."

Ben recalled that Hopper had sketched Otto Klaas in 1946.

Keeping his voice calm, he said, "Tell me more."

"Two other masterpieces were stolen from the prince's collection. Works by Leonardo and Rembrandt. In art theft circles, those two and the Raphael are known as 'The Trinity,' or 'The Great Three.' The Rembrandt and the Leonardo were recovered, but the Raphael vanished. Since then, there have been a number of reports on the painting's location. One theory even has the Germans destroying it. None of these sightings has been verified."

"How much would the Raphael be worth today?"

"Probably more than a hundred million dollars."

Ben let out a low whistle. "If the painting were found, who would get that money?"

"Can't say. Everyone this side of Hades, including the Czartoryski family and the Polish government, has been looking for the painting. Scores of international lawyers and investigators have prowled all over Europe. Presumably, the family can lay claim to the painting. But who knows? Someone is bound to say finders, keepers."

"That's a fascinating story. But how does it relate to what's in that computer?"

"The hacker got into a section of the file dealing with an individual suspected of having something to do with the painting's disappearance. That individual had close links to an international company owned by the Magnus family."

"Magnus, as in Kyle."

"Right. The same company formerly owned the Baron property. It just seemed too much of a coincidence."

"So that's why you were snooping around the gate when I saw you."

"I didn't know I was so obvious."

Ben touched his nose. "Your story didn't smell right."

"It was the best I could do. You caught me about to break into the estate."

"What did you expect to find?"

"Nothing in particular. I was hoping I'd stumble across something of interest. Was I wrong?"

"I've been inside the Baron house and the old barn on the property. If a painting by Raphael was hanging on the walls, I would have noticed."

Weber laughed. "I'm sure you would have. It's a fanciful notion anyhow. The individual we suspect had a role in the painting's theft died shortly after its disappearance."

"Otto Klaas."

A stunned expression came to Weber's face. "Who are you, *really*, Officer Dyer?"

"I'm just a lucky guy who seems to have fallen into an Alfred Hitchcock movie."

"I love Hitchcock. Tell me about the plot."

Ben wasn't sure he trusted Weber, who'd admitted he was part of the sleazy world of stolen art. A hundred million dollars could transform the most honest human on earth into a scoundrel.

He wondered if he should test Weber's newfound truthfulness by telling him he knew Otto Klaas didn't die, that he made it to the U.S. and, in 1946, was on the Baron property.

Ben's phone chirped. It was Abi calling. Speaking in a harsh whisper, she said, "Ben. Listen carefully. I'm on the *Nantucket*."

"I can hardly hear you. You're still on Nantucket?"

"Not the island. The steamship authority ferry. Meet me at the Hyannis dock. Ten o'clock. Please be there."

"What's going on?"

"Can't talk. They're after me. Look for Coffin."

"What?"

"Coffin builders!"

She hung up. Ben stared at the phone for a few seconds, then tucked it in his pocket and got to his feet. Had Abi finally gone off the rails?

"Sorry. Looks like our discussion will have to wait for now, Marty."

"But what about Alfred Hitchcock?"

"We'll go to the movies another time."

Then he was out the door and bolting down the hallway.

CHAPTER THIRTY-FOUR

BAM!

Someone pounded on the truck door inches from Abi's head. The noise snapped her out of the trance she'd sunk into since she'd wedged herself on the floor between the front and back seats. She had been lying there as still as a corpse with her pack over her face, hardly breathing out of fear that someone might hear her nervous exhalations.

Another thud came from the passenger side. Had she been discovered? Maybe not. Her pursuers were trying to flush her out of hiding. If they knew she was in the truck, they would have smashed in the windows. After a few seconds had passed, she heard the pounding again, but it was in the distance. The hunters had moved on to another vehicle.

Her ears detected a change in the sound of the ferry's engines. The boat was slowing. She checked her wristwatch. Twenty minutes to the dock. She moved her arms and legs to get the stiffness out so she'd be ready to run.

The boat slowed even more. After a few minutes there came a loud clang, and the hull vibrated. The ferry had bumped into the unloading dock. Then came the grinding sound of the descending ramp. She sat up and cautiously raised her head until she could see out the window.

A man was walking toward the truck. She stretched out on the floor again. The door was opened with a remote key and someone got in the driver's side. The engine started and the truck inched forward.

Abi wondered if Ben had made it to the dock on time. But what if he hadn't? What if he'd gotten into traffic? Or had an accident? She pushed the irrational fears out of her head. She couldn't contact him or call 911 because the phone was dead. Why hadn't she charged the damn thing while she was driving to the ferry landing?

The truck moved forward in a stop-and-go fashion. Then the wheels thumped off the ramp. The truck stopped again. Abi sat up, unlocked the door on the passenger side, and exited feet first.

She clicked the door shut behind her, mouthing a silent thank you to the driver who was still unaware he had a passenger. Then she slung the pack over her shoulder. As she joined the crowd moving toward the parking lot, she glanced around. No Ben. Instead, she saw the two creeps from the boat closing in from both sides. She whirled around and started back toward the ferry. Maybe she could ask a crew person to call for help. Someone was moving in on her right, against the flow of the passengers. She broke into a run.

"Hey Abi!" a voice called.

She glanced back. Ben was striding toward her. She stopped and threw herself into his arms.

"You don't know how glad I am to see you!" she said. "I didn't think you made it."

"I was in Provincetown when you called and had to break a few speed laws to get here. I was looking for someone who built coffins."

She remembered her panicked call. "Sorry about the confusion. My fault. I hooked a ride in a truck that belonged to Coffin Construction."

"I'm still confused. Why were you in that truck?"

She unwrapped her arms and looked around apprehensively. The crowd of passengers had thinned out. There was no sign of her pursuers.

"Two men were after me on the ferry. They wanted to kill me, but I hid in the truck. They came after me again after the boat docked."

"What did they look like?"

"Gorillas. One tall. The other shorter, both wearing polo shirts." Ben surveyed the parking lot.

"I don't see anyone like that. Any idea who these guys were?"

"No," she said. "Maybe."

"Maybe?"

She told him about Hammond's warning that her life could be in danger.

A grim expression came to Ben's face. He checked the parking lot again. The crowd was even smaller than before. "This is not the place to talk about it. Are you all right to drive?"

"I'll be fine. Can you follow me home?"

Ben said he'd be right behind her. They walked to the Land Rover. He made sure she was safely locked in before he went for his truck. He trailed Grover out of the parking lot and onto the highway. Less than an hour after leaving the dock they pulled up in front of Abi's cottage.

Abi went inside and invited Ben to take a seat on the porch while she made tea. She carried the cups onto the porch and sat in the chair next to his, staring off at the dark waters of the bay.

After a minute she began, "Let me tell you about my visit with Clint Hammond."

Ben listened to her story, asking a question here and there. When she'd finished, he said, "Hammond was right about your life being in danger. So he's probably right about everything else."

"This is getting deeper and deeper."

Ben nodded in agreement. "I talked to Weber. He admitted he's an art investigator, not a journalist. He's on the trail of the Raphael painting known as the *Portrait of a Young Man.*"

"Of course!" Abi said. "That must be the same 'young man' Mr. Hammond mentioned."

"From what Hammond told you, Otto Klaas may have been involved in the theft of the painting."

"Do you realize where this is heading?" she said.

"Yup. A missing masterpiece stolen in one of the greatest art thefts in history may have been transported to the Baron barn."

"Where Edward Hopper just happened to be with his sketchbook."

Ben chuckled softly. "I'll bet Hopper never dreamed all the trouble he'd stir up when he sketched the suspicious-looking stranger lurking outside an old barn."

"On the other hand, he'd be pleased if he had a hand in the recovery of a missing masterpiece."

"No doubt," Ben said. "First we have to recover the masterpiece. Let's go back in time to 1946. Klaas has the painting. He comes to the barn. What happens next?"

"A couple of obvious choices," Abi said. "He moves on, taking the painting with him. Or he leaves it behind."

"We've been in the barn and seen that it's empty."

"Which means he took the painting with him." She furrowed her brow. "But I don't think he did."

"Okay. You have my attention. Why do you say that?"

"Simple logic. He could have disappeared from his port of entry into any urban center in the country. Yet he came to an abandoned farm in a remote town. Why travel all the way here if it's only going to be an out-of-the way stopover on his journey? The more he travels, the more he's at risk. He could get stopped for speeding or simply because people are still paranoid about Nazi spies coming ashore from a U-boat. The farm was his destination. He was there for a reason."

"That makes a lot of sense, Abi. Maybe Hammond will come up with that reason. In the meantime, we've got to consider the matter of your safety. Tell me more about the guys who chased you around the ferry?"

"They were in their thirties. Dressed like tourists or golfers. Hair dark on the short one, blondish red on the other. Cut close to the scalp. Muscular. The tall man seemed to be the boss. Both were athletic and tough-looking. I'm calling them Big Gorilla and Little Gorilla to tell them apart. The big man called the smaller one Viktor."

"They sound like ex-military from your description."

"Why would ex-military want to kill me?"

"They were probably hired guns."

"Hired by whom?"

"Before we ponder the answer to that question, I have another.

How did they know you were in Nantucket?"

"I don't know. You were the only one I talked to before I rushed off to catch the ferry."

"Then the leak must have come from Hammond. Does it seem likely someone has been watching him?"

"That theory makes as much sense as anything. Maybe the article Mr. Hammond wrote about his war adventures caught the attention of an unfriendly eye."

"It's the only plausible explanation at this point because your visit with Hammond was under scrutiny. Those guys could have grabbed you, but they wanted the sketches first, then you."

"They would have been disappointed. I gave Hammond copies of the sketches. The originals are here at the cottage."

Ben stifled a yawn. "Sorry, but I haven't had much sleep today. Could you make another set of copies for me?"

"I'd be glad to. I'll be right back."

She went upstairs and when she returned a minute later her face was ashen.

"The sketches are gone," she said.

"What do you mean?"

She led the way up the stairs to the bedroom and opened a jewelry box on the dresser. "They were in here. I'm sure this is where I put them."

Ben looked around the room, then opened the window overlooking the deck and stuck his head outside. The scent of the sea was strong. He leaned on the windowsill and looked out over the launch site, then pulled his head back in after a few seconds. If Abi hadn't been looking in her jewel box she would have seen him run his fingers along the sill.

She closed the cover of the jewel box. "Anything suspicious out there?" she said.

"No," he said. "Nothing around the launch site." He paused, as if he were going to say something, but his watch alarm dinged.

"Sorry, Abi. I've got to get on my shift." They went back downstairs and said their good-byes. Abi was in the kitchen cleaning up when she heard a knock at the front door. It was Ben. "I know this is a last minute thing," he said, "but I'd feel a lot better after what you went through today if you spent the night at my house."

Abi didn't hesitate for a second. The harrowing chase around the ferry was still fresh in her mind. She smiled. "Thank you," she said. "I'll round up my toothbrush and jammies."

CHAPTER THIRTY-FIVE

Seamus O'Malley could have killed Viktor for spooking the woman into a run for her life, but he had learned a long time ago not to let his temper get the best of him.

At the age of sixteen O'Malley made his first kill. His ham-sized fists pounded his victim to a bloody pulp in a Dublin pub fight. He admitted at his trial that a girl and alcohol had been involved. The judge accepted neither defense and sentenced the young thug to the maximum.

Convicted as a minor, O'Malley was back out on the streets a couple of years later. He'd graduated with honors from an exclusive school that turned violent young men into hardened criminals.

His stint in jail set him up with a network of criminal contacts and taught him to keep a lid on his homicidal impulses. He learned to stay ahead of his anger and focus his attention on the matter at hand. Whether it was to smash in the face of another human being or kill, if that was the assignment. It was a paycheck either way.

Now in his thirties, O'Malley had earned hundreds of paychecks. Since walking out the prison door, he had worked as a freelance bone-crusher and killer. O'Malley's business card described him as a Security Consultant. The last few months had been the best in his career. He now worked for Sunna, a giant multi-national corporation that assigned him to jobs all over the world.

The position came with a U.S. work visa and a position

overseeing security for the company's headquarters in mid-town Manhattan. He was given a comfortable office with a view of the city skyline. An attractive secretary organized the legitimate activities that served as cover for his darker assignments. The luxuries did not come without a cost. His special skills could be called into play at a moment's notice with an order given over a special cell phone.

The telephone call earlier in the day had told him to round up a team immediately. He had called his personal travel coordinator who arranged for prompt transportation in fast-moving situations. Then, he had punched out three numbers from his contact list. He instructed the men on the other end of the line, all reliable freelancers, to meet him in the building's garage in an hour. They were told to bring their tool kits. From the basement, the elevator whisked them to the roof.

A helicopter was warming its engines as the four men stepped out onto the helipad. Each carried a duffel that held an assortment of firearms and other devices designed to kill. For this job they were dressed in standard resort wear, chino slacks and polo shirts of varying colors. The tourist disguise was betrayed by their tough-looking faces, hard bodies and military style haircuts, but it softened the edges a little bit.

The helicopter transported them to the company hangar at LaGuardia Airport where they boarded a Cessna executive jet. As soon as the plane took off, O'Malley outlined the assignment.

About a half an hour later, the jet touched down at the Nantucket airport. The Cessna would stand ready to whisk the team off the island as soon as they finished their assignment.

The travel coordinator had arranged for the rental of a Ford Explorer with dark-tinted windows. O'Malley drove the SUV on the old cobblestone streets of the town that was once the center of American whaling and parked on a street lined with historical houses.

After about forty minutes, the front door of one house opened. An attractive young woman stepped out and started walking in the direction of the waterfront.

O'Malley called up a file on his phone and compared the photo to the woman leaving the house. Then he told Viktor, to follow him. He reminded the others to contact him after their job was done.

Viktor had worked for a Russian oligarch before being hired by Sunna. O'Malley thought he was light in the brains department. What he lacked in smarts, however, he made up for with a willingness to take on any assignment, no matter how repugnant.

He and Viktor got out of the car and trailed the woman to the ferry dock. They bought their tickets and stood in line separate from one another, then followed the woman to the main deck, where they took seats on the other side of the passenger lounge. O'Malley's assignment had been clear. Get rid of the woman and make it look like an accident.

He usually had a lot of latitude in how he did his job, but this time he'd been instructed to check with his handler before making a major move. He called a number on his phone and informed the party at the other end that he planned to isolate the woman and heave her overboard.

"It's not that simple," the handler said. "She is carrying a set of sketches. Three pictures. Check her bag and make sure you have them in hand before you dispose of her."

The woman carried a backpack instead of a purse. Seamus had tried to coax the pack out of her hands with his Irish charm. Viktor's fiendish zeal screwed things up. He was weird-looking to begin with, and in his eagerness to zap the woman with the jet hypo and toss her into the cold sea, the Russian had scared her off.

Rather than handing the pack over, she held it close to her chest. When the damned tourist couple blundered into their op, the woman ran like a frightened deer. He couldn't believe how fast she was.

They'd followed her down the stairs and searched every square inch of the car deck. O'Malley suspected she was hiding in a car or truck. They tried to flush her out by pounding on vehicle doors, but that didn't work. When they couldn't find her, they were among the first off the boat. They waited in the parking lot, hoping for a second chance.

The idea was to cull her from the herd with a friendly arm around the shoulders and a knife-point pressed to the ribs. They made their move when she popped out of a truck, but pulled back when she threw herself into the arms of a police officer.

O'Malley called his handler to report what happened and to ask for further instructions. He was told his assignment had changed. Forget the woman for now. The Nantucket team would be handled directly from Central. Transportation was being arranged for him on the mainland. He would concentrate on retrieving valuable material located within driving distance of the ferry dock.

He was given the details of his task. After he'd accomplished the job he'd receive follow-up instructions. Central gave him a number to call. When he called his contact, an impossibly gravelly voice growled, "I've been expecting your call. Go ahead."

"What's with the froggy voice, mate?" O'Malley said.

"Voice-altering technology. You can't be too careful. Is that a problem?"

"Maybe. I want to be sure I know who I'm talking to when we meet up."

"You'll know," the voice said. "I've been told you're coming to pick up some merchandise."

"Yeah, that's right. You got a problem with that?"

There had been a slight pause, then the voice came back on the phone, softer in tone. "No problem. I understand completely. Let me give you directions. I'll be waiting for you."

O'Malley hung up and looked around the parking lot. He motioned for Viktor to follow him and they headed toward a man holding a cardboard sign that had the world Sunna printed on it. O'Malley told the man who he was, and was given the keys to a Jeep Cherokee.

He and Viktor tossed their bags in the back, then got in the SUV. O'Malley told Viktor to drive while he checked their destination on the cell phone GPS.

Less than an hour later they turned off the highway and followed a narrow road to a wrought iron gate between two brick pillars. In the center of the gate's metal scrollwork was a "B." Beyond the gate there was only darkness.

"We have right place?" Viktor asked.

"The GPS says so," O'Malley said, pointing to the destination marker on the screen of his cell phone.

"Maybe guy you talk to screwed us."

"If he did, we'll be the last ones he screws with. Right, Viktor?"

Viktor let out a nasty laugh, then pointed at the gates. "Look."

The iron barriers between the brick pillars slowly parted and opened to their fullest. A light blinked on in the driveway beyond the reach of the headlight beams, pointed to the ground and slowly oscillated back and forth.

O'Malley squinted at the moving light. He had learned in his work that caution was preferable to haste. He slid the pistol out of his ankle holster.

"Drive in," he said to Viktor. "Slow and easy."

Viktor put the Cherokee into gear and drove at a walking pace. The gates closed behind the SUV. The light in the driveway snapped off and someone walked into the wash of the headlights. Dressed in a tight-fitting black suit, face half-hidden behind bulbous eyes, the figure looked like a space alien.

O'Malley hit the brakes and brought the SUV to a halt. The figure pointed at the vehicle and made a slashing motion across the throat. He wanted the headlights off.

O'Malley wasn't about to leave himself in the dark. Although the figure seemed to have no visible weapon, his night vision goggles would put him at an advantage. O'Malley told Viktor to blink the SUV's lights. The figure threw one arm across its face to shield the eyes and came up to the driver's window. A black hood covered the head. Only the mouth was visible in the glow from the dashboard. The lips moved.

"Douse the lights. We don't want anyone to know we're up here."

O'Malley shifted his gun onto his lap. "You the guy I talked to on the phone?" he said.

"That was me."

"What happened to your gravel voice?"

"I washed it away with some good whiskey."

"Hope you saved some booze for us," O'Malley said. He turned off the vehicle, opened the door and got out on the passenger side, the hand holding the gun dangling by his thigh. Viktor emerged from behind the steering wheel and came around. He had his pistol in his hand as well.

The figure in black said, "You gentlemen expecting to do some target practice?"

"We didn't know what to expect," O'Malley said. He tucked the pistol in his belt and told Victor to put his gun away. "Do you have a name? I don't like to deal with strangers."

The lips opened slightly, and after a pause of several seconds, the man said, "My name is Peter Hesselbach."

"Sounds German."

"It is. What about you?"

"O'Malley. This is Viktor. That's all you have to know, Pete. Let's get moving."

The man switched on the flashlight and moved along the driveway with the others following. The Baron house loomed ahead. The building's immensity was visible against the star-speckled deep blue sky.

"Whoa!" O'Malley said. "What the hell is that thing?"

"It's a house. Don't worry. Nobody lives there."

"Who's the owner?"

"A dead man. He fell off the tower and broke his neck."

O'Malley chuckled. "You're a funny guy, Pete."

They walked past the house to the barn. O'Malley said, "What is this place?"

"It's a barn that went with the original house on the property. The material you're here for is inside."

He went over and slid the door back. Yellow light streamed from inside the building. O'Malley followed him and saw that the light came from a dozen or so battery-operated camp lights arranged in a rough circle on the dirt floor of the barn.

At the center of the circle was a hole a few feet deep. Three shovels stuck out of a pile of dirt.

Hesselbach picked up a camp light and held it over the hole. Metal gleamed through clods of dirt at the bottom of the excavation "There's your vault," he said.

He grabbed a shovel and held it out.

O'Malley stared at Hesselbach; his mouth was set in a deep

frown. He was a highly-paid security consultant, not a damned ditch digger. But his orders had been clear. Retrieve the goods. He grabbed the shovel and growled at Viktor to start digging.

The dirt began to fly. With all three men shoveling, the hole soon expanded in size. O'Malley mused that Hesselbach wouldn't be shoveling so hard if he knew he was digging his own grave. Once the goods were in hand, Pete's services would no longer be needed. He decided not to waste free labor. He would kill the guy after he had helped pull stuff out of the vault. All it would take was one swing of the shovel.

As more of the vault was revealed, O'Malley saw that the surface was smooth and unbroken. He stopped working and leaned on his shovel.

"How do we get into this thing?"

"We still have some dirt to clear away," Hesselbach said. "Maybe it's covering a hatch. I only knew where the vault was. Not how to get into it."

O'Malley stared at Hesselbach's smirking mouth, and he felt his temper rising. He couldn't wait to bash in the guy's head. His hands tightened on the handle of the shovel.

"What's that?" Hesselbach looked toward the doorway.

O'Malley followed his gaze. He cocked his ear.

"What's up?"

"I thought I heard something." The man shrugged, "Maybe it was the wind."

The three men stood around the pit, listening, but the only sound was the nighttime insect chorus.

"I'll go check," O'Malley said.

"I'll do it." He tapped his night vision goggles. "Maybe you can clear away the rest of that dirt so we can get into the vault." Before O'Malley could respond, Hesselbach headed for the door.

O'Malley glared at the departing figure, then told Viktor to keep digging. Within a few minutes they had cleared away all the dirt, revealing rectangular seams in the steel surface that could have outlined a hatch. There was no handle or hinges. A torch would be needed to cut into the vault.

He threw his shovel aside, pulled the gun out of his holster, then grabbed one of the camp lamps and stormed out the doorway with Viktor a few steps behind. He stopped and looked around.

"Hey Pete," he called out in a friendly voice. "Give us a shout-out, mate."

Beyond the puddle of light cast by the lamp, the darkness was almost complete except for the sparkle of lights from the houses along the distant shore of the bay.

He told Viktor to get another light, ordered him to walk around the barn, and started walking toward the big house. As he drew closer, he narrowed his eyes, trying to define the outline of the structure, then widened them. He had seen a section of stars blink off and on in the sky above the house. It happened so quickly, he passed it off as a trick of light.

He headed back to where Viktor's light was moving in the darkness.

Flutter.

O'Malley went into a crouch. He glanced from left to right, then up, his eyes searching for the source of the sound he'd heard above his head. He pivoted slowly, lamp in one hand, gun held high in the other, coming back to where he started. Probably a damned gull looking to crap on someone's head, he thought.

He decided to drive the SUV around the property. If he saw Pete he'd run him down. He called out to Viktor who was about fifty feet away.

"See anything?"

"No. Nothing," the Russian answered.

O'Malley told him to come over. The bobbing light had covered half the distance to where O'Malley was standing, when there was what sounded like a sharp cry of pain. The light flew through the air and landed on the ground.

O'Malley ran toward the camp light which illuminated a still form on the ground. Viktor was lying face down. O'Malley turned the body. He had dispensed violence in the form of a clean gunshot or a quick plunge of a knife in a vital organ. But he had never seen anything like this.

Viktor's forehead from the hairline down to the bridge of the nose was a bloody mash of flesh, skin and bones.

O'Malley turned slowly, staring into the darkness. He didn't know what had killed Viktor. What he did know was that he was an easy target.

He tossed the lamp as far as he could. Even before it hit the ground and blinked out, he was on the run. He blindly plunged through the darkness toward where he thought he'd left the Jeep. He stopped after a few steps, dug the SUV's keys out of his pocket and pressed the Unlock button on the remote. The vehicle's lights blinked on and the horn beeped to his left.

O'Malley set off toward the car in an easy lope. He'd stick with his original plan to get in the Jeep, find Pete and run him down.

Flutter.

It was the same sound he'd heard before. It came from above and behind him this time. He pictured Viktor's ruined face and began to run. He tripped once on a clump of grass, went down on a knee, but was up immediately, feet pounding the ground. He was rehearsing in his mind how he'd yank open the driver's door, get inside and turn on the engine and the lights.

He was almost at the car and was about to let forth a yell of triumph when he heard the weird fluttering sound again. This time it was coming not from behind him, but in front.

CHAPTER THIRTY-SIX

Abi blinked her eyes open in the morning and saw a pretty woman staring back at her. Not merely pretty, the woman in the framed photo on the bedside table was exquisite. She stood on a sandy path flanked by rippling beach grass, blue sea in the background. The breeze tossed her long blonde hair and whipped at the skirt of her ankle-length lacy white dress. An inviting smile danced on her lips. Abi knew right away that she was looking at Loren. And why Ben missed his wife so much.

The night before, Abi had been too bleary-eyed and exhausted to notice the photo. It was late by the time she packed a small bag at the cottage and returned to Ben's house. He was on duty by then. She'd wrapped the blanket around her shoulders and flopped face down fully-clothed on the bed.

She woke up in the middle of the night, found her way to the bathroom, brushed her teeth and put on a nightie. She was still jittery from the boat chase. On her way back to bed she glanced out the bedroom window. She'd been reassured to see Ben's cruiser parked in front of the house, and had slept soundly.

More photos crowded a table on the other side of the bed. The pictures showed Ben and his wife in different settings. A beach. A snow-covered mountaintop. Sitting in a sidewalk café that boasted a French name. In front of the Parthenon. As bride and groom in formal attire. The sublime expressions on their faces in every photo

216

sent a singular message: They were very much in love.

The frames were at eye-level. Ben saw Loren before he closed his eyes and when he woke up.

Abi heard a soft knock. She got up, wrapped a blanket around her body and opened the bedroom door. Ben was standing there in full uniform.

He smiled. "Good morning. Did you sleep well?"

"Very well, thank you. I saw your car out front."

"It was a quiet night. I was able to swing by in between patrols. Coffee's brewing in the kitchen. I usually hit the sack for a few hours after coming off a shift." He looked past her. "Is the bed, um, free?"

"All yours. Probably still warm. I'll head back to the cottage after I have my coffee. Maybe we can get together later to talk."

"How about chatting over lunch?"

"Good idea. Thank you for the police protection and for inviting me to sleep in your bed."

"Anytime." Color rose in his cheeks. "The police protection part, I mean. The guest room will be ready by then."

"I think I'll get that coffee," Abi said, a smirk on her lips.

She poured a cup of coffee in the kitchen and went out onto the patio, settling into a chair that gave her a view of a creek meandering through velvety marsh. Ben's ancestors had built well, situating the low-slung cottage at an inspiring location. She could see why he had returned to his roots to heal the wounds left by the loss of his beloved Loren. She was envious, in a way. The death of her own marriage had been so tawdry.

She sighed, deeply, and sipped her coffee, trying to decide whether it was too early to call Hammond. Finally, she reached into her Zen training, which teaches the archer not to think about the target; simply aim in the general direction, draw the string back and release the arrow, letting the senses tell it where to fly.

Hammond was the arrow, she mused. She had pointed him in the general direction of Otto Klaas and let fly. He said he would call first thing, but his daughter Ellie said he was forgetful. Maybe he had forgotten his promise to get back to her. She panicked. Maybe he had forgotten their entire conversation.

She took a couple of deep breaths to calm her nerves, then

glanced at her wristwatch. It was almost nine o'clock. She would call Hammond on the hour. She waited several agonizing minutes until the hands were in place, then tapped Hammond's name on her telephone contact list.

The call was answered almost immediately. "Hammond residence. This is Eleanor Hammond."

"Hi, Ellie. This is Abi. I hope I'm not calling too early. Your dad said he'd get back to me by eight o'clock. Maybe he didn't realize the time. Sorry to be a bother."

"No bother, Abi." Ellie paused for a few seconds. "Dad had a very good reason for not calling you."

Abi picked up on the sadness in Ellie's voice. "Is there something wrong?" Abi said.

"I'm afraid so. I came by the house this morning and found Dad lying on the floor in the foyer. I called the rescue squad, but he had passed."

Abi was stunned. "Oh, Ellie. I'm so sorry," she said. "This is simply…unbelievable. He was so vital and engaged when we talked yesterday."

"I was shocked, but not surprised. My father was in his nineties, after all. Having you drop by was pure serendipity. He enjoyed your visit. I haven't seen him that excited in years."

"It was wonderful seeing him." Abi paused, not wanting to seem unsympathetic, then said, "Please let me know if you'd rather talk another time. But did he leave any notes, folder or envelope around with my name on them? Maybe…some sketches?"

"I'm in his office now. Let me look at his desk." After a moment she said, "I'm sorry. Nothing here with your name on it."

"He had a metal file box. It was pretty banged up. He was putting files from the big cabinets into the box with the sketches. It was on his desk the last time I saw it."

"He's had that box for years. I tried to talk him into buying a new one. He said the box was government property and had traveled with him around Europe. It isn't anywhere in his office. I'll look in his bedroom. Hold on." She came back on the line after a time. "No sign of it. That's curious."

Abi thought it was curious as well. She said, "That's all right.

I'm sure it will turn up somewhere. You say you found your father in the foyer? Do you know what happened?"

"Dad refused to subscribe to a personal alarm system. I think he may have become ill during the night and rather than calling 911 he instinctively headed for the front door. Maybe he was confused, or in a daze and collapsed before he could call for help."

"That's probably it. As you said, he was in his nineties. Thank you for bringing me up to date. Please let me know when you've arranged a memorial service."

Ellie said that family was flying in to help with the preparations and she would be sure to let her know. Abi hung up and stared into space. She wished she could be sure Hammond died a natural death, but a picture flashed in her mind of the Little Gorilla man brandishing a shiny metal cylinder while his companion tried to sweet-talk her out of her backpack.

Her assailants would have had time to get back to the island and go to Hammond's house but transportation options were limited that time of night. Which left open a scary possibility. The men on the boat weren't working alone. The ferry chase was part of a larger operation.

It still didn't explain how complete strangers knew she'd be on the boat. And what she carried in her bag. Someone had known that she was visiting Hammond and why they had met. Abi felt overwhelmed by the whirling onrush of questions with no answers. She got up, went back into the house and knocked on the bedroom door.

"Ben. It's Abi. Are you still awake?"

There was a rustling sound, Ben opened the door. He was dressed in T-shirt and sweatpants that were as rumpled as his face. "Everything okay?" he said.

"I'm so sorry to wake you up. I'm…." Tears welled in her eyes. She wrapped her arms around his waist and put her head on his chest.

She felt him tense up, then he relaxed and returned the embrace. "What's wrong, Abi?"

"Mr. Hammond is dead. And I'm responsible."

His bleary eyes snapped fully awake. "Whoa," Ben disentangled himself from her embrace. "Let's talk in the kitchen."

He poured ice water into a pitcher and grabbed two glasses. Taking her gently by the hand, Ben led Abi to the kitchen table. After they'd both had some water, he asked her what had happened. She told him about her talk with Ellie Hammond and her suspicions of foul play.

"He never would have died if I hadn't called yesterday and led those people to him."

"Are you saying he was murdered?"

She nodded.

"Why would someone want Hammond dead?"

"The same reason they came after me. We know too much about Otto Klaas."

Ben said, "Let's stop right there. If someone killed Hammond—possible, but still a big *if* at this point—the murderers are to blame. Not you."

"Yes, I know. But—"

Ben touched her lips with his fingertip.

"No buts. You said Hammond was going to look for something in his files. What was it?"

"When I showed him the sketches he could hardly believe what they suggested, that Klaas didn't die at the end of the war. What really got him excited was the fact that Klaas's picture was drawn here in Truro, on property once owned by the Sunna Industries. And we know who owns Sunna."

"The Magnus family."

She nodded. "The Monuments Men knew about a suspicious trip Klaas made to Norway not long before he was supposedly killed in the air raid. Clint thought he had additional correspondence about that Norway trip in his files."

"What was so special about Norway?" Ben asked.

"It was the ancestral home of the Magnus clan."

"No big surprise that Klaas was friendly with the Magnus family. He taught the youngest one to fly at the glider school."

"Those Magnuses were in the U.S. Remember, there was still a war going on. Klaas visited the family patriarch who was active in the Norwegian fascist movement, and close to his counterparts in Germany. I asked his daughter about the file box. It's missing."

Ben stared at Abi, his lips slightly parted, as if he were about to say something. She thought that he was stunned by the news about the file, but he said, "We have a larger problem than those files."

"Larger than murder and attempted murder?"

"Those things couldn't be possible if someone weren't following your every move. How can that be?"

"I don't know, Ben," she said with a mixture of anger and exasperation. "I simply do not know."

"Neither do I. So let's backtrack to where you called Hammond."

"Okay. We read the mention of Otto Klaus in the newspaper article. I gave Mr. Hammond a call. He was eager to meet; so much so, that he asked me to come to Nantucket as soon as possible."

"Who else knows about this conversation?"

"You're the only one who knew I was taking the ferry to Nantucket to see Mr. Hammond."

"Apparently I *wasn't* the only one," Ben said.

"Damn. How could anyone know that? And how did those two creeps learn I'd be on the late ferry?"

"Maybe your cell phone has been compromised. Or there was a leak from Hammond's phone. Someone who read his newspaper article could have been listening."

"Here's my problem with that, Ben. The article came out weeks ago. Nothing bad happened until I called him. A few hours later, he is dead."

"There's a lesson to be learned here. Don't use the phone and when you do, watch what you're saying."

She nodded. "Is it time to go to the authorities with this story?"

"Sure, we could call in State Police Lieutenant Curran, who is already suspicious about me being too chummy with Hank Aldrich. What would we tell them? That we found an Edward Hopper sketch of an old Nazi. That a couple of goons chased you on a ferry boat and someone may have killed a Monuments Man from World War II? That the bad guys appear to be organized and well-financed, and can hear every word we say?"

Abi sighed. "Yes, I see what you mean. What, then?"

"We can't do this alone. I've got another idea. We go to Weber."

"How could he help us?"

"He's an experienced private investigator. Will he help? That's another question altogether."

"Why wouldn't he? We're amateurs. He's the pro."

"You nailed it. We're amateurs. A village constable and an art historian. He's afraid we'll screw things up."

"So what? He needs us. Tell him that, please."

Ben saw from the fire smoldering in Abi's eyes that she would accept no excuse. He looked up Weber's number and called him. The call went to voicemail. He left a message asking Weber to get back to him, then he called the number for the Provincetown Inn and asked to be connected to Weber's room.

"Mr. Weber has checked out. He said he's going home to Europe."

"When did he leave?"

"A taxi picked him up about ten minutes ago."

Ben thanked the desk person, hung up and called Weber's phone again. As before, he was transferred to voicemail. This time, though, he left a different message.

"This is Ben Dyer, the village policeman, with a message for Mr. Weber. There's something very important you don't know about Otto Klaas. Call me."

CHAPTER THIRTY-SEVEN

Weber was on his way to the airport when he got the call from Ben. He'd been staring out the taxi window at the rolling dunes of the Province Lands, thinking he was going to miss this strange, sea-girt desert that was so unlike the solid mountains of Switzerland.

Maybe he had given up too soon. He still didn't know if Kyle Magnus had hacked into the stolen art database. All he had to show for his investigation was a puzzle with so many pieces missing it was impossible to complete the whole picture. And a bruise on his head that was extremely tender to the touch. He had simply run out of leads. He'd debated canceling his flight and had put off his departure from the inn until the last minute. In the end, he decided it was time to go back to Zurich and regroup.

The chirp of his cell phone had cut into his ruminations. The caller ID showed that Ben Dyer was calling. He let the call go into voicemail, listened to the brief message, then clicked off. Weber liked the town cop. He was an interesting guy, and Weber shouldn't have been so patronizing, but Ben didn't know what he was getting into.

The phone chirped again minutes later. Again, out of curiosity, he listened to the voicemail. Only this time he called back.

Leaning into the phone, he said, "What's this important information about Otto Klaas?"

"Let's get together and I'll tell you what I know."

"Sorry, Officer Dyer. I'm on my way to catch a plane to Boston and a connecting flight to Zurich. I'm already running late."

"You might not want to leave town after you hear what I have to say."

"You will have to make it quick. The taxi is almost at the airport."

"I'll sum it up in one sentence. Otto Klaas did not die in the war."

A stunned expression came to Weber's face. "That's not what the official records say. He died in an Allied air raid."

"The official records are wrong. Klaas was in Truro the year after the war ended."

Weber chuckled, unsure what his response should be. "Now you're really stretching credibility."

"I'll stretch it even further. Months before Klaas supposedly died in a raid, he was in Norway as a guest of the Magnus family."

"Where did you hear this?"

"From a very good source. A Monuments Man who investigated Klaas."

The taxi pulled up in front of the airport terminal. Weber opened the door and swung his foot out. "This Monuments Man told you this personally?"

A woman's voice answered. "Mr. Weber. This is Abi. We're on speakerphone. I talked to the Monuments Man about Klaas."

"I'm familiar with the work of the Monuments Men. What was his name?"

"Clint Hammond."

"And if I spoke to Mr. Hammond, he would tell me the same thing about Klaas?"

"No, Mr. Weber. He would tell you nothing. Mr. Hammond was murdered last night."

Weber's leg froze halfway out the cab door. Lowering his voice so he wouldn't startled the driver, Weber said, "Hammond is dead?"

"Yes. He was very much alive when I went to see him in Nantucket yesterday. I believe he was killed a few hours after I talked to him."

Weber glanced at his watch. "Where are you now?"

"On the way to the airport. We can be there in ten minutes," Ben said.

"I'll wait for you at the entrance."

Weber paid the driver, got out of the taxi, retrieved his bag from the trunk and stood on the sidewalk. He was still trying to digest what Ben and Abi told him when the white pickup truck pulled up to the curb. Ben rolled the window down.

He said, "Hop in. We'll go somewhere less public to talk."

Weber got in the back seat with his bag and Ben drove a half mile to the parking lot near the Race Point Coast Guard station. They got out and Ben led the way down a boardwalk that ran between sand dunes to the ocean. A few surf fishermen were tending their lines. Some young people of college age were tossing a Frisbee around.

"This private enough for you?" Ben said.

"It's fine, thank you," Weber said. "I might still be able to make my flight to Boston unless there is a compelling reason not to. You have three minutes to make your case."

"I can give you more than one compelling reason," Abi said. "A few days ago I discovered some sketches by the artist Edward Hopper. The drawings were dated 1946 and indicated that a man we have since identified as Otto Klaas was in Truro." She handed Weber the article from the Nantucket newspaper. "This prompted my trip to see Mr. Hammond in Nantucket so I could show him the sketches."

Weber scanned the article and passed it back. "What was Hammond's reaction when you told him the report of Klaas's death had been false?"

"He was shocked, but he said it made sense. He didn't think Klaas would be dumb enough to die like that. He felt that he had overlooked something important, and he would find it in his Monuments Men files. He promised to get back to me after he had a chance to look into his papers."

"Any idea what was in these files?"

"Only that it had to do with the trip that Klaas made to Norway."

Weber gazed off at the sea, and after a moment of thought, he said, "Let's go back to these sketches, since they prompted this whole adventure. Can I see them?"

"I'm afraid not. They were stolen," Abi said. "Someone got into my house while I was in Nantucket."

"Who would do such a thing?"

"I don't know."

"What about copies?"

"I left them with Mr. Hammond. They're missing, along with his files."

She recounted her conversation with Eleanor Hammond earlier in the day.

"And on the basis of that exchange, you concluded this ninety-two-year-old man did not die of natural causes."

"No," she said. "On my own basis. Someone tried to kill me."

Weber listened politely to the story about the ferry chase.

"You have a great eye for description."

"I was trained as an art historian and spent years running a gallery, so I am used to looking at the details of a scene, especially when it is so vivid."

"These two men you evaded sound like creatures from a Stephen King novel. Little Gorilla and Big Gorilla."

Making no effort to hide her weariness, Abi said, "I can deal with skepticism, but not ridicule. The men who were out to do me harm were flesh and blood. Maybe the nicknames are my way of dealing with how frightening they actually were. I can call them Needle Man and Scary Sweet Talk if that pleases you more."

Weber looked as if he had been slapped in the face by an invisible hand. "That was unprofessional of me. I'm taking my own frustrations out on you. I don't mean to minimize your terrifying experience. And the death of Mr. Hammond does sound suspicious, but only an autopsy will show evidence of foul play."

"That's not going to happen. As you pointed out, he was an old man with a medical history. There's nothing to suggest his death was due to anything other than natural causes."

Weber looked up at the sound of airplane engines. A Cape Air plane had taken off from the airport and was passing overhead. He watched the aircraft gain altitude and fly in the direction of Boston. "I think I was supposed to be aboard that plane," he said.

"I'm sorry you missed your flight," Abi said. "Especially since you don't believe anything I've told you."

"I believe some of it. You must admit it would be better if I could see the sketches and talk to Mr. Hammond."

He squinted at the plane, now a dot in the sky, but he was thinking that Abi's story was more impressive than he let on.

Abi took his silence for disapproval. "I don't blame you a bit," she said. "You may have to take some of this on faith."

"I have been an investigator far too long to accept what I hear on faith or at face value. Even honest people make mistakes. You can easily persuade me, however. Now that I have time, I'd like to look at the barn. It's the epicenter of all you say happened and may offer evidence that supports what you've told me."

"Thank you." Abi turned to Ben. "Well?"

He shrugged. "No time like the present."

Ben led the way back to the truck. Less than twenty minutes later he stopped at the entrance to the Baron estate. He used the keypad on the post to open the gate, and pulled into the driveway. As they went past the big house, Weber said something in German that was clearly an exclamation.

Shifting back to English, he added, "This place looked large from a distance, but I never realized how massive it actually is."

"Ugly, too," Ben said. "Proves money can't buy good taste."

He parked close to the barn and they all got out of the truck. Like a hound sniffing the air for a scent to follow, Weber walked around the building and came back to where the others were standing.

"It's a rather ordinary structure in poor condition. Why wasn't it torn down when that monstrosity was built?"

"The town insisted that the barn be preserved. The last owner, Mr. Baron, was engaging in what we lawyers call demolition by neglect." Ben got a flashlight from the truck, went to the door and slid it back on its runners. "What else do you notice, Mr. Detective?"

"The door moved easily and without noise. Someone oiled the runners recently."

"Good call, Marty." Ben patted him on the back. "You have the makings of a village constable." He stepped into the barn and flashed his light at the floor.

Abi came up beside him. "This excavation is new," she said.

"Someone has been busy."

Ben picked up one of the shovels from the dirt pile. "Three someones from the looks of things."

Weber crouched at the edge of the hole and dropped athletically into the excavation. His shoes made a hollow grating sound as he walked on the exposed metal. The surface had been cleared off except for a section at the far end partially covered by dirt.

He asked Ben to pass down the shovel, and used it to clear away the remaining dirt, revealing seams in the metal that outlined an elongated rectangle.

"Is that a hatch?" Abi said.

"It looks that way, but there's no knob or lock on the outside," Weber said.

He inserted the tip of his shovel into a seam but couldn't leverage the hatch open. He tossed the shovel onto the pile of dirt next to the hole and extended his arms. Ben and Abi grabbed his hands and helped him climb out.

"Detective work can be dirty," he said, brushing his palms and the knees of his slacks. "You said this is new to you. What did you mean?"

"We've seen evidence of activity around the barn, but we had no idea someone was looking for that vault," Ben said.

"The diggers found it, but they didn't know how to open it," Abi added.

"Neither do we," Weber said with a smile. "May I borrow your light?"

Ben handed him the flashlight. Weber methodically explored the barn, moving from stall to stall. After he'd checked the ground level, pausing to read the glider school sign, he leaned the rickety ladder against the side of a hay loft, climbed onto the wide shelf and walked the length of the barn. He stopped short suddenly and clicked off the flashlight.

"Well," he said.

"What's wrong?" Abi asked.

Weber stuck the flashlight in his pocket and climbed back down. "It's stuffy in here," he said. "Let's get some fresh air."

They went outside and Weber kept walking, finally stopping a short distance from the barn. "Avoid looking back," he said. "There's a camera inside the barn above the vault, and there may be other surveillance devices watching us from the outside."

"Are you sure?" Abi said.

"I'm pleased to see I'm not the only skeptical one in this crowd. But yes, it is attached to a cross rafter. I only saw it from several feet away, but it looks like an advanced model I've used in my own work. It's a combo camera and recording device. The audio function is another reason we needed to get out here to talk."

"That's not good," Abi said. "We don't know how long that thing has been there. Someone could have been watching us every time we stepped foot in the barn. There could be cameras all over the property."

"It would be best to operate on that premise," Weber said. "I considered removing the camera or disabling it, but whoever installed it would know the device had been discovered. It's possible someone was recording every detail of our visit. I think it's best we stay out of the barn."

"Damn," Ben said. "I was hoping we'd figure out a way to get into that vault."

"I've been thinking," Abi said. "Maybe the hatch was not meant to be unlocked from the outside. Opened maybe, but not unlocked."

Weber was learning to pay attention when Abi voiced an opinion. "I'm listening."

"What if access is from another point? Someone gets into the vault and opens the top from the inside."

"That makes sense," Ben said. "We'd have to dig some more to expose the sides of the vault and that would put us in view of the camera."

"There may be an easier way," Abi said. "Follow me."

Weber glanced at Ben, who shrugged. They trailed Abi to the thicket of trees at the base of the slope behind the house. She stopped at the tree line and pointed toward the house.

"This is about where Hopper stood when he made the sketches. At the time, there was a well between him and the barn. He liked to paint patterns of light on exteriors, so he sketched the scene without the well, the way it looks now."

"Why is this important?" Weber said.

"An access tunnel could have been run from the well shaft to the vault, allowing someone into the vault to open it from the inside."

"That's brilliant, Abi," Ben said. "How did you know about the well?"

"I've seen a photograph taken of the house and barn about the time Hopper painted them. There were two wells—one close to the barn, the other near the house."

"Could a tunnel have been run from the well closest to the house?"

"I don't see why not," Abi said. "The distance isn't much greater than that separating the other well from the barn."

"Any idea what happened to the wells? I don't see any sign of them."

"They were covered when town water mains were brought in from the road. The one near the barn was re-opened in 1945."

"Why would the well be reopened if there were water mains?"

"The timing is certainly interesting," Abi said. "Let's take a look."

They trudged back to the barn. Weber studied the building's sides and eaves and said there were no cameras that he could see, although they might be hidden. At Ben's suggestion, they walked three abreast along one side of the barn, turned and followed a parallel path back, eyes glued to the ground, but found no trace of a well, past or present.

"We need a pike or something similar to poke the ground with," Ben said.

"There are also instruments that can detect what's under the surface," Weber said. "Unfortunately, all we have for now is our eyes."

"Let's give it another try," Ben said.

As the two men scoped out another row, Abi wandered over to the house. Weber looked up just in time to see her drop to all fours.

He went over to where she was kneeling next a depression in the grass. At the bottom of the depression was a circular well cover made from weathered boards.

"What do you have?"

"This may be the house well. Can someone get me a shovel?"

Ben trotted back into the barn and retrieved a shovel. He pushed the blade into the edge of the cover and lifted it off. Abi got down on her knees and pointed the flashlight into the well. There was no reflection of water. The well was dry, but it was far from empty.

"Dear God," Abi said.

"What's wrong?" Ben said.

Abi handed him the flashlight and backed away from the well.

Ben got down on his knees and directed the flashlight beam into the well, which was around thirty feet deep. At the bottom of the well was the face of a man. Judging from lack of expression in the eyes and the bloody mess where a forehead would have been, the man was very dead.

"Damn!" Ben said, handing the light to Weber, who pointed the beam down the well where it illuminated the grisly scene.

"Damn indeed!" he said. "Who is he?"

"I think I know," Abi said. "It's hard to tell from his face, but he's wearing the same color shirt as the tall man who chased me around the ferry."

"His friend may be down there with him," Ben said. "There's a foot sticking out near the dead guy's face."

"This is crazy!" Abi said. "The last time I saw those men was on a boat in the middle of Nantucket Sound. How did they get *here*?"

"I don't think they jumped in on their own." Weber glanced around at the barn and house. "Whoever killed them may still be around, so I'd like to make a suggestion. First, let's cover up the well. Second, let's get the hell out of here."

CHAPTER THIRTY-EIGHT

"Well, another fun trip to happy hollow," Ben said as the gates to the Baron property closed behind them.

It was a lame joke, meant to lighten up the grim atmosphere. The only response was an unintelligible grunt from the back seat where Weber sat. Abi was silent.

Ben hoped she hadn't gone into shock. In the last twenty-four hours she had narrowly avoided being tossed into Nantucket Sound, had an old acquaintance die under suspicious circumstances, and discovered the bodies of the two killers who had chased her around a car ferry in the dead of night.

He glanced to his right. To his surprise, Abu was smiling.

"Are you all right, Abi?"

She nodded. "I'm fine, thanks. I was just thinking about the time before I moved into the quiet little flower cottage on the hill, when the worst things in my life were divorce and bankruptcy. Silly me. That's kid stuff compared to what I've gone through since I arrived in this bucolic little town. I don't think anything would faze me now."

"Not even a lawyer?" Ben said, grinning.

She smiled. "Not even a lawyer."

Weber frowned in puzzlement at their laughter. "I don't want to break up your party, but what do we do next?"

Baring his teeth in an alligator grin, Ben said, "Hell, Marty,

232

what do I know? I'm just a village constable. Maybe I can give the killer a ticket for littering."

"Hah!" Weber said. "You have every right to put me in my place. I'm sorry for my rude comment. It was especially stupid because I started my career as a village policeman in Switzerland. I'd like to apologize to you as well, Abi. I fully believe your story."

"Apology accepted," Abi said. "But Marty has a valid question," she said to Ben. "What *do* we do next?"

Ben yawned. "I don't have a clue where we go from here, except to bed maybe."

"Are you saying you want to go to sleep?" Weber said.

Ben yawned and nodded at the same time.

"How can you think of sleep at a time like this?"

Abi cut in. "Ben was awake most of the night making sure I was safe."

"My apologies again, but there's a murderer on the loose. It would be in all our interests to figure out a plan of action," Weber said. "We don't know if there's stolen art in the barn, but evidently it was something worth killing for."

"You're right about that," Ben said. "And the murderer will know from the camera or cameras that we're getting close to him. Which could place us in danger."

"Thank you," Weber said. "So may I offer a radical solution? We go to the police and tell them what we have found."

"Great suggestion," Ben said. "But not now."

"Why not now?"

"Let's say we tell the police about the bodies in the well. The cops investigate. They even get into the vault. All good. Only it scares the perpetrator into hiding. Ownership of the artwork—if that's what's even in there—gets tangled up in legal battles for years."

"I don't disagree," Weber said. "But what's the alternative?"

"We delay bringing in the police for twenty-four hours. We stake out the property, and when the bad guy comes back for the loot, we call in the state police, tell them that there's a possible drug deal going down. If nothing happens tonight, we go directly to the authorities with the whole story."

"Interesting. And where would we be for this stakeout?"

"The tower at the Baron mansion. We can get onto the property through a back way. The top of the tower is a perfect observation post. If someone gets too close, I'll be armed and we'll have a radio to call in backup."

"Hopefully, it won't get to the shooting stage." Weber sighed. "Okay, I'm in. It's better than returning to Zurich to face my boss."

"I don't like the idea of you going back to that awful place," Abi said.

"Neither do I," Ben said. "We'll be careful."

"I still don't like it. I don't mean to insult either one of you, but you're not exactly a SWAT team. Ben is a lawyer by trade and you're an art investigator, Marty."

"Good point," Weber said. "Which is exactly why neither one of us is inclined to take foolish chances."

"Promise me not to push things to the last minute."

Ben said, "I promise, Abi. As soon as I see someone poking around the barn, I'll call in the cavalry."

"Okay," Abi said, sounding unconvinced. "Now tell me where I fit into this mad scheme."

"You'll be our communications backup on the outside," Ben said. "We'll keep in contact so you'll know exactly what's going on while we're up in the tower."

"I'm going to be on tenterhooks the whole time, but I'll do it."

At Weber's request, Ben drove him to the inn to re-register and arrange for delivery of a rental car to replace the one he had turned in. He also had to untangle his flight arrangements and contact his office in Zurich to bring them up to date.

Ben asked him to come to his house at midnight. Then he drove home to pick up the Land Rover. As she went to get into the vehicle, he touched her arm.

"Before you go, I've got a favor to ask," he said.

"Sure. How can I help?"

"It doesn't have to do with me. I'd like you to consider moving out of the cottage and into my spare room until this thing is resolved." Seeing the dead bodies in the well had persuaded him this was a dangerous game they were playing, and he worried about Abi being up on the hill alone.

Abi had put such a premium on self-sufficiency and being independent, he'd expected a quick, polite brush-off. Instead, she returned the arm touch.

"Thanks, Ben. Let me give it some thought while I straighten out a few things at the cottage."

She leaned forward and pecked him on the cheek, then got into the Land Rover and drove off. Ben gave his head a shake. Abi was one of the most amazing women he'd ever met. He felt the stirrings of something that had deserted him when Loren died. The capacity for affection.

He was feeling something else as well. Bone-tired. He needed a nap before he fell asleep on his feet. He went into the house, stripped his uniform off and was headed for the bedroom when his cell phone chirped.

He answered the call and a voice said, "Hello, Officer Dyer. This is Hank Aldrich. Remember me?"

"Of course I do, Hank. How are you doing?"

"I'm okay. Can we get together to talk?"

"I'm going on duty in a short while. I can't get to the jail to see you right now."

"I'm not in jail. The DA dropped the charges. I've been released. I'm sitting in a car outside your front door."

Ben rubbed his eyes.

"Okay," he said. "C'mon in and tell me about it. No guarantees I'll stay awake."

Ben pulled on a pair of shorts and T-shirt. He opened the front door. Hank was waiting on the steps. He vigorously pumped Ben's hand.

"Don't know how to thank you," he said.

"You can thank me by explaining how you got out of jail."

Ben led the way into the kitchen, got a couple of bottled waters out of the refrigerator and gave one to Hank. They sat down at the kitchen table. Ben took a sip of water and said, "Okay. Explain please."

Hank said, "Your friend is a great lawyer, to begin with. And in addition, the evidence against me was mostly circumstantial."

"That's not unusual. Eyewitnesses to a crime are rare and

unreliable. Most evidence is circumstantial, but people have been executed because of it."

"They would have loved to have hanged me, too. Especially that hard-ass state cop."

"Why didn't they?"

"The strongest piece of forensic evidence they had was the remote I supposedly used to set off the blast that wrecked the glider. I proved I used it to control experimental model planes. I even got someone from the Navy to testify that I was working on a project that involved wing lift tests."

"What about the allegations involving possession of explosives?"

"That's all they were. Allegations. The cops searched my room, my car, my workshop and house. Never even found a firecracker."

"Good thing. Possession would have sent you away for life. You were the last person with access to the glider."

"Another red herring! The DA couldn't prove I was the last one to touch the Darmstadt. Remember, the aircraft sat on that hill all night with no one watching it. My lawyer argued that anyone could have walked up the driveway or climbed the bluff to do their dirty work."

"Is that what killed their case?"

"It should have, but the DA said I could have come back during the night. What really drove the stake into the heart of their argument was lack of motive. The DA said I killed Magnus because he won the lucrative Navy contract. When Kyle called from the plane and offered me the partnership he didn't say he had put a contract in the mail. My lawyer showed it to the judge and pointed out that Kyle wanted me to be an equal partner on the job. He needed my expertise. The DA's case went up in smoke."

Ben chuckled. "I would have loved to have seen the look on Curran's face when Kyle torpedoed his case."

"I didn't tell him that Kyle said he was going to make some powerful people unhappy and needed friends."

"What powerful people was he talking about?"

"He didn't say. I haven't thought about it with all the legal crap that's been going on."

"For the record, I never thought you were guilty."

"Thanks for that, and for your legal advice."

"Consider it *pro bono* in the interests of science. What happens now with the contract?"

A thoughtful expression came to Aldrich's face. "Kyle felt really bad about the screw-up on the glider flight—lucky for me. He said he was having a thing with Melissa, but she was the one who pushed to have him fly, which is probably why she feels so bad right now. He also wanted to make up for the money I had put into the Darmstadt and he saw the Navy contract as a way to do it. He was a damned good pilot, and he was an even better aeronautical engineer, as it turned out. He won the contract fair and square."

"I'm curious about that contract. Is the project classified?"

"The general outlines of the thing were in the solicitation for bids. The Navy wanted a way to insert SEALs behind the lines for specialized missions. Kyle and I had similar designs. I have to admit his was far better. The Navy thought so, too."

Ben's eyes were drooping. "I'd love to hear more about it, but I'm starting to fade. Got to hit the sack or I'll keel over. Can we talk when I'm more alert?"

"Hell, yes. In the meantime I'll send you the blueprints. Keep them to yourself. You'll be amazed how smart Kyle was. We can talk later."

They got up and said their goodbyes. Aldrich thanked him again for his help, then he was off. Ben headed for the bedroom to make another try at getting some rest. He set the alarm and as he crawled under the sheets, he thought that Hank's innocence left open the question of who killed Kyle Magnus. Maybe it was someone who hated Kyle, or feared or envied him.

After talking with Hank, though, a new category could be added to the lists of suspects: Unhappy Powerful People.

CHAPTER THIRTY-NINE

Abi pushed the Land Rover around a curve faster than even a newer version of Grover would have tolerated. The old vehicle protested with squeaks and squeals.

"Sorry, Grover," she said, easing off on the gas pedal.

Good Lord, she thought. *Now I'm apologizing to an old SUV. That's what comes from getting too close emotionally to a lawyer.* She was confused and annoyed. Confused because she wasn't sure how to react to Ben's sweet invitation to bunk out at his house; annoyed that he assumed she needed his protection.

She was also irritated at herself for putting Ben off, not taking his offer of a place to stay for what it was. A gesture of concern from someone who cared about her well-being. She did some Zen archery breathing to calm down. Maybe she should go home and clear her head with a few twangs of the bow-string. Instead, after her *Kyudo* breathing exercise, she picked her cell phone off the seat, went to her contacts and tapped a name.

"I've been expecting to hear from you," Weber said.

"Really. Why is that?"

"I saw the way your head jerked around and the hard stare you gave me when Ben was outlining his plans for tonight. You weren't pleased."

"I didn't know I was so obvious. But yes, Ben seemed to be pushing me aside."

"I've only known you two for a little while," Weber said. "But it would not take a detective to see that he has some feelings for you. Maybe he simply didn't want you placed in any danger."

"I like Ben a lot as well, and that's why I worry about him, too. Do you think we can talk?"

"Just tell me when and where."

"How about now? There's a vineyard off the main highway. It should be quiet there this time of day."

She gave him directions and a short time later she turned off Route 6 onto a section of two-lane blacktop that used to be part of the main road to Provincetown. A few hundred yards further, she pulled into a driveway next to the sign that said Truro Vineyards and parked near a historical, two-story white house built at the edge of an expansive lawn.

Leaving Grover, she strolled over to a table and chairs near the gnarled and twisting trunk of a spreading mulberry tree. A wine-tasting was in progress in the pavilion, so only a few people lounged on the chairs around the lawn.

No sooner had she taken a seat before Weber arrived. He came to her table. She pointed to the bar located in a small, open-sided building on the other side of the lawn.

"They've got wine, of course, and rum and gin. I'm buying. It's a small payment for making you cancel your travel plans."

"Thank you. I'll go for the gin. With lime, on the rocks."

Abi ordered the gin and a glass of Cabernet Franc wine. He sipped from his cup, closed his eyes and smiled, then opened them and gazed at Abi.

"Well, what can I tell you?"

"Everything that you know about this thing we've gotten ourselves into. It's very big, isn't it?"

Weber nodded. "Much bigger than you and Ben could ever have imagined." He let his words sink in, then continued, "You're aware of the political situation in Europe, particularly the rise of neo-fascism?"

"I read the news. It's not only a problem in Europe. We've got a growing number of homegrown nutcases in this country, I'm ashamed to say."

"Yes, but we have a sorry history to remind us of the consequences of extremism. Europe lay in ruins the last time the anti-democracy forces took control. Many worry that it could happen again, fueled by immigration and austerity measures. Nationalistic movements have had electoral successes in a number of European countries, and other places around the globe. Each success makes these movements stronger. Extremists in Europe have reached out to their American counterparts, so the situation is becoming increasingly dangerous. Groups have formed to counter these trends. One of them is a client of the organization I work for."

"I thought your job is to recover stolen art."

"That's correct. We look into contemporary art thefts and World War II art plundering."

"You're confusing me. What does art theft have to do with the growth of fascism?"

"Certain industrialists are behind the nationalist trend. They are secretly financing charismatic candidates whose elections would be the tipping point for a political wave. It will be called something else, but underneath it all is good old Nazism. If the flow of money is stopped, those candidates can be defeated."

"That makes sense, but again, where do you and your clients fit in?"

"We all have an interest in bringing down the biggest source of European extremist funding. A company called Sunna Industries."

"Owned by the Magnus family."

"Sunna was started by a Magnus and run by the generations that followed. Sunna is the Norse goddess of the sun, which tells you something about how the Magnus family viewed itself. The last Magnus to be involved in its operation was Knute, whose father was Karl, the boy in the glider school photo. Like his ancestors, Knute was a lover of fine art."

"Clint Hammond said the family kept a fabulous collection in the Magnus castle in Norway."

Weber nodded. "It is rumored that the Magnus collection is bigger than many art museums. Knute carried on the family tradition of acquiring art, so it is probably even more impressive."

"Is Knute still alive?"

"He passed away a few years ago, supposedly, but you can never be sure about the family. They are like a black hole that absorbs all light."

"Who runs the company, his children?"

"He had none, thank God. The company is run by a board of directors with a rotating chairmanship. They were handpicked by Knute, and all bear the same Magnus hostility toward democratic government. They are also unanimous in their response to any perceived threat to Sunna. When you started snooping around the old barn, you had to be squashed."

"You make me sound like a bug."

"You and Mr. Hammond were no more than insects to them. They knew somehow that you had discovered the secret of Otto Klaas. And that you shared it with Hammond. You had to be eliminated."

"Sunna sent the men who chased me on the ferry?"

"That's the logical conclusion."

"But who killed them?"

"One of many unanswered questions. We may know more after tonight. But Sunna has a lot to lose if word gets out that stolen art was hidden in an underground vault buried on property they previously owned."

"This may sound cynical," Abi said. "Do you think a fuss over stolen art is enough to derail a family as rich and powerful as the Magnuses?"

"Yes, if it involves a masterpiece whose disappearance has captured the imagination of people around the world. The *Young Man* is the Holy Grail of plundered art. My organization and others would open their files and demand an investigation into the entire Magnus collection."

"You'd have to get past legions of lawyers to enter the Magnus castle."

"True, but at the very least, we could link the family's evil past with their neo-Nazi activities. Sunna would be forced to pull back its global funding for extremist candidates, creating a domino effect that would discourage others."

"They could always try again."

"They probably will, but by going after their stolen art, we will strike at the beating heart of the Magnus Empire."

Abi placed her hands to the sides of her head. "Excuse me, but this whole thing is simply mind-boggling."

"Yes, but this is the state of the world we live in."

"I'm not talking about the politics. It's the possibility that a missing masterpiece is under that old barn."

"Sunna owned the property. It makes sense, particularly with the Otto Klaas and Norway link."

"What guarantee do we have that someone hasn't already recovered the art?"

"None. Klaas disappeared. Karl's father Gunnar died of a stroke within days of the war's end. Someone else might have known of the art cache, but the recent interest leads me to believe that the secret has remained intact up to now."

"We know about the vault because I found the sketch. Whoever has been digging around the barn must have had another source of information. Why now? Could Kyle have known something through his family ties?"

"I'm not sure where Kyle fits in. He was not part of the inner Magnus circle. He could have come across new information. I'm here because the hack of our network was traced back to Kyle's computer. Unfortunately, we can't ask him about it because he's dead."

"I would have been dead, too. But I run fast when I'm scared."

"Your unfortunate experience tells us whoever sent people after you and Hammond had money and resources."

"Like Magnus and Sunna."

"Those are reasonable guesses."

Abi looked around at the peaceful vineyard scene as if to reassure herself she wasn't in a bad dream. "You realize what we're saying? That the fate of western civilization rests on a village constable, an art theft detective and an art historian."

"Not the entire fate," Weber said. "Only part."

"Sorry, but that doesn't make me feel better. I'm going to be a nervous wreck while you're at the Baron house."

"Please don't worry. It's not a bad plan, actually. Ben and I can watch unobserved. We'll be in a good defensive position in case we're discovered, and Ben assures me he will have backup standing by."

"Thanks for all your help."

"And thank you for the gin." Weber got up from his chair. "Try not to worry. We'll all meet here tomorrow to celebrate the conclusion of the mission, the toppling of the neo-Nazi movement in Europe and the recovery of one or more masterpieces."

"You're making me nervous again."

"Do you trust me?" Weber said.

"Yes. You've been very forthcoming."

"And do you trust Ben?"

"I should never have doubted him. Yes, I do trust him."

"Then you'll have to have faith that we can carry out this surveillance operation. We are both professionals and quite capable, despite being former and current village constables."

"I wouldn't want anything to happen to Ben. And you too, of course."

He gave her a quick, tight smile.

"I'm glad to hear that. I'm supposed to meet Ben at his house at midnight. I will see you tomorrow morning."

"Maybe sooner. Ben has asked me to stay at his house for safety's sake."

"So much the better."

They walked to their cars. She went to shake hands, then changed her mind and gave him a shoulder hug instead. He grinned and said "*Danke* schön."

Weber got into his car and drove off. Abi slid behind the wheel of the Land Rover and went to put the SUV in reverse. She paused as her eyes fell on the vineyard building and she marveled at the size and beauty of the mulberry tree that blocked the view of the house.

During her Hopper tour the guide said that Hopper had brushed out the tree in the final painting because it blocked the house. She got out of her car and leaned against the hood, trying to picture the house without the tree. In her mind's eye, she transposed the scene of the Snow barn as Hopper sketched it, as it would have looked without a well.

The grainy photo of the Snow farm she had seen in the Proctor office showed two wells. The one close to the house, which had been used as an improvised cemetery. The other well had been a few steps from the barn where it could be used for watering livestock.

She had paid little attention to the farmhouse sketch because Otto Klaas had drawn her interest. She wished she had the drawing in front of her. But it seemed clear that Hopper had ignored the barn well in his aim to sketch the exterior wall.

Her theory about the vault access from the barn well wasn't so far-fetched after all. A company like Sunna would have had the resources to dig a tunnel from the barn to the newly-opened well and bury the vault so it would be ready for Klaas. She was eager to take another look, but that would screw up Ben's plans. She got back into Grover and drove to the flower cottage hill, where she discovered she had company. A car was parked near the cottages and a lone figure stood at the edge of the bluff.

Abi parked Grover and walked out to the cliff. She said hello. Melissa turned, a sad expression on her face, but she smiled when she saw Abi.

"I'm saying a last goodbye to Kyle," she said.

"That's a nice thing for you to do." Abi didn't know what else to say.

"Thank you. He was so excited about the flight. It wasn't just the glory, he said. He wanted to redeem his family name."

"What did he mean?"

"He didn't say. Only that he hoped good would come out of bad. Well, I've got to get moving. It was nice meeting you. I'm going to miss this beautiful place."

Abi looked out at the bay. The setting sun was painting the clouds in gold and pink.

"Are you leaving Cape Cod?"

"Yes. The rest of the crew has gone ahead, so I'm the only one left."

"Sorry to see you go. I'm also sorry I didn't get to know Kyle better. What next?"

"I'm meeting the crew in Boston and we'll take the shuttle to New York. Then it's back to work getting out the magazine and editing the documentary." She glanced at her watch. "I'd better go."

"It was good to see you again. Best of luck."

They exchanged hugs. "Thanks," Melissa said. "Enjoy the rest of your stay here."

"I will," Abi said, thinking that her stay would be short. She had made up her mind about Ben's offer.

CHAPTER FORTY

Ben bustled around the house as if he were back in his legal days prepping for a big case. He was surprised at how calm his nerves were. He checked off items on his mental list with little thought of the long, and possibly dangerous night ahead, despite what he'd told Abi.

He screwed the cap tight on a thermos full of coffee and tucked it into a pack. Seconds later, he heard a knock at the front door. The kitchen clock showed that it was exactly midnight. He went to the door and let Weber into the house. The detective was dressed in jeans and a navy hooded sweatshirt. A Boston Red Sox baseball cap was pulled down over his unruly locks.

"Right on time," Ben said.

"I'm Swiss," Weber replied laconically. "We invented time."

"And the cuckoo clock as well, as I recall."

"Thanks for reminding me. Anything I can help you with?"

"I'm all set, thanks, but I've got something for you."

Ben led the way into the dining room. A canvas bag lay on the trestle table. Ben unzipped the bag and lifted out a shotgun. He hefted the weapon, then handed it to Weber.

"Sixteen-gauge double-barrel Remington. My grandfather gave it to me when I was a teenager. We used to go deer hunting together in the woods around Truro before the town got too built up with summer houses."

"Hunting is part of the culture in Switzerland even if no one does it much anymore." Weber took the gun from Ben, ran his fingers over the embossed barrels, then he put the stock to his shoulder and sighted at a window. He lowered the gun, opened the breech, looked down the barrels, and closed it up. He handed the gun back to Ben. "Clean, even by Swiss standards. When was the last time it was fired?"

Ben smiled. "A long time ago. But I'm sure it still works."

"Do you actually think we'll need this cannon?"

"I hope not," Ben said. "But there's a good reason you're riding shotgun. We don't want to end up at the bottom of a well."

"Good point. I'll do my best to see that doesn't happen."

"I've got my police Glock 9mm in my backpack along with some buckshot loads for you."

Ben zipped the shotgun into its bag and handed it to Weber. Then he grabbed the backpack and they went out to the truck. Fifteen minutes later, Ben drove past the gate to the Baron property, kept on going and tucked the pickup onto the wooded road at the end of the cul-de-sac. They got out of the truck and Ben told Weber they'd be following a path that would get them onto the property without being seen.

Hoisting the backpack onto his shoulders, he advised Weber to stay close behind because he wouldn't be using a light. They were both dressed in dark clothes, making it even harder to see each other, but they'd be invisible to others as well.

Their progress through the pine forest was slow and erratic, but eventually they made their way to the fence.

"It gets a little trickier from here, especially in the dark," he told Weber. "There's a fallen tree crushing the fence. Feel your way along the trunk and keep the shotgun bag close so it won't catch on a branch. Just follow my lead."

"That would be good advice if I could see your lead to follow."

"We can't use a light this close to the property. Take your time."

Ben pulled himself up onto the trunk and worked his way along the fallen tree until he was on the other side of the fence. He climbed down the tree branches to the ground and waited for Weber. He could gauge Weber's progress by the string of grunts and curses in German coming out of the darkness. The mutterings grew even stronger when Weber had to weave his big body through the network of branches.

He finally joined Ben on the ground and they struck out through the pine forest, breaking out into the open after a few minutes of walking. Ben headed toward the massive house with Weber close on his heels until they came to the base of the tower—an ominous silhouette against the blue-black sky.

"There's a staircase directly in front of us," Ben said. "I'll guide you to the stairs and we'll climb to the next level." He took Weber's hand and placed it on the stair railing. They made their way quickly to the top of the stairs.

"Good job, Marty," Ben said, "But I should warn you—"

"I know. It gets even trickier from here."

"Correct. The exterior ladder runs up the side of the tower from the patio," Ben said. "You're from Switzerland, so you're probably not afraid of heights."

"On the contrary. I'm probably the only person in Switzerland who gets a nosebleed climbing a step ladder, but I'll be fine."

Ben led Weber to the tower and guided his hand to the first rung of the ladder.

"Stay close. I'll try not to step on your hands."

He began to climb. Weber was right behind him. Ben stopped halfway up to check on Weber. He whispered that he was doing fine, but had to adjust the shoulder strap of the shotgun bag. He paused again at the top of the ladder and stretched his arm out to Ben, who had climbed to the top of the tower.

Ben grabbed Weber by the wrist and pulled him up. Weber belly-flopped onto the observation deck. Then they both stood up and looked around. Although the Baron property was shrouded in darkness, they had an unimpeded view of the long curve of the Cape. The distant lights of Provincetown sparkled like diamonds.

Anticipating the coolness of the night, Ben had dressed in jeans and a windbreaker and he wore a baseball cap on his head. He took insect repellent out of his pack, applied it on the exposed skin of his hands and face, and handed the bottle to Weber.

Then he produced a set of binoculars from the pack and looked through the lenses in the general direction of the barn. He could see the faint gray outline of the building. He tried not to think about the bodies at the bottom of the well.

Satisfied that they had arrived ahead of potential intruders, he turned on a hand radio, then opened the thermos and poured two paper cups full of coffee.

"Any idea what we're waiting for?" Weber said.

"If I knew that I might not be here waiting."

"I understand."

"Good," Ben said. "I'm glad someone does."

CHAPTER FORTY-ONE

Three hundred feet above the beach in front of the flower cottage hill, a lone gull was out for a nocturnal snack—the equivalent of a human raiding the refrigerator—when it suddenly snapped its wings and peeled off in a sideways dive that took it safely over the waters of the bay.

The source of its alarm was a long, dark shape, many times bigger than the bird, that had invaded its airspace.

The shape circled above the cottages several times, then climbed even higher, balancing on an updraft before it broke out of the pattern and went into a long, shallow dive in the direction of the big house with the tall tower.

As it neared the tower, it gripped its single talon, readying to sink it into human flesh. The first kill would be easy. The victim would be totally unprepared for the attack. The second would be slightly more involved because the prey would be aware of the threat.

The operation would take less than thirty seconds.

Then back to the hill cottages to deal with the other problem.

CHAPTER FORTY-TWO

Abi had organized the last of the boxes and stacked them in alphabetical order in the office. She surveyed the results of her labors, recalling the jumble of paper and files she had first seen in the professor's office.

With the filing done, she could go up to her bedroom and pull together her personal belongings. She hadn't yet told Ben that she'd decided to accept his offer to move in. *Move in.* Simple words, but the enormity of her decision hit her. It wasn't exactly moving in with someone, she reasoned. She was simply taking a room.

Her phone chirped, notifying her of a FaceTime call. Ben's face came onto the screen.

"Communications center," she said.

"You're coming in loud and clear," Ben said.

"You are too. Are you in position?"

"Weber and I are at the top of the tower."

"See anything suspicious?"

"Not yet. We're taking turns checking the barn at fifteen-minute intervals. Keeping an eye on the perimeter in between. Any news at your end?"

"I've finished with Professor Waldstein's files and I've decided to move into your house, if the offer is still good."

"Of course it is! That's great, Abi. Key's under the doormat. When can you make the move?"

"As soon as I pack my personal stuff, I'll close the cottage and shift the communications center over to your house."

"Which means your smiling face will be there to greet us at the end of our mission."

"Don't know how smiling it will be after staying up all night," Abi said, "but I'll have the coffee pot going."

"Thanks, Abi. We'll be looking forward to it."

"Remember what we talked about, Ben. If you see anyone moving around the barn, you have standing orders from the communications center to call the police immediately and let them do all the work. Please don't mess around."

"Don't worry. Marty and I are both cops. We know the drill. We've got the barn in our sights."

"I'll be here if you need me. Speaking of the barn, I think I figured out how to get into the vault."

"No kidding! Are you going to let me in on the secret?"

"Not quite yet. I want to do a little more research. Concentrate on your stakeout for the time being."

"Will do. I'll call in a little while."

She went upstairs to her bedroom. Packing didn't take long. She carried her bag downstairs to the office.

As she sat at the desk doing a mental inventory, Abi picked up the diagram she had drawn of the house and the two wells. She recalled the bodies in the house well and thought about Ben and Weber at the top of the tower. Abi knew they were capable, but despite Ben's assurances, she couldn't help feeling a sense of unease. There were so many unknowns swirling around the Baron house and barn. One thing she was sure of, though. This was going to be a very long night.

CHAPTER FORTY-THREE

Suspended between its diaphanous wings, the shadow stopped its long dive and swooped up into a hover. The hand slid the climbing ax back into its leather holster. The men hunched down on the top of the tower would live a while longer.

With a soft rustle of wings the shadow drifted out over the bay in a wide turn, then started back toward the cottage hill.

The Birdman thought back to his first clumsy attempt to get into the air, like a fledgling eagle pushed out of the nest by its parents. But the wings had done the job they were designed to do, and the dips and twists and near crashes had evolved into smooth transitions from one maneuver to another. He could float, motionless, like a milkweed seed, held in the sky by invisible strings; or, with a slight shift of his body, drop from the sky to pounce on unsuspecting prey, like an owl on a field mouse.

As his aerial skill evolved, the cold-blooded godlike sense of power grew with it. Flying was not simply a technical exercise. The flier had to think like a raptor, letting his humanness go.

The ruthlessness that had driven his every move before he sprouted wings had been replaced by an unrelenting hunger.

Like a bat, he could see in total darkness. And like the emotionless force of nature he had become, he could drop almost silently from the sky and make the kill.

CHAPTER FORTY-FOUR

"Anything happening out there?" Ben said. He was sitting on the deck, using the pack for a cushion, his back against the railing.

"Quiet as the grave," Weber replied.

"Could you use a less spooky comparison?"

"Of course. Quiet as a cathedral." Weber leaned on the opposite railing and raised a pair of binoculars to his eyes.

"Okay. My turn in five minutes," Ben said.

"Maybe this will all amount to nothing," Weber said.

"In that case all we'll have lost is a good night's sleep. We'll sneak off the property and call the police on the way home. Abi thinks she knows how to get into the vault."

"Really? How would that be possible?"

"She wouldn't say. I'll call her back."

Ben was elated at the news Abi was moving into his house. He slipped the phone out of his pocket. An email message had come in from Hank. The subject line read: Here it is. Project Icarus.

Ben tapped the first attachment to the message. A diagram popped up. He could make no sense of the intricate lines and technical writing. He scrolled down and began to see a pattern to the drawings although it was hard to comprehend the details on the small screen. He tapped in Hank's phone number.

Hank answered after a couple of rings. "Get my email?" he said.

"Yes, but I don't know what I'm looking at."

"Check out the video in the second attachment."

"I'll give it a look."

He clicked on the attachment labeled 'Flypack Test.' The video lasted thirty seconds, and it showed a human figure gliding through the air under silvery wings. The helmeted figure came to a stop, hovered in place, then swooped, gained altitude and flew off until it was a pinpoint.

"Impressive. Is that for real?"

"Very real. The video shows a test of the Icarus flypack developed by Kyle Magnus. The flypack is a combination flysuit and parasail, only far more sophisticated. Kyle was a genius. My design was more of a glorified sports parachute, but he integrated the latest space age materials into computer technology. The flier straps on the pack and jumps into the air; the wings pop out, and he rises and descends at will. Same principle Hesselbach used to set world records."

"Magic wings," Ben said with wonderment.

"That sums it up."

"Was that Kyle in the video?"

"No. Kyle could fly a conventional glider, but the wings are controlled by body movement; more like a hang glider. Phil Mead had lots of experience flying hang gliders and parasails, and he's an ex-Navy SEAL. Kyle hired him to do the initial tests at his farm in Vermont. You're probably surprised to hear he was working on the Navy project."

"Surprised isn't the word for it. What happened to the prototype Mead is flying? Did the Navy take it back?"

"There were actually two prototypes: the original model, and a backup rig. The Navy has one. I don't know about the other. Maybe Mead has it."

"Have you spoken to him about it?"

"I did. He said no when I asked him. Then I became otherwise occupied. I never liked the guy. Seemed a little wacky. Probably from doing that sneaky stuff for the Navy. Smart though, even with that redneck drawl of his."

Speaking in the calmest voice he could muster, Ben said, "I'm going to have to get back to you. Something just occurred to me."

"No problem. Catch you later."

Ben hung up without saying goodbye, then stood and did a slow, 360-degree pivot.

As he gazed at the cloud-streaked sky he was thinking about Abi's unease, her feeling she was being watched, the "wrinkling" of the sky, the break into her office, the theft of the sketches and the scratches on the bedroom windowsill.

He remembered how Mead seemed to be everywhere, and knew everything. He recalled being puzzled at how someone could come and go to the barn without being seen.

"What are you looking for?" Weber said.

"That was Hank Aldrich on the phone. He said Kyle Magnus invented a device that works like a personal glider. It was designed to drop Special Ops right on top of unsuspecting victims."

"Like us?"

"Yes. Like us. Mead was the test pilot for the pack."

Weber mumbled something in German. "Should we be worried?"

"Very worried. We're sitting ducks up here."

Ben popped two shells into the shotgun and handed it to Weber. They stood back-to-back on the platform, their eyes scouring the sky.

"I don't see anything," Weber said. "Maybe no one knows we're up here."

"Don't count on it. You said microphones and cameras could be everywhere."

"Yes, but we were careful and moved away from inside the barn."

"What if there were listening devices and cameras in locations other than the Baron property?"

"That would be a problem. It's a simple matter to install cameras in a house or a car and transmit signals to a cell phone. It depends where the devices were planted, but someone could have heard everything we've said. Every time we said it."

Ben had already gone beyond Weber's conclusion. He explained what he wanted, then called Abi using FaceTime.

"Command central. Abi here."

"Hi, Abi. I see you're in your office; good."

"What's going on?"

Without responding, he passed the phone to Weber, who said, "Hello, Abi. Please show me what is on your desk, then the corners of the ceiling, slowly turning around with the phone camera so I can see what's on the shelves. Especially the higher parts of the office, that are out of your line of sight."

"Got it," Abi said.

There was no mistaking the seriousness of Weber's tone. She followed his instructions without question. When she got to the bookcase, he said, "Stop. That book with the ornate scrolling on the binding. It's different from the others. Please slide it out carefully and open the cover."

Abi put the phone down on the desk, slid the book out and opened it.

"That's weird," she said.

"Please show us what you've found," Weber said.

She picked up the phone and pointed the camera at the book. A rectangular hole had been cut in the pages. In the hollowed-out opening was a small black box made of hard plastic. A green light glowed on the side of the box.

"Is this what I think it is?" she said.

"Probably."

"What should I do?"

"Hold on. I'll let Ben handle it."

"Just one second. Someone's at the door."

Ben took his phone back but it was too late. She was gone. Her phone looked up at the ceiling. He heard her voice, then a man talking. "We've got to go," he said to Weber "Grab the shotgun."

"Go where?"

Ben pulled the backpack over his shoulders and headed for the ladder.

"To the cottage hill. Abi's in trouble."

CHAPTER FORTY-FIVE

Abi paused with her hand on the doorknob.

"Who is it?" she called out.

"It's Phil Mead," a voice said. "Got something important to talk to you about."

She sighed and unlocked the door. Mead stood on the porch holding a canvas bag in his hand. He was wearing a tight-fitting black workout suit that showed off his muscular arms and legs.

"This is a big surprise. Melissa said everyone had left town."

"Heading out tomorrow, which is why I came by tonight. Saw your lights were still on. You got a minute?"

Abi had no desire to get into a discussion with Mead.

"I was about to turn in for the night."

"Sorry about that. But I've got a lead on a big story. As an art historian, it's right up your alley."

Mead wasn't going away. "Have a seat on the porch and enjoy the fresh air. I'll get us a couple of glasses of seltzer."

Abi regretted cutting Ben off to answer the door; the seltzer was just an excuse so she could retrieve her phone. The sooner she dealt with Mead, the quicker she'd get rid of him.

She went back inside, pushing the stop under the door with her toe. On the way to the kitchen she popped into the office and grabbed her phone. Ben had hung up. She folded the Baron barn diagram and slipped it into her shorts pocket along with the phone.

When she carried two glasses of seltzer onto the porch Mead was in a rocking chair. The canvas bag was on his lap. She put the glasses down on the table and sat in another rocker. As she looked off at the bay, she realized that her Land Rover was the only vehicle on the hill.

"How did you get here?" she said. "I don't see your truck."

"Danged thing crapped out at the bottom of the hill," Mead said. "I've called Triple A, but they can't be here for another forty-five minutes. I'll walk down in about half an hour and meet them."

"Tell me about your big scoop," Abi said, pleased that Mead's visit had a time limit.

"I appreciate that. Lemme give you some background. Dunno if you're aware that I was the one who came up with the idea to do the reenactments of Hesselbach's flight."

"It was a brilliant idea."

"Thanks. I'd been researching a story on the original flights. The editor's job at the magazine was vacant. I thought that coming up with the reenactment would put me in line for a promotion. Didn't happen. Publishers were real excited, but they brought Melissa in to run things and made her editor."

"Sorry. You must have been disappointed."

"Big-time, but I get it. She photographs better than me. Smart, too. She assigned me to do the bios for the two glider pilots who'd been picked to fly. When I met Kyle, he tells me he volunteered to fly the glider because he'd heard his family had a history of promoting gliders in the U.S. He even tried to get the Magnus company, Sunna Industries, to sponsor the reenactment."

"That was a smart move."

"It would have been, but he never hears from them."

"I'm surprised they'd treat a member of the family like that."

"Kyle was a bottom feeder. He's got a small family trust fund, but he's a poor relative of the moneyed folks in the Magnus clan. He hoped the glider event might bring him into the family business. He asked me to dig into some papers that had been passed down the line. Box in the attic had stuff left over from his grandmother's estate. He thought maybe that would help me write a story that would get their attention."

Abi took a sip of seltzer to suppress a yawn. She was wondering if she could get rid of Mead before the repair truck arrived.

"So you did the story on the Magnus family."

"Yeah, but not the one Kyle wanted. See, the paperwork had belonged to his grandfather, who worked in Sunna's PR department. A lot of what was in the box was press clippings. His job was to bury bad publicity under a pile of puff pieces."

"That's not unusual, a big company polishing its image," Abi said.

"True, but Sunna's reputation needed serious scrubbing. They were involved in slave labor and working people to death."

"That's disturbing to hear," Abi said. "How did Kyle react?"

"Real bad. He asked me to keep the nasty bits out of the story. He was bidding on a Navy contract and was worried the government might pull out if they heard his family was in the thick of the death business."

"That must have put you in an ethical bind as a journalist."

"Actually, it put me in a very good position once I laid it out for him."

"I'm not sure I understand."

"I'm just a low-paid, middle-aged hack writer for a dinky magazine hardly anyone reads. I asked what he could do to remedy that situation. He offered me a job working on the Navy project. If he got the contract he'd make the arrangement permanent. I took him up on the offer."

"And the story about his family?"

"I wrote a puff piece about the Magnus family and their business. Done deal, or so I thought, until I dug a packet of letters out of the box having to do with a certain collection at Magnus castle. Maybe you know what I'm talking about."

"Not at all."

Mead chuckled softly. "The letters were sent to the Magnus family from a guy named Otto Klaas. I went to language school in the Navy and knew enough German to read what it said."

Abi managed to keep her voice level, responding, "That was a lucky coincidence."

"Finding those letters changed everything for me."

"In what way?"

"The letters talked about the delivery of art supplies to Truro. Now, what do you think that was all about?"

"I don't have a clue," Abi said. Her mouth was so dry she could hardly get the words out.

He grinned. "I think you know they were talking about moving stolen art to the old Magnus property. That batch of sketches you found showed Otto delivering the loot."

"How did you—?"

He raised a finger to his lips. "Same way I know you and your friends were at the barn today. And that they're up on the tower keeping a lookout for me. I also know that you figured out how to get into the vault."

He took a cell phone out of the pouch hanging around his neck and tapped a screen icon. The image showed Abi from the back, sitting in the office and studying the diagram of the wells she had drawn earlier.

"*I think I figured out how to get into the vault,*" she was saying.

"You probably also figured out that it was me who's been sniffing around the barn. Finally found the vault with a metal detector." He slipped the phone back into the pouch. "We don't have a lot of time to waste, so I'll make this quick. I was planning to cut the hatch open from the top, but that could damage what's inside. You've got information I want. We can trade."

"Trade what?"

"You give me the diagram showing how to get into the vault. I give you your life." Mead laughed at the expression on her face. "Just kidding. Use your head, hon. What do you think I'd do with all that art? Especially the young guy?"

"The Raphael."

"That's the one. Can't just put it on eBay. So instead I'm going to collect rewards. Stuff gets back to its rightful owners. Rewards come in. I'm just a Georgia cracker. I need someone with art know-how who can help me sort the stuff and get it to the right people. Whaddya say?"

"What about my friends?"

"Oh hell, we'll cut them in. Ben's a lawyer. He'll come in real handy. We'll figure out what to do with the other guy."

"Okay," she said.

His eyes narrowed. "That was fast. You sure you're not pulling my chain?"

"There's a lot you don't know about me. I lost my business. I'm broke. I don't even have a place to live. My husband screwed me out of every cent I owned. Something like this could restore my career and pay the bills."

"Wow! You've got more motivation than I have. I just want a bundle of money."

"I got kicked out of my Boston apartment. Maybe I can buy it back. The diagram that shows the vault access is in the house."

She stood with her glass in hand. Mead was on his feet and would have cut in front of her, but she dropped the half-full glass. It splashed seltzer and ice onto his feet. He looked down, then up. His brow was knitted in a scowl, but the toothy grin that came to his lips a second later was even more frightening.

She probably would have frozen in place if he hadn't growled, "Cute move, darlin'."

He reached down for his bag. Abi quickly stepped into the house and kicked the doorstop aside on the way in. The door slammed and locked shut behind her.

Mead yelled, "Hey! Open up. We're partners."

She ran for the stairs that would take her to the bedroom. As she started to climb the stairs she heard a crash. Mead had thrown his weight against the door, but it wasn't going to give.

Then one of the panels splintered, a metal point came through the door and a hand reached in and groped for the door handle.

Abi raced up the stairway, ducked into the bedroom and slammed the door.

CHAPTER FORTY-SIX

Ben practically fell down the ladder in his haste to get off the tower. He stepped off the bottom rung, got a flashlight from his bag and pointed it up the ladder so Weber could see where to place his feet. When Weber finally neared the bottom of the ladder, Ben grabbed him by the arm and pulled him down.

"We've got to hurry," he said.

"Maybe it's time to call the police," Weber said.

"Not now," Ben said, breaking into a run.

"When?" Weber said as he tried to keep up with him.

"No more talk. If you can't run faster, I'm leaving you behind."

Ben was open to calling in help, even if he hadn't figured out how to explain that a winged murderer was flying over cliffs and dunes. His first priority was Abi. The microphone in her office would have picked up Abi's statement that she knew how to get into the vault. Mead would do anything necessary to get the information out of her.

And once he did that, he'd have no more use for her.

CHAPTER FORTY-SEVEN

Abi slid the latch shut and put her ear against the bedroom door. Silence. She pictured Mead in the office, looking for the diagram of the Baron property.

Moving stealthily in the darkness, she knelt down, rolled the shag rug back in the closet, and lifted the hatch, tensing at the soft creak of the hinges. She felt around the edge of the rectangular opening and found the top of the ladder. Then she swung her legs around, stepped on the ladder, climbed down a few steps, and then stopped. She listened.

Still nothing.

Maybe Mead had gone around behind the house and was waiting for her. She talked her way out of her panic. Mead wouldn't know about the fire escape. Even Ben didn't know about it. She had to get away from the cottage. If she didn't move now she'd be sticking halfway out of the floor when he bulled his way into the bedroom.

She descended another few rungs and closed the hatch cover behind her. As she reached the bottom of the ladder her foot bumped against something and she heard a soft thump. She had left her archery case leaning against the ladder after her last shooting session.

She groped in the darkness for the case, picked it up, and reached out in the general direction of the door until the fingers of her free hand touched wood. She felt for the latch, opened the door, and stepped out into the night.

The moonlight was bright enough for her to see the start of the path that ran from behind the house into the moors. A mist had moved in from the bay and was creeping across the heath. She listened intently, but the only sound was the night chorus of insects.

Without thinking, she tucked the archery bag under her arm. She dashed across the backyard, pausing at the edge of the grass, thinking it was like a scene from *The Hound of the Baskervilles*. She took a quick look back, then set foot on the fog-shrouded path.

If she could make it across the hilly grasslands, she'd head to the nearest occupied house and ask someone to call the police.

Guided more by instinct than sight, she struck out into the swirling mist.

CHAPTER FORTY-EIGHT

Ben and Weber followed the bobbing flashlight beams back through the woods to the fallen tree in a fraction of the time they had spent getting to the Baron house. They climbed up through the tree limbs, ignoring the branches that tore at their faces, slowing only to make their way down the trunk.

Ben was first to reach the pickup. He had the engine started by the time Weber got in the cab. The detective was gasping like an asthmatic steam engine.

Alarmed at the sounds coming from Weber's throat, Ben said, "Are you all right?"

Weber was out of breath and unable to reply. He nodded vigorously and tapped his wristwatch. Ben dropped the gear shift into drive and nailed the gas pedal.

The truck fishtailed on the sandy road. Ben almost lost control as the pickup skidded around a couple of curves. He eased off the gas pedal after coming out of a sharp turn, when the truck seemed dangerously close to a rollover.

It only took a few minutes to get to the cottage hill, but to Ben, bound by the laws of physics and time, it seemed like hours. He pulled up to Abi's cottage and slammed on the brakes.

Abi's Land Rover was parked outside. Ben's sense of relief vanished as soon as he and Weber got out of the truck and saw that the front door of the cottage had been smashed in.

He slid the pistol from its holster and gestured at Weber to follow him, first cautioning him to keep the shotgun pointed off to the side. With his pistol clutched in both hands, arms extended straight ahead, he stepped onto the porch. Broken glass crackled underfoot. An undamaged glass with clear liquid in it sat on the table.

One of the door panels was in splinters. He turned the knob. The door was unlocked.

Nudging the door further open with his gun, he stepped into the cottage.

The light was on in the office. He told Weber to cover him, then edged his way around the jamb. The fake book used to hold the security camera lay open on the table. The camera was nowhere to be seen. He came out of the office and motioned for Weber to follow him to the bottom of the bedroom stairs.

"I'll check the upstairs," he said. "Stay here and keep an eye on the front door."

Ben went up the spiral staircase. The door was open and the latch broken. He flashed his light around the bedroom, then into the closet. He noticed the hatch in the closet floor. Lifting the cover, he pointed his flashlight into the opening and spotted a ladder. He climbed down, into the storeroom. Cool air was coming through the partially-open door. Throwing it wide, Ben stepped into the night.

There was no sign of Abi. Behind the cottage the mists drifting over the moors had blocked all but a few of the lights from distant houses. Fingers of fog were starting to obscure parts of the sky.

He went back into the garden shed, climbed the ladder to the bedroom then descended the spiral stairs. Weber was in the dining area, the shotgun cradled in his arms.

"No one's in the house," Ben reported. He headed toward the smashed front door.

Weber hustled to keep up with him.

"Where are we going?" he said.

"We've got to find Abi before it's too late," he said, wondering—even as the words left his mouth—whether it was *already* too late.

CHAPTER FORTY-NINE

Mead circled above the cottage hill like an owl looking for prey.

After ransacking the office in a fruitless search for the diagram, he had followed Abi's route up the stairs and thrown his shoulder against the door. Once in the empty bedroom, he discovered the closet hatch and climbed down the ladder to the storage shed, the same route Ben would follow later.

This clever little mouse had found an escape route.

He went outside to look around. The mist had thickened at ground level. She could have broken off in any direction. He would have to cover a lot of ground in a short time.

He could cover it even faster from the air. Rather than retrace his steps up the ladder and through the cottage, he went around to the front, retrieved his bag from the porch and trotted to the cliff where he'd left the flypack.

Mead slipped his arms through the elaborate vest, unzipped the bag and slid the climbing ax into its specially-made holster. Then he clipped the belt holding the holster around his mid-section.

Next, he took night goggles and the helmet from the bag. He placed the goggles over his eyes and the helmet on his head. He was ready to fly. He activated the switch in the front of the vest, and braced himself. Seconds later, fabric wings sprouted magically from the sides and back of the vest.

Once he was well-balanced on both feet, he ran several paces and jumped off the edge of the cliff.

The fluttering wings caught the updrafts coming up the side of the cliff and lifted him in the air above the beach. He kept his legs tight together. Using shifts of his body weight and tugs on the shrouds controlling the wings, he maneuvered himself until he was moving parallel to the edge of the cliffs where the updrafts were the strongest.

Gaining altitude, he flew back and forth over the beach, then angled inland to scour the landscape around the cottages.

Magnus had been a true genius. Too bad he had to be dispensed with. Hesselbach's Darmstadt was primitive compared to this marvel of modern engineering. He needed no noisy propellers or jets to keep him aloft. Only a feel for the updrafts and breezes, and a strong body to shift the angle of the diaphanous wings that extended from the flypack.

He wheeled over the cottages and saw another vehicle parked next to the Land Rover. He dropped down a hundred feet and was surprised to see Ben's truck. He thought Ben and Weber were still on the tower roof. He glided out to the edge of the cliff, gained altitude and rose even higher over the cottage colony.

Behind the row of cottages a blurry form was moving across the moors. Even more interesting were the two shapes following the first. The lone figure had to be Abi, followed by Ben and his friend. He adjusted his body, and slid off at an angle. From its holster he drew the ax and clutched the handle tightly in his hand.

He would come in from behind, swinging the ax like a polo player driving a ball with his mallet. That would take care of the first one. The second target would spin around, instinctively looking for a threat from behind, but by then he'd rise, make a quick turn and attack from the front. Then he'd take care of the woman.

CHAPTER FIFTY

Ben trudged along the winding path through the heath, intent on finding Abi, yet completely aware of the danger that lurked above.

He walked a few steps, stopped and slowly pivoted. His eyes scanned the sky through breaks in the mist, and then he walked a short distance and went through the same routine. It was slow going, but the only way he could think of to avoid an aerial attack.

He had finished another rotation when he saw movement on the path ahead. He called out.

"Abi?"

"Is that you, Ben?" Abi's voice.

"Yes. Stay where you are. Mead is a killer. He's flying around out there on high tech wings. Keep watch on the sky. I'll come to you."

In his haste, Ben failed to go through his stop, look and listen routine.

He felt a tingling in his scalp. Probably some primitive warning reflex that went back to the time humans were low on the food chain. Reacting instinctively, he went into a crouch, drew the Glock from its holster and clasped it, and the flashlight, in both hands.

He aimed at the sound and switched on the flashlight. What he saw was almost beyond belief.

Swooping down on him through the fog was what looked like a big-eyed mythological creature. It was too late to get off a shot. He ducked and tried to protect his head. Something hard struck his raised forearms and glanced off his head. The blow knocked the gun and the light from his hands and he fell over backwards. He rolled over, reached for the flashlight with his good arm and was getting to his knees when a double explosion echoed across the heath.

He pointed the light at the sound.

Caught in the beam was Weber, who was fumbling with the shotgun. Ben guessed he had fired both barrels at the same time. He had broke open the shotgun breech, but in his haste to reload he dropped the shell.

Ben kept the light trained on Weber, who got down and groped in the grass. He found the shell after a few seconds, and successfully loaded the gun, only to stand there, bewildered, as if he were unsure of where to aim.

Ben swept the sky with his flashlight beam and saw Mead, who hovered fifty feet above the fog-shrouded moors. He had a climbing ax in his hand and he was angling his body, readying himself to swoop down like a dive bomber on the unsuspecting Swiss journalist.

CHAPTER FIFTY-ONE

Abi had been keeping watch on the sky as Ben had advised.

So she was startled, but not surprised when the winged figure suddenly appeared in a bull's-eye of light above the low-lying fog. Goggles obscured his face, and his mid-section was wrapped in what looked like an elaborate vest.

She had gasped as Mead began his attack, arm raised, the ax swinging. Then Ben had dropped the flashlight and she didn't know what happened. But seconds later, the tremendous double-boom of what sounded like a shotgun echoed across the moors.

She hit the ground on her belly, clutching the archery bag like a child holding a rag doll. But instead of fear, all the anger and frustration of the last few years welled up in her throat.

Not. Going. To. Be. Pushed. Around. Any. More.

Her hand felt for the tab and she slowly unzipped the bag. Then she rolled over on her side and slid the bow out and bent the bamboo to string it. Next, she removed an arrow from the exterior pouch. She got onto her knees, stood on shaky legs and slowly pivoted.

The mist was thick close to the ground, but when she elevated her gaze she saw a break in the murk that allowed a glimpse of the star-filled sky.

There was a patch where the stars were blacked out, like the strange phenomenon she had seen from her bedroom when she'd first moved into the cottage.

Keeping close watch on the shadow moving across the sky, she stood and yelled out:

"Mead. It's me, Abi. I've got the vault diagram. You want it? Come and get it."

She reached into her pocket, pulled out the paper and held it in the air.

The dark patch remained the same. Mead was hovering.

"Still want to be partners? It's yours for the taking."

She waved the paper.

The patch moved slightly to the right, then to the left, then descended, putting it into the mist. Mead had taken the bait and was making his move, but she could no longer see him.

Flutter.

He was closer now, and from the sound of his wings, she knew he was circling.

The circling stopped. He was making his move. She reached down, picked up the bow, notched the arrow to the string…and waited. She pivoted, keeping pace, and at the same time lifted the bow over her head. She slowly lowered the bow, pulled back on the string, holding it as the Master had said, like a child holding a proffered finger, firmly and without purpose.

She brushed aside all thoughts of aiming, as she had been taught, sweeping her mind clean, concentrating on her hands. She pulled the arrow back, trying to keep the bow steady, although it was difficult to do so because of the resistance from the taut string drawn to its highest point of tension.

Abi remembered how her Zen master had hit the bull's-eye in complete darkness to prove that an archer shoots with the mind, not the eye. She could hear his voice whispering in her ear.

The hitter and the hit are no longer two opposing objects, but one reality.

She resisted the temptation to aim, letting herself drift into a state of where she was no longer conscious of herself, where she and the target were a single entity.

You must let go of yourself; wait for fulfillment or you will fail.

Abi pushed away the mist clouding her mind.

The rustle of wings…directly above her.

Relaxing, she released the arrow. The shot was clean. No jerking of the bow in recoil. One second the arrow was there; the next, it was simply gone. She remained in a rigid position and was still frozen in place until she heard an animal-like shriek of pain.

Only then did she lower the bow.

She ignored the moaning that came out of the darkness and called out Ben's name.

"We're over here," Weber called. "Ben's been hit."

The bow slipped from her fingers and she ran toward the sound of Weber's voice. She found him kneeling beside Ben, who lay on his back, holding his arm close to his chest. His eyes were squeezed shut. She knelt and put her face close to Ben's.

"Ben, can you hear me?"

After a moment, his eyes slowly opened and his lips widened in a smile.

"Yeah. I can see you, too. Nice."

From the direction of the cottages came the sound of engines, car doors slamming and shouting voices.

CHAPTER FIFTY-TWO

State Police Lieutenant Curran arrived with a squad of troopers in SWAT gear. He was expecting a drug gang. Instead, he found a man, dressed like a giant bird, who lay in the grass with an arrow in his shoulder.

"What's with the Halloween costume?" he asked Ben. "I thought this was a drug bust."

"This case is worth more than a hundred drug busts," Ben said.

He advised him to take Mead into custody after they patched him up. When Curran asked what Mead should be charged with. Ben said: "Charge him with multiple homicides, attempted murder, grand theft and assault and battery."

"Not bad for starters."

"Oh yeah. I forgot about trespassing."

"Surprised you didn't add littering. Witnesses and evidence?"

"He tried to kill me," Ben said.

"He tried to kill me, too," Abi said.

"And me as well," Weber added.

"Busy boy. That'll do for now. Anything else?"

"Yes. You can call in the FBI. Tell them this involves grand larceny across international lines and ask them to get in touch with me."

Curran raised an eyebrow. "We'll need statements. I'll see you later," he promised.

"We're not going anywhere," Ben said. "One more thing, I suggest you talk to the police chief about posting a guard at the Baron property."

"What the hell is that?"

"Related crime scene. There are two dead bodies there at the bottom of a well."

"You've got to be kidding."

"I wish I were, Lieutenant Curran."

Ben and the others got in the truck and drove back to his place. Abi suggested that Ben see a doctor. He thought his arm was bruised rather than broken. He had a headache but didn't think he had a skull fracture. Back at the house he popped painkillers and ran cold water on his arm. Abi fashioned a makeshift ice pack for his head. Then they rustled up breakfast of bacon and eggs. Weber left after breakfast, saying he'd be back after he'd had a long nap.

Abi wanted to change into clothes that were in the overnight bag she had left at the cottage. Ben said the cottage was now a crime scene and he'd better go with her. Holding the ice pack against his arm, Ben got in Grover and Abi drove them to the cottage.

At the bottom of the driveway Abi stopped to pick up a FedEx envelope tucked behind the flag on the mailbox. The envelope was addressed to her. Even more surprising was the sender: Clint Hammond. On the back of the package was a neatly written note from Ellie who said she found the package in the foyer with instructions from her father to overnight it to Abi.

She tucked the envelope next to her seat and drove up the hill.

A couple of SUVs with state license plates were parked in front of the cottages next to a town police car. A police officer got out of the cruiser and smiled when he saw Ben.

"What's going on?" Ben said.

"Team from the state crime lab is working the field behind the cottages," the officer said. He pointed to the front porch wrapped in yellow police tape. "I'm keeping an eye on this place."

"The lady left her suitcase inside," Ben said. "Okay if we grab it and run?"

"No problem. They took the front door to the lab to check for prints. Someone's coming by in a little while to seal the doorway with plywood."

"I'm glad to hear that," Abi said. "There are some valuable papers in the office."

"I'll make sure they're safe."

Abi stepped over the shards of glass and into the house. The suitcase was where she'd left it in the kitchen area. She picked up the bag and headed out, after making a quick check of the office. The professor's files appeared to be undisturbed. A minute later she was driving off the hill. Back at the Dyer homestead, she showered and changed.

By then, Ben was on the phone. He saw her and mouthed the letters 'FBI.' Abi gave him a thumbs-up. She stared at her name printed in big block letters on the FedEx envelope, sighed, and pulled open the tab.

Inside was a single-spaced letter from Hammond. She began to read.

"I should have known Otto Klaas pulled a Houdini. There was no reason for him to be at that air base. He was a skilled glider pilot and was in the Luftwaffe, but had nothing to do with planes or flying. He was a thief on a grand scale. Before the war he scouted art for the Nazis to steal. As an aide to *Reichmarschall* Hermann Goering, he helped them plunder the world's great masterpieces.

"Stolen art was divided into six categories. Hitler got the first pick, of course. Then Goering. Third, came the German museums, and so on down the line. Klaas, who was close to Goering, would have seen him for what he was. Greedy. Without morals. Insatiable and easily duped. As the war went on, Klaas watched Goering lose battles and prestige, and hitched his star to the wealthy and connected people he had come to know at the glider school.

"I believe that in the confusion toward the end of the war he diverted masterpieces destined for Goering to his new patrons: the Magnus family. I direct your attention to the note written from Klaas to Magnus. The one my faulty memory was trying to recall. My German has gotten rusty through the years, but I think I've done a reasonable translation. Please give it a read and get back to me so we can talk about where it fits into the fascinating story you told me."

Ben hung up the phone and said, "The FBI is going to call me back after they figure out how to handle the case. Anything important in the FedEx pack?"

She handed Ben the letter.

"It's from Mr. Hammond. Let me know what you think."

Ben plunked down on a chair and quickly read the letter.

"He confirms the link between Klaas and the Magnus family, but I don't see the bombshell we hoped for."

"*I* do. Read the translated note Klaas wrote to Magnus."

Ben cleared his throat:

"Dear Mr. Magnus. I'm pleased to inform you that I'm in Poland working with a young man and others who may be able to provide you with the services you need in regard to lead shipments."

"Well?"

"The first part of the letter is intriguing, but I'm not sure what lead shipments is all about. Something to do with the Sunna metal business?"

"Possible. But it also might refer to lead artists once used in their paint as pigment. Lead helped a painting dry faster and resist moisture."

"Would it have been used in Raphael's time?"

"All the great artists used it, even later, and many suffered from its effects. Van Gogh used to lick his brushes and some people think the lead he ingested contributed to his physical and mental decline. Raphael died in 1520, at the age of thirty-seven. Cause unknown."

"This places Otto in Poland, where the Raphael was last seen in 1945," Ben said.

"The Polish government says the *Young Man* is in an unknown bank vault in an unknown country. But what I found equally intriguing was the reference made in the letter to 'others.'"

Ben furrowed his brow. "Meaning there may be more masterpieces buried under the barn?"

"We don't know if anything is buried in that vault," Abi said, "but the note raises an exciting possibility, doesn't it?"

Ben nodded. "Yes, it does. All those years that Raphael's famous boy may have been stuck in that vault, he may not have been alone."

CHAPTER FIFTY-THREE

The female FBI agent wielding the metal pike had only probed the ground near the barn a half-dozen times before the point struck something solid.

A couple of male agents carefully shoveled the turf, creating a round hole about a foot deep and a few feet wide, revealing a circular well cover made from wood planks fastened together with rusty nails.

The agents pried up the cover using the tips of their shovels. One of the agents pointed a flashlight down the hole.

"All clear," he said.

"No bodies?"

"Nope."

"Lovely," said the female agent. Her name was Danielle and she was in charge of the operation. "Let's take a closer look."

Another agent lowered a video camera with a high-powered light into the shaft at the end of a cable connected to a monitor.

"Well's dry. There's an opening at the bottom of the shaft."

Danielle wore a snug-fitting jumpsuit. She slipped on knee and elbow pads, goggles, a construction helmet with a headlamp and radio. She stuck a hammer and small crowbar in a tool belt, then covered her nose and mouth with a mask connected to a small air tank on her back.

While she was getting ready, the other agents backed up a Tahoe

SUV close to the hole and attached the top of a rope ladder to its bumper. They pulled up the video camera and the agent began her descent. At the bottom she explored the opening and interior with a flashlight.

"Tunnel's constructed of corrugated steel," she said over the radio. "Pretty good condition. Interior is unobstructed. Big enough to for me to crawl through. Room for you, too, Mike, if you care to join me."

"Be right down," the agent said.

"Okay. I'm going in."

By the time Mike reached the bottom of the well, Danielle had crawled into the tunnel.

"Okay so far," she said. "About twenty-five feet in. Mike is behind me. Coming to the end." After a pause, her voice came on again. "Metal door. Circular. Marine type. Flush to metal surface. T-Bar turning handle." There was a grunt, then an expletive. "Damned thing is stuck. Glad I remembered persuader."

She inserted the crowbar through the turning handle. The sound of hammering came over the radio. Then a triumphant: "Got it! Prying door off." Then, after a few seconds, "Going in."

She kept up a running commentary, but the muffled words were hard to understand.

Abi stood inside the Baron barn with Ben and Weber, looking down into the hole that had been excavated in the floor.

Standing on top of the vault, now fully exposed, were two agents in jumpsuits. One held a hand radio. Danielle's voice was coming through but it was faint and garbled. The radio transmission was silent for a few seconds, then the barn echoed with a loud metallic knocking from the vault.

The pounding continued until one edge of the rectangular hatch rose about an inch above the surface of the vault. The agents got down on their knees and inserted the fingers of their gloved hands into the space between the hatch cover and vault surface; then, they lifted.

The hatch cover was heavy, but they opened a space of six inches. Two more pairs of gloved hands appeared from under the cover. With four people pushing and pulling, the cover was quickly moved aside.

Danielle's face appeared in the opening. She removed her helmet, goggles and mouthpiece. "Your diagram was right on the mark, Abi."

"Thanks, but please don't keep us in suspense. What's down there?"

The smile on Danielle's lips grew even wider. "You guys nailed it on that, too. Give us a hand."

She moved aside. The opening was filled with the top of a narrow wooden box secured with metal strapping and hinges. Lifted from inside the vault, the box rose through the opening to a height where the other two agents could pull it out. They passed the box up to Abi and the others, who hauled it out of the excavation and leaned it up against a stall. The box was identical to the one Otto Klaas was holding in the Hopper drawing. She could hardly contain herself at the prospect of what might be inside.

Her excitement only grew as five more containers came out of the vault. They were carefully wrapped in thick quilting and loaded in the back of the Tahoe.

"That's it," Danielle said. "Except for this. Might be important."

She handed Abi a thick leather bound book, then extended her hands. The other agents lifted her out of the vault and helped Mike climb up. Danielle said they found the boxes side-by-side in a vertical position in an airtight steel storage bin.

Abi had predicted that the latch for the cover on top of the vault would be on the inside. The last person in the vault had locked the hatch from the inside, crawled through the tunnel and climbed up the well shaft.

She opened the ledger. The pages had been divided into columns, each titled with words neatly written in German. She showed the book to Weber.

His eyes widened. "This looks like a list of artwork. There are designations for the original owner and the name of the piece. Most interesting is the column with the disposition of the artwork."

"Otto's second set of catalogues," Abi said.

Before she and Weber could dig into the ledger, Danielle came over and asked for the book.

"Anything of value here?" she said.

"It could be of immense value," Weber replied. "It looks like a record of stolen art. I'd suggest you get it into the hands of an expert in international art theft."

"I'll be sure to do that." Danielle shook hands with everyone. "Thank you so much for all your help, folks."

"Thanks for letting us watch the operation," Ben said.

"It wouldn't have been possible without the information you provided," Danielle said.

"When will we know what's in the boxes?" Weber said.

"Could be a while. We've got to open the boxes without damaging the contents. After that, we'll report to the higher-ups. They'll have to figure out who owns the property and where it goes from there. This is a big deal. The State Department is chomping at the bit. We'll let you know as soon as we can."

"Who's doing the conservation and preservation?" Abi asked.

"We came out of the Boston office, so we'll be heading directly to the lab at the Museum of Fine Arts."

She got into the Tahoe with a driver. The other agents piled into two similar SUVs. With the vehicle carrying the boxes in the middle, the SUVs headed off down the driveway away from the Baron property.

Weber watched the caravan leave. "Bureaucracies are the same around the world. I had hoped that we'd know more about the contents of the vault before I headed back to Zurich."

"I could put on my lawyer's hat and try to see what I can do," Ben offered, "but these are the feds we're dealing with."

"Don't give up hope," Abi said.

She tapped her cell phone screen. "Celine? Abi here. I'm fine. That young man we talked about earlier? That's right. He's coming your way with a shipment of lead."

CHAPTER FIFTY-FOUR

Three Weeks Later

Mead looked a lot better than the last time Ben saw him lying in the grass with an arrow in his shoulder.

He sat at a metal table across from Ben in a room at the Plymouth County Jail reserved for inmates and their lawyers. He was dressed in orange and had grown a neat goatee. His arm was still in a sling. The man in the dark suit sitting next to Mead was his lawyer who had set up the interview.

Ben had asked to meet with Mead after many sleepless nights lying awake in bed with unanswered questions swirling around his head. When he'd found out Mead's defense attorney was a former colleague, he asked to meet with his client. To Ben's surprise, Mead agreed to see him. No preconditions.

"You're looking good," Ben said.

"Thanks," Mead said. "They're treating me okay. The officers say they haven't had a celebrity like me since Whitey Bulger." He grinned. "Guys here call me the Birdman. Shrink calls me a sociopath."

It was hard for Ben to believe the genial man sitting across from him was a cold-blooded killer.

"How's your shoulder?" he asked.

"Sling's coming off this week. Tell your girlfriend she's one hell of a shot."

"I'll tell her, but she's not my girlfriend."

Mead winked. "Whatever. Sorry I gave her a big scare. Nothing personal."

"I'm sure she'll be happy to know you're contrite. Would you have killed her if you got the chance?"

"Dunno," Mead said. "Like the counselor here likes to say, it goes to state of mind."

"And you were in a murderous state."

"I wouldn't have liked it. Same with you. I'm kinda glad you ducked when you did."

"Yeah, me too. Is that why you agreed to see me, to apologize?"

Mead turned to his lawyer who said, "My client has pled guilty to murder charges. Since there's no death penalty in Massachusetts, he figures he's in for the rest of his life in any case and doesn't want to go through the hassle of a trial."

"I'm surprised you didn't try an insanity defense."

"I would have," the lawyer said. "Mr. Mead didn't want me to."

"That's right," Mead said. "I'm as sane as you are."

Ben's head still ached from time to time and he felt a twinge of pain in the arm Mead had bruised. "Sure, Phil," he said. "Nothing crazy about dressing up like a bird and killing people."

"Like I was saying a minute ago about state of mind. Gotta admit I was crazy some of the time." He stared off into space. "Something about strapping on a pair of wings, jumping off a cliff and flying around in the dark. You kinda feel like a god. I kept thinking I was a big ol' hawk." Mead chuckled. "Turns out I was a sitting duck."

"Too bad," Ben said. "Those wings would come in handy right now."

The far-off look faded from Mead's eyes. "My flying days are over. This thing was never about anything more than greed."

"Greed I can understand better than flying gods. I know how it ended. Tell me how it started."

Mead nodded. "You've gotta go back to Andscar Magnus. He emigrates from Norway to the U.S. and gets into the metals business. He makes a ton of money selling stuff to both sides in World War I. His son Gunnar developed a lot of connections in

Germany. He saw a big market once the Germans started to build planes again."

"Gunnar would have been running Sunna when Hesselbach arrived in the U.S. in 1928."

"Right. He had been keeping an eye on Hesselbach. Figured he might loosen up things in Germany for powered airplanes. He heard Hesselbach and Penney wanted to set up a school on the hill where they launched the flights. He bought another property, thinking he could sell it to them, but when a syndicate decided on a third site for the school, he sent his son Karl there to learn how to fly."

"Which is where they met Otto Klaas."

"Klaas had come over from Germany to be an instructor. He and Gunnar became friends. They both liked art and didn't care how they got it. They stayed pals after the school closed in 1929. Klaas went back to Germany. The Nazis were taking over the glider clubs. He joined the Luftwaffe and met Goering who gave him a job."

"Scouting out art collections to steal."

"Otto was all over the place tracking down art for his boss, but he kept his own set of catalogues listing pieces that might interest his pal Gunnar."

"That must have been risky."

"He'd be dead meat if Goering found out. Way he worked it, he'd be right behind the troops when they moved into a country. He'd snatch up the stuff on his lists, and in the confusion he set aside one batch for the Führer and his gang and another for the Magnus castle in Norway. When it looked like Germany was on the ropes, Klaas faked his death and, with the help of the Magnus family, snuck into the U.S."

"And ended up at the old Snow property."

"The farmhouse was still in the Sunna's real estate portfolio. Otto knew his way around from his earlier time in the States."

"Too bad he didn't know someone was sketching his picture."

Mead whistled softly. "That artist didn't know how close he came to getting killed."

"If Otto had murdered a famous artist like Edward Hopper, police and news people would have been all over the Snow property.

How did you get involved in this deal?"

"Dumb luck. I pitched the reenactment of the Hesselbach flights to the magazine. Kyle and Aldrich were picked to build the plane and make the flights. I did profiles on both guys to promote the project. Aldrich was easy. Techno-nerd who ran a small company that designed and built recreational gliders. Magnus was a lot more interesting."

"In what way?"

"His family connections to Sunna. I got in touch with their PR people who sent me piles of info. I was looking for an angle that would connect Kyle with the family. He remembered seeing a box full of family papers in the attic and got it down for me."

"This was the box you told Abi about."

"Yeah. One of Kyle's relatives worked in the Sunna PR department years before. He had a special job keeping bad news about the family from circulating."

"What sort of bad news?"

"Sunna did business with the Nazis during the war. They sold Germany parts for the same war machine that was killing U.S. and allied soldiers."

"A lot of companies and their subsidiaries kept business ties with Germany after hostilities began. What was different with Sunna?"

"The barracks near their factories were really death camps. Thousands of slave laborers were worked to death. Men, women, kids. Didn't matter."

"Kyle knew none of this?"

"Not until I told him. He didn't believe it until he read the files himself. Which is when he got really upset."

"I don't blame him."

"The info was nothing I could use for the profile. I put it aside. Things changed when Melissa got named as editor."

"The job you were angling for."

"On top of that she took over the Hesselbach project. I could see that I'd be on my way out after the reenactment. Who's going to hire a middle-aged hack writer?"

"You must have been pretty angry."

"Yeah, broke, too. I dug the Sunna files out. Told Magnus I was going to do a story on his family and hoped it wouldn't hurt his chances with the Navy."

"You were going to blackmail him with the material he'd given you."

"That was the idea. I figured as a Magnus he'd have a big stash somewhere."

"What was his reaction?"

"He laughed. Said he was low on the Magnus totem pole and didn't have much money."

"A blackmailer's worst nightmare. A mark who doesn't care."

"Even crazier than that. He remembered what I said about my SEAL background and offered me a job as test pilot for his flypack. He said he'd cut me in if he got the Navy contract."

"Seems like a good deal for you."

"Hell yes. I took the job. When he got the contract I figured I was all set. Magnus screwed that up. He'd been doing some research of his own and found out that the Magnuses were financing neo-Nazis in Europe. He decided to go public with the stuff on his family."

"When did Otto Klaas come into the picture?"

"The attic files had folders laying out each of the crimes Sunna committed and the PR strategy for burying the story. Sunna was suspected of dealing in stolen art. Klaas was mentioned. Kyle got desperate and tried to break into the stolen art network of an outfit in Switzerland."

"It's called The Restitution Registry. Marty Weber works for them. He was following up on Kyle's attempt to get into their file on Otto Klaas."

"Kyle shouldn't have done that. He was signing his own death warrant."

"What are you talking about?"

"Kyle was getting too close to learning the truth about Otto Klaas. The Magnus family didn't like that."

"How would they know Kyle was snooping around?"

Mead gave Ben a lopsided grin. "I told them."

Ben stared at Mead. "You never cease to amaze, Phil. How did you hook up with the family?"

"I had some names of PR people from my research for the

magazine story. I told them I was doing a story on the death camps. High-priced lawyer called and threatened to sue me. I told him I'd hold off on the story if he got word to the Magnus family that I knew how to get my hands on their property that went missing in 1945."

"You needed someone to fence the goods."

Mead nodded. "Guy got in touch. No name. Said to call him Central. He said his employer was interested in recovering the property. He wanted proof that I knew where it was. I said I'd get back to him. The problem was getting onto the property. The place was like a fortress and Baron was always there."

"Strange that he died suddenly."

Mead shrugged carelessly. "No great loss from what I heard. I came out to take a look at the launch site and figured I'd give my wings a run. I dropped in one night to look around. He heard me, so I took care of him. Then I could snoop around without being interrupted, until your girlfriend showed up."

"Abi must have complicated things."

"Big-time. I'd located the vault with a metal detector and dug down to it. I couldn't figure out how to get in without messing up any art inside. Meanwhile, Sunna was getting on my case. Central called and threatened to cut me from the payroll. So I tossed them a nugget. Said Kyle wanted to set the record straight about his family. Central told me Kyle had to have an accident."

"The glider flight?"

"It was a perfect set-up. I flew onto the site before the flight and planted a small explosive charge near the controls. I triggered the blast from the top of hill."

"Too bad for you the Coast Guard got the glider out of the water before traces of explosive were washed away."

"Best I could do on short notice. Your turn now. I've got a question for you."

"Fair enough."

"Was the Raphael in the vault? I have to know. It's driving me crazy." He chuckled at his unintended joke. "Hell, Ben. You know what I mean."

"I'm afraid I do. The painting the FBI found in the vault was a portrait of a young man."

In his excitement, Mead missed the odd wording of Ben's answer.

"I knew it!" Mead said. "Damned Raphael was sitting under that old barn all these years."

"I said it was *a* painting, not *the* painting."

"A fake? Crap. That can't be."

"Sorry for the bad news. The lab at the Museum of Fine Arts confirmed that it was a forgery. A good one, but a fake nonetheless."

"I'll be damned. You suppose Otto Klaas knew the painting was a fake?"

"Hard to know. Klaas went through a lot to move the painting out of Europe to its hiding place. I can't see him doing that with a fake. Dishonest people can be the easiest to fool because they figure they're smarter than everyone else."

"Guess the joke is on me."

"It's even funnier than you know. There were a dozen other paintings in the vault that weren't fakes. They were lesser known but still valuable masterpieces by famous artists: Vermeer, Holbein, even a small Rembrandt. They're worth millions."

"Hell! That score would have set me up for life."

Ben glanced around at the small room and the guarded door.

"Looks like you're already set for life, Phil."

CHAPTER FIFTY-FIVE

Museum of Fine Arts, Boston:
Later the Same Day

Abi took the long way from her office through the Impressionism galleries, stopping at every Renoir or Monet that caught her eye.

For an art historian, working at a job steps away from some of the greatest masterpieces in the world was as good as it gets. *An art museum is so incredibly civilized*, she thought. *And peaceful.*

The wheels of justice had started grinding the morning after the FBI got into the vault. For days, Abi, Ben and Weber were busy with phone calls and police and FBI interviews. On top of everything else, Abi got official word from the professor about her new job and Celine called to ask when she was moving in.

While she moved back to Boston, Ben stayed in Truro. He hadn't wanted to let the chief down. They had a few phone conversations, but hadn't seen each other. Abi was delighted when he called that morning and said he'd like to see her later in the day.

She gave him a big hug when he entered her office.

"It's too nice a day to sit inside." She grabbed a couple of bottles of water from a small office refrigerator. "Let's go out for a walk," she said.

They left the museum and after a short stroll, sat on a bench in The Fens—enjoying the garden that winds along a marshy section of the Back Bay.

Abi gazed at the stately museum building. "I can't believe I'm getting paid for being here. I'm living with Celine now and we go jogging along the Charles every morning."

"I'm happy to hear that," Ben said.

"You're wearing a dark suit that fits you very well, by the way, so I guess you accepted the job offer at your old law firm."

"The chief fired me when I told him I'd been asked to go back to the firm. Said I'd be stupid not to take the deal and that he didn't hire dumb cops. I've moved back into my town house on Beacon Hill. My first case is the Baron land acquisition."

She clapped her hands. "Bravo. Let me know what I can do."

"I will." He paused. "Weber called me yesterday. He got into Kyle's computer and found a file with the announcement he planned to give after the flight. It was an apology for the misdeeds of the Magnus family."

"Kyle had a lot of courage. It would have gone against every evil tendency in that horrible family."

"Unlike Icarus, he said he knew better than too close to the sun."

"He was talking about Sunna Industries."

"Yes, but Kyle never fully appreciated that he had been drawn into a conspiracy that went back to 1945. Sunna and Klaas had an unsigned covenant. They'd help him escape from Europe if he brought the stolen art with him. Mead was part of the same deal, only decades later. And by then, Sunna had upped the ante. It wasn't only about the artwork: Mead would have to kill Kyle if he wanted to be paid."

"So that's what it was all about? The money?"

"That's what Mead says, but I suspect there was a darker reason than the pursuit of fortune. Even he doesn't know."

"Where is he now?"

"He's had his wings clipped and is grounded in the Plymouth jail waiting transfer to prison. His lawyer is an old friend of mine. I asked if I could talk to his client."

Ben gave Abi an account of his conversation with Mead. "He said to tell you that you're a good shot with a bow and arrow."

"If I'd been a good shot I would have hit him in the heart instead of the shoulder. I can't believe that jerk had been watching me from the very beginning."

"He'd put the camera in the barn to keep an eye on the art stash. After he saw you snooping around, he broke into your cottage and installed another camera in your office. He heard all your conversations, and saw your computer screen."

"Which is how he knew I was going to Nantucket."

"Mead heard you talking to Hammond and figured he needed help before things fell apart. He called Sunna, they sent a team out to deal with you and Hammond and retrieve the sketches. After you got away they came to Truro for the artwork. Mead figured they'd kill him after they had the loot, so he took care of them first."

"That reminds me," Abi said. "What's going on with the Hopper sketches?"

"The FBI has them. They're part of the evidence."

"The professor wants to give them to the museum eventually. The paintings are in the museum vault until the rightful owners can be determined. It could take years."

"Any news on the *Young Man* forgery?" Ben asked.

"The origins of the fake may be an even greater mystery than the whereabouts of the real Raphael."

"And the whereabouts of Otto Klaas as well."

"He left the ledger, which suggests he was coming back. After he stored the art in the vault his job was done. He'd await word from Gunnar. Maybe he never got it because Magnus died of a heart attack a few months after Otto arrived in the country."

"He could have gone anywhere."

"True, but a pilot like Klaas would never get flying out of his blood. I asked my historian friend at the glider museum to research glider schools and clubs with the name Darmstadt that were set up in the U.S. between 1945 and 1955."

"Sounds like a long shot."

"I figured Klaas wouldn't have been able to resist flying and teaching. I may have hit pay dirt with a news story. A member of the New Darmstadt soaring club in upstate New York died in a glider accident. His name was Oskar Klamperer. Initials O.K."

"You think that was Klaas?"

"The news clip had almost nothing about his background. No photo. Not even an address. That's revealing in itself. I'll keep working on it."

"No," Abi said. "Let it lie. You'll have enough to do with the Baron acquisition. Don't get back into your workaholic routine."

"Thanks, Abi. Hard to break old habits. Please pinch me if I ever start talking like that again. I put my work above Loren. I don't want to make that kind of mistake the next time."

"Next time?"

"Sorry. I should have said, *if* there is a next time."

"Oh, I think there will be," Abi said. She kissed him playfully on his cheek. "In fact, I'm sure of it."

EPILOGUE

Ben picked up the framed photo of Loren from the table next to his bed and carefully tucked it between sheets of bubble-wrap into a cardboard box packed with other pictures. He carried the box out to his truck and put it on the floor of the cab. On his walk back to the house he heard the beep of a horn. A postal truck had pulled up to the mailbox for its daily delivery. He ambled over to say hello. Ben had known the driver since they were in kindergarten.

"Morning, Ben," the driver said, handing him a packet of mail wrapped in a rubber band. "Guess this is the last batch of mail I'll be delivering here for a while."

"Thanks," Ben said, taking the mail. "Don't know why I didn't think of having it forwarded before now. "

Ben knew he was being disingenuous. He had waited so long to fill out the mail forwarding form because having his mail go to Boston would have been one less excuse for returning to the house. And by extension, letting go of Loren. So at least once a week, he got up early and drove to Truro to collect his mail. He'd make a perfunctory check of the house, and be back in his law office for the afternoon.

"When will we see you again?" the driver asked.

"In the fall after all the tourists are gone and we can have the town to ourselves again."

"Sounds like a plan," the driver said. Giving Ben a thumb's up, he added, "Good luck."

As the truck drove off to the next delivery, Ben riffled through the wad of mail. It was mostly bills and bulk mail, like supermarket sales or coupon packs. A mustard-colored padded envelope caught his attention. The name on the return address was that of Phil Mead's lawyer.

Ben used his Swiss army knife to slice open the envelope. He pulled out the folded slip of paper and read the message:

"My client wanted you to have this. He said he will have no use for it where he is going."

In with the note was something in white tissue. Ben unwrapped the paper and stared at the object cupped in his hand. The last time he had seen the three-gull glider school badge was on Mead's baseball hat. It was probably his imagination, but he felt a twinge of pain in the arm he had used to fend himself from Mead's air attack.

Ben's lips formed a frown. He dropped the badge to the ground and went to crush it under the heel of his work boot.

Something made him stop. Instead of stomping the badge, he reached down, picked it up, and stuffed paper and all into his pocket. The house check only took a few minutes. He did a room-to-room survey to make sure the windows were shut. Everything was in good shape. It always was.

After locking up, he backed the truck out of the driveway. Rather than follow the road to the state highway, he headed for the bay beach. It was a perfect sunny day. The beach was crowded with sun-bathers and swimmers. Burdened with coolers, blankets and chairs, beach-goers clustered near the parking lot. A walk of a quarter mile took him away from the crowds to a deserted section of beach.

He walked to the water's edge and reached into his pocket for the badge. He stuffed the paper back in his pocket and gazed for a couple of seconds at the three gulls frozen in flight in the palm of his hand. Then he cocked his arm and threw the badge as far as he could. He used all the power in his arm and shoulder, but the light weight of the pin, coupled with the fresh southwest breeze, conspired to drop the badge far short of where he wanted it to be. It went *ploop* into a gentle wave, hardly making a ripple.

He shrugged at the disappointing result of his mighty pitch. The badge would tumble in the waves for a while before burying itself in the shifting bottom sands. A kid digging in the beach one day might find the corroded remnants of the flying award and puzzle over what it was.

But maybe, just maybe, the enamel birds would release their spirit to soar among the clouds with the souls of Peter Hesselbach and Kyle Magnus. They were the real bird men. Mead was a fraud. He strapped on the wings of Icarus and used his god-like power to satisfy his craving for power and riches.

Ben was past the physical pain Mead had caused, but he wasn't entirely free of the psychological scars. On the walk back to his truck he stopped suddenly when a shadow crossed the sand in front of him. He looked skyward, only to see a gull soaring against the sun. He smiled, and gave the bird a thumb's up.

"See you in the fall, pal."

That's when he'd be back to oversee the demolition of Fort Baron by the Loren Dyer conservation trust. As Ben had drawn up the papers, the goal of the trust was to return the dunes and heath to their natural state in the tradition of Edward Hopper. Abi would be by his side. And so would Loren.

*

ABOUT THE AUTHOR

PAUL KEMPRECOS is the author of eight novels in the *Aristotle "Soc" Socarides* private detective series, including *COOL BLUE TOMB*, winner of a Shamus award from the Private Eye Writers of America for Best Paperback, and *SHARK BAIT*, nominated for a Shamus in the same category. Grandmaster of Adventure writer Clive Cussler blurbed: "There can be no better mystery writer in America than Paul Kemprecos." Paul became the first fiction co-author to work with Cussler when they created and wrote the *New York Times* bestselling *NUMA Files* series. After collaborating with Cussler on the first eight books in the *NUMA Files*, Paul wrote two adventure novels including *THE MINOAN CIPHER*, nominated for a Thriller award by the International Thriller Writers. His short story *The Sixth Decoy* was included in the anthology *NOTHING GOOD HAPPENS AFTER MIDNIGHT* and will be part of the 2021 edition of *AMERICA'S BEST MYSTERY STORIES*. Paul lives on Cape Cod with his wife Christi, a financial advisor.

To learn more about Paul Kemprecos, check out his website at www.paulkemprecos.com.